SILENT SECRETS

A Whispering Pines Mystery, Book Seven

Shawn McGuire

OTHER BOOKS BY SHAWN MCGUIRE

WHISPERING PINES Series
Missing & Gone (prequel novella)
Family Secrets, book 1
Kept Secrets, book 2
Original Secrets, book 3
Hidden Secrets, book 4
Rival Secrets, book 5
Veiled Secrets, book 6
Silent Secrets, book 7
Merciful Secrets, book 8
Justified Secrets, book 9
Secret of Her Own (novella)
Protected Secrets, book 10
Burning Secrets, book 11
Secret of the Season (novella)
Blind Secrets, book 12
Secret of the Yuletide Crafter (novella)
Wayward Secrets, book 13

HEARTH & CAULDRON Series
Hearth & Cauldron, book 1

GEMI KITTREDGE Series
One of Her Own, book 1
Out of Her League, book 2

THE WISH MAKERS Series
Sticks and Stones, book 1
Break My Bones, book 2
Never Hurt Me, book 3
Had a Great Fall, book 4
Back Together Again, book 5

SILENT SECRETS

A Whispering Pines Mystery, Book Seven

Shawn McGuire

Brown Bag Books

This book is a work of fiction. Names, characters, places, and events are products of the author's imagination or are used fictitiously. Any resemblance to actual events, locales, or persons, living or dead, is entirely coincidental.

Published by Brown Bag Books
ISBN-13: 9781098742171

For information visit:
www.Shawn-McGuire.com

First Edition/First Printing May 2019

For those who see the beauty and value of silence.

Chapter 1

THE DREAM . . . NO, THIS ONE was squarely in the nightmare realm. I'd had it every few nights for the first week, then every other night. This week, it came two nights in a row, so I tried hard to stay awake. Around one thirty, my eyes refused to stay open, so I crawled into bed, hoping I was tired enough to sleep without dreaming. No such luck.

I stared out the windows, trying to get a fix on what time it was, and shivered at the sight of the frost-covered pine trees. The temperature wasn't getting above forty during the day now that we were into late November and dropped below freezing at night. Ice had started to form in the shallow areas and permanently tree-shaded coves of Whispering Pines' lake. The still unfrozen water looked colder, like it was starting to gel or stiffen in preparation for the thick layer of ice that would soon cap it and trap in all the lake's secrets.

"Are you awake?" My boyfriend, Tripp Bennett, sat on the edge of the bed and rested a hand on my hip. He knew I'd been dreaming a lot lately, but he didn't know it had been the same nightmare on replay. He pushed a lock of hair away from my eyes, a look of concern on his face.

"I'm awake." I pushed myself up to sit, propping my

pillow between my back and the headboard.

"Good. I wasn't sure if I should wake you up or let you work through it."

It had been three weeks since I'd moved out of the boathouse and into the main house. Tripp and I now shared Pine Time Bed-and-Breakfast's all-white main floor bedroom. It was beautiful with its traditional raised-wood paneling and a wall of windows that provided an amazing view of the lake.

"You were having another nasty dream," Tripp told me. "This has been happening a lot. Do you want to tell me about it?"

I rubbed the grit from the corners of my eyes. I wasn't sure I wanted to talk about it. What if telling him made it worse? Then again, remaining mute about things rarely helped. What the heck.

"It only lasts a few seconds. I'm on one of the backstreets in Madison. Not sure where exactly. Probably the University area."

"Are you a cop?"

I'd spent four years serving as a patrol officer and then one more as a detective for the Madison Police Department. A lot of that time was spent in the University area of town, so good guess on Tripp's part.

"Yeah. I'm standing near my squad car, and Lupe is confronting Matt. As in, she's yelling at him."

Confusion creased Tripp's brow. "Matt? The guy who died here last month? What was Lupe saying to him?"

"I couldn't hear the words. She was angry, though. Or maybe scared." I hadn't considered that second possibility. The line between anger and fear could be blurry at times. "Whatever it was, she wanted him to do something, and when he wouldn't do it, she shot him."

"Oh, babe." Tripp leaned in to comfort me with a hug, and I placed my hands on his chest to hold him back.

"That wasn't the worst part." I turned and stared out the

window while Tripp waited for me to continue. "After Lupe shot him, Matt turned into Frisky. And then Lupe turned into Randy. I became Sheriff Brighton."

Tripp immediately grasped the significance. "Do you really need to analyze this to understand it?"

On the single worst day of my professional life, my partner, Detective Randy Ketchum, shot and killed our unarmed informant, Frisky Fox. But why was I dreaming about that incident now? And why was my mind combining that day with the events of last month?

"No, I don't need to analyze it," I snapped. "My subconscious is letting me know, over and over, what can happen if I trust people when my gut tells me—"

In a flash, I understood why the events combined. No wonder I was having nightmares about Frisky.

"What's the matter?" Tripp asked.

I sighed before saying, "This week is the one-year anniversary of Frisky's death."

"That could have something to do with it. You're upset about Lupe in the present and thinking about Frisky in the past."

Great. Now he was analyzing me.

"Wait. You said, 'over and over.'" Tripp adjusted positions on the bed, scooting in a few inches so he wasn't perched quite so precariously on the edge. He enveloped one of my hands in both of his, resting them on the goose-down comforter covering my legs. "Have you been having this same dream every night? That would explain why you're so tired and short-tempered lately."

I almost said, *sorry my distress is putting a smudge on your perfect little life.* Where had that thought come from? Glad I stopped those words from coming out of my mouth.

"Not every night." Not until this week at least. "I've had it a lot, though."

"Maybe you should go over to Unity and talk to someone?"

I'd had a nightmare. It's not like I was in the midst of a mental breakdown. Although, the nightmares and lack of decent sleep were getting to me. As was this conversation. Done talking about myself and my nightmare, I mentally changed direction and noticed Tripp was dressed for the day in jeans and a T-shirt.

"What time is it?" I reached for the alarm clock on my nightstand. Eight thirty-six. I never slept this late. The kitchen was just outside our bedroom and the faint aroma of toast hit me. "Did you eat already?"

No one was staying in the B&B right now. Only the two of us, my West Highland White Terrier Meeka, and our long-term renter River Carr. There was no need for Tripp to make a big, fancy breakfast, but I thought we'd still eat together like we always did.

"Yeah, I ate. Just something quick. River and I need to run to Wausau and get more supplies for the attic. Maeve also asked that I pick up another turkey, big as I can find. I guess Sundry sold out."

More to myself than him, I grumbled, "So I'm spending the day alone again."

He ignored the complaint. "Seriously, babe, do you need to talk to someone about this dream?"

His unsaid statement was loud and clear. *You haven't left the house in a week. You've barely left this room. Now you're whining because I have to go buy supplies so I can keep working on our apartment?*

"I thought I was talking to you." I nudged him out of the way with my legs then rolled out of bed and headed for the bathroom.

"Jayne."

"No, that's fine. Go do your thing with River."

They'd been hanging out together constantly lately. Not a big deal under normal circumstances, but the summertime flood of tourists to the village had dried to barely a trickle. This meant my sheriff responsibilities had also all but evaporated. I had plenty of time on my hands. Too much, really. The plan had been that Tripp and I would work on the attic renovation together. Then River moved in with all his knowledge of carpentry, and now our renter got to spend more time with my boyfriend than I did.

He caught my arm and tugged me toward him. "What's wrong?"

"You mean other than that I just shape-shifted into a crooked sheriff in my nightmare? Or that I saw an innocent man I didn't protect die and turn into an innocent woman I also didn't protect?"

"Matt's death wasn't your fault." He sighed and took a half step back. "It's not just the dream. You've been like this for days."

"Like what?" I snapped.

"Irritable. Quiet. Depressed. Look, I get it. The whole Lupe thing—"

"Nope. Not going there."

His shoulders dropped. He wanted me to talk about how Lupe had duped us all for weeks. Possibly months. There wasn't a whole lot to talk about. It was simple, really. All the clues to her deception had been right there. I either didn't see those clues or I ignored them, and a man died. Protecting the public was my job and I had failed in the biggest way. For the second time in a year.

"I know there's not much for you to do right now." His approach was gentler now. "There are practically no tourists, and the villagers are behaving themselves. You don't have to go anywhere, that's fine, but you can't just sit here all day. You need to do something."

It's not like I couldn't have left the house over the last week. It's just that getting dressed and going somewhere felt like too much work.

"What do you think I should do? Take up knitting?"

The smallest of smiles turned his mouth. "Not exactly what I was thinking, but a hobby of some kind is a good idea. I'm sure Ruby would be happy to give you lessons."

Ruby McLaughlin owned The Twisty Skein, Whispering Pines' hobby shop. She was like the Energizer Bunny on speed. I wasn't sure taking a knitting lesson from her would be relaxing, but it would for sure be entertaining. I chuckled at the image that presented.

"There's my girl."

He pulled me in for a warm, comforting hug. I fought the embrace at first, then let myself relax into it. Why was I fighting him so hard lately?

"Please, get out of the house today. As great as this place is, you need a change of scenery every now and then. God knows I do after days on end of taking care of guests. Jola's been asking you to come in for a massage. Call her and see if they can fit you in today."

"You're really pushing me to get over to the health center."

"That's because I'm worried about you. It's crisp but beautiful outside today. Soon enough, the weather will keep us inside."

"Together?" I waggled my eyebrows and glanced at the bed.

"You're reading my mind."

He moved in to kiss me, and I held my hand over my mouth. "Morning breath."

He kissed my forehead instead. "Thanks for telling me about your nightmare. I wish you would've said something sooner, though."

"Didn't want to bother you."

"You never bother me." He opened the bottom dresser drawer and pulled out the thick olive-green hoodie I gave him as a moving in together present. It had *Wayfaring Stranger . . . no more* printed in bold ivory lettering. It signified that his days of wandering and looking for a permanent home were over. He loved it as much as I'd hoped he would. "Seriously, are you okay? We do have to go to Wausau, but if you need to talk more—"

I put a finger over his lips, stopping him from offering to stay. I knew he really wanted to get on the road with River. "I'm fine. Go. I promise I'll leave the house today. Maybe Maeve needs help with the Thanksgiving prep."

I'd been looking forward to tomorrow for weeks. Many of the villagers would stay home and have Thanksgiving dinner with their families. Others were going to gather at the village pub Grapes, Grains, and Grub for a Thanksgiving smorgasbord and the Packers game.

"Good." He tugged on the sweatshirt. "You're looking cheerier already."

By the time I was showered and dressed, Tripp and River were long gone, leaving only Meeka and me to rattle around in the big seven-bedroom house. I found the little Westie lying in a patch of sun by the patio doors. As soon as she saw me, she rushed to my side and leaned against my leg. She could tell that I'd been having a rough couple of weeks and had been hovering near me constantly. Tripp drew the line at her sleeping in our bed between us, though.

"I thought we'd go into town today." I'd said this as though it would be a major trek. It took all of five minutes to get from our driveway to the far side of Whispering Pines. "We can go visit Briar and Morgan."

That set her tail wagging double time. She loved the mother-daughter green witch duo.

After a quick breakfast of toast with peanut butter and a drizzle of honey, an orange, and plenty of coffee, I loaded the two of us into my SUV and started for the Barlow cottage.

At the intersection of my quarter-mile-long driveway and the highway that divided the village in two, I had to wait for cars to pass. First, a silver-blue minivan and then a beige sedan. A rusty, beat-up and faded olive-green Excursion was next and caught my attention. It was loaded to capacity and driving slowly, a good five miles per hour below the speed limit. That was unusual. People usually flew through here. A man was driving, hunched over the wheel, hands at ten and two, gazing around as if looking for someone or something. The woman in the passenger's seat next to him had bleached-blonde hair. While I couldn't clearly see the people in the back, I was able to make out the heads of four more passengers between the second and third row of seats.

A newer model, two-door, royal-blue Nissan pickup truck followed the Excursion. They were close enough that either the pickup's driver was a tailgater or the two were together. I counted only two people in the pickup, but the bed of the truck was filled with duffel bags and backpacks and what appeared to be camping gear. That couldn't be right. Camping in northern Wisconsin in late-November? It might have been hunting equipment. It was deer hunting season, after all.

Neither vehicle was doing anything wrong, but something about them made my gut twist. While I couldn't pull them over on the grounds of giving me a funny feeling, I could issue the Frontier a citation for the tailgating thing.

Meeka barked from her cage in the back.

She was right. They were headed out of town anyway.

"All right, I'm going."

I turned right out of the drive, headed east on the highway, and was about to turn north onto the gravel road that led to the Barlow cottage when my walkie-talkie squawked.

"Sheriff O'Shea? This is Violet. Are you there?" She sounded frantic.

Damn. After days of doing nothing, I was finally ready to get out and have a little fun. Of course this was the time an incident would come up. I pulled to the side of the road, pushed the hazard lights button, and reached over to the passenger seat to retrieve my walkie-talkie.

"This is Sheriff O'Shea. What's going on, Violet?"

"You've got to get over to the Grinder. Flavia and Reeva are about to go nuclear."

Chapter 2

I PULLED MY JEEP CHEROKEE into my parking spot behind the sheriff's station and let Meeka out of her cage. She studied me with her head cocked to the side as I stood there for a moment debating how to proceed. I wasn't in uniform but was semi-prepared. It was a deeply ingrained habit to always have my badge on me, and it was currently in my inside jacket pocket. Having an easily accessible weapon was also a longstanding habit, so I had grabbed my gun case when I left the house and slid it under the driver's seat. Around here, the Glock was rarely necessary. I'd only drawn it twice in the six months I'd been here.

It was highly unlikely Flavia and Reeva were doing something that would require me to need my weapon. I couldn't take a chance with the villagers' safety, though, so I shrugged out of my baggy fleece jacket, slid my shoulder holster into place, and retrieved my Glock from its case.

"Sheriff O'Shea for Violet," I announced into the walkie-talkie. "Be there in two minutes." To my K-9, who was also out of uniform and wearing only her collar today instead of her harness with insignia, I said, "Violet never gets freaked out. This can't be good."

We ran around to the front of the station and onto the Fairy Path, a wood plank path that wound through a thick grove of trees. As we jogged, I noticed squirrels racing around the grove, grabbing small pine boughs off the forest floor and scampering up trees to finish padding out their nests. Before we knew it, the temperature would be permanently below freezing during the day and in the single digits or subzero at night.

We exited the Fairy Path and, like cars merging onto a freeway, entered the red brick walkway that circled the pentacle-shaped garden at the center of the village commons. Ye Olde Bean Grinder was the third cottage past the trailhead, so it took no time at all to reach. I climbed the stairs and nearly collided with a man wearing a brown jacket and a white hat coming out of the shop.

"Sorry." I gave a distracted wave, turned back toward the door, and nearly got trampled by Violet.

"Thank the Goddess you're here." She stepped out onto her porch, practically vibrating with anger.

"Are they inside?"

"They are. Basil is making sure they don't destroy my shop or kill each other."

"It's that bad? Was there a physical altercation?"

"Not yet, but there is a sister altercation in progress." She inhaled deeply and blew out the breath. "Everything was fine. Flavia was there drinking tea and talking to that man who just left. Everything about that was weird."

"Why?"

"Multiple reasons. First, Flavia never comes to the Grinder. Second, she was having an actual conversation with a stranger. Third, we rarely serve tea."

I gave her a blank stare at the third point. "Tea is a weird thing?"

"This is a coffee shop. Except for chai, we only keep a

small amount of Earl Grey and Chamomile on hand. Tea is Morgan's thing. Anyway, Reeva came in a couple minutes after Flavia started talking to that guy, ordered a cappuccino, and sat down to read a novel. She'd been there for nearly ten minutes before Flavia noticed her. When she did, she went nuts." Violet made explosion hands next to her head.

"What are they fighting about?"

"Martin."

Not a surprise. The entire village knew a fight over Reeva trying to be more involved with her nephew's life was coming. With Violet hot on my heels, I entered the Bean Grinder to find Reeva sitting in one of the comfy overstuffed leather chairs in the corner by the fireplace. A fire crackled happily in the hearth while Reeva attempted to ignore Flavia, who was hurling insults like only a sister could.

"Couldn't manage to have a family of your own, could you?" Flavia taunted and tried to pull free from the firm grip Basil had on her upper arms. When Reeva didn't give her a response, she added, "Do you really think you can steal my son from me? Do you honestly think he will prefer an aunt who's been absent his entire life to the mother who's always been here and always will be?"

Big words. I knew their history, which meant I knew why Reeva had been absent for the last twenty years. It involved a night of Flavia and Reeva's husband comforting each other after Flavia's husband had died in a bear attack. Shockingly, things got worse from there.

"Flavia?" I approached with caution like I would an angry animal. "You're causing a disturbance."

She glanced up at me with a crazed look in her sharp-blue eyes. She said nothing to me but spun back on Reeva.

While Basil, Violet's twin brother and business partner, detained Flavia, I turned to Reeva. "What's going on?"

Reeva held up a finger, indicating I should give her a

moment to finish reading her current passage. She flipped the page, placed an intricately embroidered linen bookmark in the crease, and closed the book. Before answering, she took a sip from her cappuccino.

"It appears my sister has found out that I am providing the land for Martin's cottage."

In a move that few villagers fully understood, Reeva had decided to divide the six acres she rented from the village and give half of them to her nephew and my deputy, Martin Reed. I had written it off as just another way to get back at her sister for that night of comfort twenty years ago.

"Didn't she already know Reed was building a cottage?" I asked.

"She knew he was building but not where." Reeva took another sip, her eyes sparkling as she looked at me over the cup. Then she sighed contently and set the cup aside.

Sibling rivalry at its best. Or maybe at its worst. "Now she knows and wants to make you pay?"

"That's my guess."

Flavia strained against Basil's strong arms. When she couldn't get away, she kept verbally attacking Reeva from across the room. "Everything was fine until you came back to the village. I was patient while you cleaned out Karl's house."

Reeva's eyes narrowed and darkened at Flavia's mention of Reeva's recently deceased husband.

"I said nothing when you announced you were staying in the village," Flavia continued. "I said nothing when you took that seat on the village council. I didn't even say anything when you decided to finally act like an aunt to my son. In fact, I encouraged him to spend time with his only other living relative."

Reeva made a scoffing *phfft* sound.

"But now, I find out that you have betrayed my generosity. Not only have you convinced him to leave my home, you're moving him into your backyard."

Flavia looked at me as though expecting me to do something about this outrage. Then Reeva threw me under the bus.

"It wasn't my idea for Martin to move out on his own. Jayne planted the thought in his head first."

"He's twenty-three years old," I objected, "and can't even do his own laundry. It's well past time for him to have his own place." I scowled at Reeva. "I never said he should move into your backyard, though."

Flavia made a violent lurch forward, finally breaking free of Basil's hold. In a flash, she was across the room with her long bony fingers wrapped around Reeva's throat.

"Jayne, do something," Violet insisted as the two women grappled. "They're going to break something."

"As in, each other?"

She shrugged as though that was possible but not her primary concern.

I physically pulled the two apart and stood between them with arms spread wide, keeping Flavia from charging again. "You need to calm down."

"She's stealing my son."

"Your son is an adult. He's free to live wherever he wants. You, however, are going to be charged with assault if you don't settle down in the next two seconds."

I stood, with my hand literally on Flavia's upper chest, holding her back, and turned to Reeva. "Are you okay?"

With a hand to her own throat, Reeva coughed and gasped, trying to get her breathing under control. There were red marks on her neck from Flavia's assault, and her eyes were watering. Her voice came out raspy when she spoke. "I'm fine. Or I will be."

"You're probably going to have a nasty sore throat. Do you want someone at Unity to take a look?"

She shook her head and whispered, "I'll make myself some healing tea when I get home."

I'd had my fair share of Morgan's special Wiccan blends. That would do the trick better than any medical treatment the village clinic could provide.

I asked Basil to keep Flavia from going ballistic again while I continued speaking with Reeva.

"Do we need to be worried about her? I mean, I realize she's upset with you but to attack you this way?"

Reeva, whose eyes were the same piercing shade of blue as Flavia's, stared at her sister with a look I couldn't define. There was a glint of something nasty and almost triumphant that made my breath catch. My sister Rosalyn used to get the same look when I would get in trouble while she walked away from a situation unscathed.

"Honestly," Reeva whispered, "I was prepared for her to do something like this. You were exactly right. Martin should have moved out long ago. She's had him so tight in her grasp for so many years, I'm surprised I didn't need to break him out." She clamped her hands together in a representation of Flavia's stranglehold on her son. "I'm proud of him for finally taking action."

"Do you know how he's doing? I know he comes back every weekend to work on that cottage—"

"He's been in the village?" Flavia screeched. "Every weekend? He hasn't come to see me." She glared at her sister. "He's been staying with you, hasn't he?"

Flavia made another lunge for Reeva, but Basil stood in front of her this time like a bodyguard denying entry to the town's hottest nightclub.

"Have you apologized to him for the things you said about Lupe?" Reeva asked her sister.

"I only said the truth," Flavia insisted, sniffing and looking away. "I don't have to apologize to my son for telling him what he needs to hear."

"He loved her," Reeva said, making Flavia flinch.

"He *loves* me. I'm the only woman he needs in his world."

"That," Violet said with a look of disgust, "is all kinds of messed up."

The Grinder's door opened, and a few villagers walked in. They froze in their tracks and walked out again when they realized the sister feud had ramped up another notch.

"Answer my question," Flavia demanded. "Has my son been in the village and no one has told me?"

Reeva's mouth turned in a wicked smile. "Yes, he's been in the village every weekend since Samhain. And he didn't come to see you. What does that tell you about how your son feels about you right now?"

With that, Flavia darted past Basil with a spin move any NFL running back would be proud to master. She went for Reeva's throat again. I attempted to pull her off, but in the process, she shoved me into a small table full of coffee condiments and accessories. A thermos of half-and-half dropped, broke open, and spilled all over the floor. A shaker of cinnamon joined it, creating a reddish-brown stream in the middle of the white puddle. Cardboard sleeves to put around paper cups went flying, fell into the creamer, and became ruined as they soaked up the liquid. Well, some of the liquid. Meeka was lapping up the non-cinnamon flavored portion.

The sisters, Basil, and Violet all stared at me, sprawled out on the floor with stir sticks stuck in my hair.

Violet rushed to my side and helped me up. "Are you okay?"

"I'm fine. Just embarrassed and a little fed up."

"You're not the only one." Violet turned, pointed first at Flavia and then at the door. "That's it, get her out of my shop before I press charges."

I took hold of Flavia's upper arm while indicating Reeva

should stay where she was by the fireplace.

"You need my help with her?" Basil asked.

"I'm not sure." I stared Flavia in the eye. "Are you going to come with me quietly, or do I need to find something to handcuff you with?"

In addition to always having my badge and my Glock with me, I would now always be sure I had at least one pair of zip-strip cuffs in my pocket.

"I believe I've made my point." Flavia stood tall with her nose in the air, once again her normal prim self.

"Honestly, Flavia," Violet said while dropping soggy paper sleeves into the nearest garbage bin, "I can't remember the last time you were in my shop. You finally come, and you do this?"

Flavia had the decency to look ashamed and nodded at the mess all over the floor. "I will repay you for the damages I have caused."

"You sure will." Violet was still fuming. "I intend to send you a bill. And I'm going to pad it out for the lost business from customer's you scared away."

"What about you, Reeva?" I asked. "Would you like to press assault charges?"

The vindictive side of me hoped she'd say yes. It wouldn't result in more than a fine and a night in jail, but oh, how satisfying would that be?

"Can I think on that for a bit?" Reeva asked. "I wouldn't want to make an emotional decision. I mean, if Martin was my son, I'd be upset too."

At the wicked gleam in Reeva's eye, Flavia lurched again. I had a good hold on her, though.

"If I don't hear from you by the end of the day," I told Reeva, "I'll assume you're passing on charges."

Before anything else could happen, I escorted Flavia out of the Bean Grinder and toward the Fairy Path entrance.

Villagers standing in pairs and small groups around the commons paused their conversations to stare. Shop owners stood on their porches with questioning looks and smirks hidden behind hands. Naturally, word had spread in record time about the commotion the sisters were causing.

As we passed Shoppe Mystique, Morgan caught my eye from where she stood on her porch. I shook my head, indicating I couldn't stop now, and continued to guide a muttering Flavia. I had no idea what she was saying, probably trying to put a hex of some kind on Reeva. Or maybe on me since I had initially encouraged her son to leave her house. She didn't seem to even notice where I'd taken her until I opened one of the holding cell doors and put her inside.

"Are you arresting me?" she asked.

"No. Lucky for you, no one's pressed charges. Yet. I'm putting you in time out. I want you to sit here for a while and cool down. I understand you're upset, but I cannot believe you just attacked your sister in public. Oh, I will be issuing a fine for disturbing the peace. Just to you, not Reeva."

Flavia stood there with her arms crossed. "Reeva always comes across as the innocent one." She sounded like a little girl whose sister just got away with breaking a prized family heirloom by blaming it on the cat. "She's fooling you, Jayne. She's fooling everyone. You'll see."

I pointed at the cot bolted to the wall. "Sit and chill."

As I crossed the room to my office, Meeka squeezed between the bars of the other cell, jumped up onto that cot, and stared at the crazy angry lady.

It had been more than a week since I'd been in the station, so this was a good opportunity to go through my emails and sort through the mail that had been shoved through the slot on the front door. As I figured, there was nothing urgent and only a few things of any real importance in my inbox, but it was full and needed sorting.

While I was on the computer, as I did every time, I checked on the status of the APB on my scummy and until recently unknown half-brother, Donovan Page. He'd escaped custody four months ago after being arrested on various charges surrounding my grandmother's death. Unfortunately, there was nothing new to report there. Not that I had expected to find anything. Deputy Atkins at the county sheriff's office had promised to contact me with any updates, no matter how small.

"Are you done in there yet?" Flavia demanded from the other room. "I have cooled down, as you requested, and would like to go now. I have an appointment."

"It's only been a half hour," I called back. "I still have a stack of mail to sort through."

As with the emails, ninety-five percent of the paper mail ended up in the recycle bin. There was one envelope that stood out, though. It was the size of a postcard and had only "Sheriff O'Shea" typed on the front. Someone had hand-delivered this card. Instinct took over, and I slid on a pair of latex gloves before opening it. Not wanting to smudge any possible fingerprints, I held it gently and only by the edges. I sliced the envelope open with a letter opener and slid out a plain white card. It looked to be standard cardstock that could be purchased at any office supply store and fed through a printer. As on the outside, I found only a single line of text when I opened the card.

I know what you did.

Was this a joke? What did I do? Then my mind went to everything that had happened surrounding Lupe Gomez last month. Was this related to that? It could have been a member of the Hernandez-Jackson family unhappy with how I'd handled things with Jacob and Matt. The card had been hand-delivered, though. Maybe it was a villager upset that I'd given Lupe so much leeway in the village all summer.

"Are you done with your mail yet?" Flavia asked. "You can't possibly have that much."

How long had I been sitting there going through the possibilities? My mind tended to run amok with options in situations like this. I looked down to see Meeka sitting in the office doorway. It seemed watching Flavia had become boring.

"You're right," I told my dog. "It's one envelope. For all I know, it could be some bored local kid looking to cause trouble."

Meeka cocked her head to the side, confused.

I slid the envelope and note into a plastic evidence bag, just in case, and placed it in the evidence locker on the far side of my office. I wrote out a ticket for disturbing the peace and crossed the building to Flavia's cell.

"It's about time," she said, gathering her possessions. "I think you've embarrassed me enough."

"Oh, Flavia. You know me better than that. If I wanted to embarrass you, I wouldn't do it in the privacy of the station." Before inserting the key in the lock, I handed her the citation.

"What's that?" She looked down her pointy nose at the offending paper.

"I told you I'd be fining you for disturbing the peace. Pay your ticket, and I'll let you go."

Flavia sniffed and dug into her small bag. Then she shoved some bills out through the bars at me.

"Thank you." I counted the cash and then asked, "What's going on with you and Reeva?"

"You heard it all." Her narrow, bony face flushed a medium pink, like she'd suddenly gotten a sunburn. "She's trying to steal my son, and I won't tolerate that."

"You do remember that I know all about your past, right? I know what happened between you and Karl and where

Yasmine came from." Her sunburn deepened. "I also know what you did to your sister's marriage."

Flavia had gotten pregnant by Reeva's husband the night of the comforting. After bribing Karl and Reeva with other damning, scandalous secrets, Reeva left Whispering Pines with the baby and raised her as her own in a small town north of Milwaukee. Then six months ago, twenty-year-old Yasmine returned to the village and turned up dead on my property.

"What's done is done," Flavia said dismissively.

"Maybe. Have you and Reeva ever talked about those events?"

Flavia sniffed. "Don't get all touchy-feely with me, Sheriff. My relationship with my sister is none of your concern."

"It is when it's the reason you're causing a scene in the middle of my village."

"Your village?" She laughed while tugging on her long leather gloves. "Someone is getting mighty big for her britches."

"My job is to maintain the peace. When you're physically attacking people in a public place, it's my job to stop it." I unlocked the cell door and held it open for her. "If it happens again, I'll gladly throw you right back in here. Don't doubt that for a second. And I'll press charges on behalf of the village."

She secured her drab-gray wool cloak around her neck and left the station without another word. She and Reeva were nowhere close to having dealt with their past, which meant more troubles. As I had been for the last six months, I would continue to keep an eye on her.

Alone now with nothing to do and nowhere near ready to go home, I looked at Meeka. "Let's go find Morgan."

Chapter 3

THE MOMENT WE ENTERED SHOPPE Mystique, Meeka paused for a pat from Morgan and Briar and then trotted straight to the reading room at the back of the building. Smart dog. It was toasty warm in there due to the fire roaring in the fireplace. She jumped up on one of the wingback chairs next to the hearth, curled into a ball, and promptly fell asleep.

"What was going on earlier?" Briar was arranging books about the Christmas/Yule season on the top shelf of the bookcase. "I went over to see if everything was okay. Violet had quite a mess to clean up."

I filled them in on the details while Morgan removed small pumpkins, gourds, and dried leaves from the mantel over the hearth and replaced them with pine boughs, pinecones, and red pillar candles.

"We knew this was coming," Morgan said. "I'm only surprised it's taken this long to boil over."

"The problem is," I said, handing her a dinner-plate-sized grapevine wreath with a pentacle woven into the center, "I don't think this is anywhere near the boiling point. Flavia was doing her best to get a rise out of Reeva—"

"And Reeva wouldn't take the bait?" Briar guessed.

"Reeva has always had the ability to stay calm and collected during the worst storms. Figuratively. I have no idea how she stands up to an actual storm."

I chuckled at the feisty lady as Morgan asked, "Did you handcuff her?" An evil little grin played across her mouth.

"I warned her that I would, but I didn't have any cuffs with me. I did give her a timeout in a jail cell for about an hour." I followed the pair out to the main room. "The topic of Flavia and Reeva is wearing me out. Can we talk about something else, please?"

"Sure we can. I'm glad to see you out and about," Briar said in that mom way that made me feel simultaneously proud of myself and ashamed. "The Lupe incident hit you hard, didn't it?"

"I guess." This topic wore me out even more, so I shifted to yet another one. "I almost went out to your cottage. Good thing Morgan was out on the porch earlier. I thought the shop was only open on weekends now."

"We're not open for business today," Morgan confirmed. "We're making sure everything is stocked and ready for our after-Thanksgiving customers." She took hold of the three-foot-tall and six-foot-long cornucopia sitting across from the door and dragged it out onto the front porch. It had been on display in that spot since Mabon Fest in late September. "We'll repurpose that as kindling for our fire pit. Now it's time for a Yule display."

"I can hardly wait." It was worth stopping into Shoppe Mystique just to see Morgan's decorations. "Can I help with something?"

"Are you bored, Jayne?" Briar asked.

"I'm trying not to be. There was a little excitement with the sisters this morning, but I haven't had anything real to do for the last three weeks."

"Is that why you're out of sorts?" Morgan drank from the

huge mug of water that was always at her side, staying hydrated for her growing baby.

I hesitated before telling them about the nightmare I'd been having. "What do you suppose that's all about? Other than that this week is the one-year anniversary of Frisky's death."

"Your subconscious is preparing you for something," Briar said with certainty.

When I arched a skeptical eyebrow, Morgan added, "The Universe provides in unexpected ways. You simply need to listen and watch for the messages. The list of unresolved issues you made during Samhain, was the incident with Frisky on it?"

"Of course. It's the event that led to everything else in my life changing. But how do I resolve it? It's not like I can talk to her."

Briar made a *phftt* sound. "I know some pretty talented fortune tellers who would disagree with that."

"What does Tripp think about this dream?" Morgan asked.

"That my present Lupe issues are melding with my past Frisky issues. I don't really get it."

"It's possible," Morgan suggested, "that the dream is more symbolic than an attempt to merge the two. There's nothing more you can do regarding Lupe. Perhaps her becoming Frisky means it's time to let that incident dissolve and finally deal with the Frisky event."

Anything was possible. If I could figure out why my brain thought the things it did, life would be a lot easier.

Morgan placed her hands to her lower back, winced, and stretched. "I'm already aching. I can only imagine how I'll feel toward the end of this pregnancy."

I studied her belly. "Has the baby grown since the last time I saw you . . . ten days ago? Significantly, I mean."

Morgan moved her hands to cover her visibly larger baby belly. "She has grown. We've officially entered the second trimester, and she's starting to make her presence known."

I tried to envision the small human tucked beneath the surface. "Is she kicking?"

"It's less of a kick and more of a flutter right now." Morgan smiled, looking peaceful and maternal. "Almost like a tiny butterfly flapping its wings in my womb."

We got back to work then. The Barlow women gave me the task of dusting shelves and sweeping out corners. Not very exciting, but it kept me busy and was far better than sitting at home alone. They also let me restock the "Amulets, Charms, and Talismans" table as long as I did it mindfully, which meant holding each piece in my hands and infusing it with a positive thought before putting it in its place on the table.

While I worked on my tasks, Briar strung pine and berry garlands around all the display cabinets, and Morgan set to work replacing the cornucopia with a five-foot Yule tree. Rather than strings of traditional Christmas lights, she used lights shaped like tiny candles and decorated it with pine cones and clove-studded oranges. There were also small pentacles made of twigs and secured with strips of raffia to little grapevine wreaths. My favorite ornaments were adorable six-inch tall Yule goddesses. Their arms, faces, and hair were made from corn husks; their skirts from pine needles, holly leaves and berries.

After a couple of hours adding touches to every area of the shop, they declared it ready for holiday business, both looking pleased with the festive appearance. Or rather, the new festive appearance. Shoppe Mystique was always festive.

"Are you going home?" I felt like a little kid who still wanted to play but all her friends got called in for the night.

"We are. It's been a long day." Morgan yawned as though

offering proof. "We'll see you tomorrow."

"Tomorrow? Does that mean you're coming to Triple G for the buffet?"

"River asked to spend time with us tomorrow, so Mama and I are planning an intimate dinner for three." She sighed but with less irritation regarding River than usual. He was clearly wearing her down with his suave charm and smoldering good looks. "We'll try to come to the pub afterward."

I roused Meeka from her nap, and we were all about to leave when I remembered the card I'd received.

Morgan frowned as I described it. "What are your instincts telling you about that?"

"That either someone is not happy about the way I dealt with the Jacob and Lupe thing or someone in the village is playing with me."

"Both situations are possible." Morgan closed her eyes and touched her thumbs and forefingers together like she did when she meditated. From the slight tilt of her head, she appeared to be tuning in to a frequency only she could hear. After a couple deep breaths, she opened them again. "It could also be related to something entirely different. Proceed with caution."

"The baby is enhancing her intuition." Briar patted Morgan's belly. "You'd be wise to listen."

I shivered. "I guess it could be someone I busted for something in Madison. Rosalyn has been talking up the B&B like crazy around town, which is great but not if the wrong person hears about it."

"Funny, isn't it?" Briar asked as she pulled on a deep-purple stocking cap with a matching pompom so big it spanned the width of her head. I had to smile. "Just when we think the road is clear, the Universe tosses in a speedbump. You're being tested, Jayne. Get through all of these little hiccups, and you'll be rewarded with a good life in the end."

"Keep in mind, though," Morgan added, "the life you think you want is not always the life you need. All will turn out as it is meant to, but it may not be anything like the one you've been planning for."

I had no life plan, so my world couldn't get too upset.

I zipped my fleece and headed for the door. "Is that what River is for you? A speedbump?"

The Barlow women had a tradition of raising their daughters—and they only had daughters—on their own. River, however, had decided he wanted to be involved with his baby's life and was refusing to leave.

"What if you get to the other side of this test," I continued, "and find out that life with River is what the Universe had in store for you?"

Morgan pointed a dagger-like black fingernail at me. "Don't make me put a pox on you."

"That baby is making you wicked." I giggled. "Ha! You're the wicked witch."

"Darling," Morgan purred, "that broom jockey has nothing on me."

"If anything," Briar stated, "baby girl is making her sassy. Thank you for the help, Jayne. If I have the energy, I'll wander down and watch a football game with you tomorrow too. That might be fun."

I hoped all three of them made it. Tripp was right. I was used to being around people. It would be different if my sheriff-ing responsibilities were quiet but I still had plenty to do at the B&B or vice versa. Having nothing on either side wasn't working so well. I needed to ease into this quiet Whispering Pines winter lifestyle.

Meeka and I said goodbye to the witches and turned east toward the station. We'd gone a few feet when I noticed a group of four women sitting in a circle on a blanket near the negativity well at the center of the Pentacle Garden. Probably villagers I'd never met yet. Many of them stuck close to their cottages during the tourist season, only venturing out to go to Sundry, the general store, in the early morning hours. More curious than concerned, I figured I'd wander over and say hi.

We made our way toward them, crunching along one of the gravel pathways, when the oldest of the four, an older woman with distinctive rectangular red glasses, looked up at us with a smile. She appeared to be their leader.

Late fifties or early sixties, twenty-five pounds overweight, short Afro haircut, light-brown complexion.

"Good afternoon," I called out as Meeka trotted over to the group. "I'm Jayne O'Shea, sheriff of Whispering Pines."

The woman got to her feet, groaning as she did, and topped out at five feet. "You're probably wondering what we're doing in the middle of your beautiful garden."

We glanced around the mostly barren plot. There were still a few patches of plants hanging on. Morgan called them "cold lovers"—pansies, kale, something called sedge, and witch hazel. Since the plants weren't ready to cash it in, the village green witches left them where they grew.

"Well," the woman reconsidered, "maybe it's not so beautiful right now, but I'm sure it's eye-popping in the warmer months." She held her hand out to me as she stepped forward. "I'm Octavia Smith, but everyone calls me Tavie. Pleased to meet you, Jayne. Or should I call you Sheriff?"

I glanced down at my jeans and lake-blue fleece jacket and realized I didn't look much like a sheriff. "I'll answer to either. What are you ladies doing out here on such a chilly day?"

"Let me introduce my girls first," Tavie said and pointed at one. "This is Gloria."

Early twenties, large round dark-brown eyes, olive complexion, apple cheeks, pointed chin, long messy black-brown hair.

Gloria raised a hand, fingers splayed wide in a wave. In a tiny but confident voice, she greeted, "Nice to meet you, Sheriff."

I had an overwhelming desire to pinch those cheeks. Fortunately, I controlled myself.

Tavie pointed to the next girl, who dutifully stood. "This is Melinda."

Five foot four, deep-auburn pixie-cut hair, twenty pounds underweight, chestnut-brown eyes, reddish freckles beneath both eyes and across her nose.

Her age was hard to determine because she was so little, but eighteen or nineteen seemed about right. She stepped forward and held a hand out to me as though closing a deal and, with a slight southern accent, said, "Good to meet you, ma'am. Hope we're not disturbing anything here."

"Not at all," I assured. "Just seems a little cold for you all to be sitting out here like this."

Melinda hugged a two-sizes-too-big quilted flannel shirt closer around her. "It is a bit chilly, but we're just about done."

Done with what? What had I interrupted?

Melinda took her seat between Gloria and the other girl.

"This is Silence," Tavie said of the third girl in jeans and a heavy beige sweater.

Nineteen or twenty, five foot seven, honey-blonde wavy hair halfway down her back, crystal-blue eyes, blindingly white teeth, scrubbed-clean ivory skin.

She immediately reminded me of a girl in the high school class above mine who would walk into the lunchroom, "accidentally" drop something, and three guys would swarm around her to pick the thing up. Inevitably, one would ask if she had plans for Friday night.

"Her name is Silence? That's unusual." Then I thought of where we were. Not much was considered unusual in Whispering Pines.

"Silence doesn't speak," Tavie explained as the girl gave a little curtsy and grinned at me, deep dimples piercing both cheeks. "She communicates with us through writing."

Tavie pushed the girl's hair over her shoulder as Silence held up a small whiteboard with *Pleasure to meet you, Sheriff* written on it.

I nodded, smiled at her, and to the group in general, stated, "Melinda said you're just about done. Done with what?"

Tavie gave Silence a fond smile, and the girl obediently took her seat again. Meeka padded over and sat at Silence's side, but not in an *I like her* way. Her attitude was more *She needs someone*. Weird, Meeka wasn't a trained therapy dog.

"We live in the Milwaukee area, just north of downtown," Tavie explained. "I run a boarding house for these girls. We heard about the troubles you all were having up here with the deaths and the kidnapping last month. We were just sick about it and have been praying for you."

Praying for us? An image of Tavie standing at a pulpit beckoning villagers to gather around flashed in my mind. "And you decided to come up and pray right here in the middle of the village?"

"Exactly." Tavie held up her hands. "Don't worry, we're not zealots. We didn't come here to try and convert anyone. The girls and I simply take comfort knowing that a higher power is watching over us. I'm not sure what it is, but there's something strong surrounding your village. We all sensed it as soon as we got here."

The girls nodded.

"It is okay that we sit here, isn't it?" Tavie had been nodding her head the whole time she spoke. Subliminally trying to convince me to agree with whatever she said? "We just felt . . . summoned, I guess, to be here and do what we know to do to help. And that is to pray."

A shiver shot up my spine. "Summoned?"

Tavie narrowed her eyes as she stared at me. "That's been happening, hasn't it? Others have said the same thing, haven't they?"

River Carr two months ago. My sister last month. Various visitors who stopped for lunch and stuck around for a few days. Tripp arrived shortly before I did in May and decided to stay.

"There have been a few occurrences," I acknowledged.

"Being called to a place doesn't always mean you're going somewhere good. Sometimes, it means you've got work to do."

I swallowed. "I understand that." I almost told her that's why I stayed in Whispering Pines after initially coming to sell Gran's house. It's not that I felt summoned, but once I got here, I knew this was where I was meant to be. That's how it was for my grandparents, too, which was fortunate since they'd bought the two thousand acres sight unseen. "Where are the four of you staying?"

"We don't have a place yet," Melinda said with a touch of irritation and a quick glance at Tavie.

"We got here about an hour ago," Tavie explained, "and have been walking around exploring the place." She pointed at the white marble well at the center of the garden. "This felt like the strongest spot, so we decided to sit and offer our prayers here first. Finding somewhere to stay was the next item on our agenda. Do you recommend anywhere in particular?"

Biting back a grin, I said, "Since you asked, I happen to own a bed-and-breakfast and have plenty of room available. Our prices—"

Tavie waved me off. "Doesn't matter what your prices are." She turned to the trio sitting on the ground and looking hopefully up at us. "What do you say, girls? Should we take the sheriff up on her offer?"

All three agreed.

"I was just about to head home. Where did you park?"

Melinda and Silence pointed northwest as Tavie said, "In the parking lot just past the campground."

"I'll meet you there. I've got to get my car."

Feeling suddenly revived and excited for the first time in a week, with the exception of looking forward to the upcoming Thanksgiving buffet and football game marathon, of course, I noted a little skip in my step as Meeka and I made our way back to the station.

Chapter 4

IT WAS ALMOST EMBARRASSING HOW excited I was to have these four ladies come stay with us at Pine Time. Picking up on my mood, Meeka was excited, too, and pranced around me as we walked along the Fairy Path. I understood now why Gran was so eager and willing to let others stay when they showed up on her doorstep. That big house needed to have lots of people in it.

Ten minutes after leaving the quartet, I pulled into the west side lot to find Gloria and Melinda piling into the back of a little black Mercedes SUV.

"The house isn't far from here," I told Tavie. "Only about a two-minute drive."

"I can't tell you how happy we are about this," Tavie said as she slid into the driver's seat. "We knew we'd find a place. We just hadn't expected our host to come to us."

They followed me west along the highway and then south onto the short road that became my long driveway. I slowed as we passed the Whispering Pines campground. It had been closed for the season since the beginning of the month, so the olive-green Excursion and royal-blue Nissan pickup truck that had caught my attention earlier today stood out like cats at a mouse gathering. Guess I'd been right about them wanting to camp. They'd made themselves comfortable with pitched tents and a big campfire.

I stopped my vehicle and motioned for Tavie to pull up next to me. When she did, Silence lowered the passenger's side window.

"I need to make a quick stop here and find out what's going on," I told them. "The bed-and-breakfast is at the end of this drive. I won't be long. One of the patio doors in the back should be open, so go on inside and make yourselves comfortable."

Tavie gave me a thumbs up and continued down the drive.

I backed up, pulled into the campground, and took a right onto the one-way path that wound past the campsites. The group stared at me as I came to a stop near them.

"Hey there," I said with as much Whispering Pines friendliness as I could muster. "Can I help you with something?"

The man I'd seen driving the Excursion earlier stepped forward. *Five foot eight, mid-thirties, goatee, short wavy medium-brown hair, scrawny and sickly looking.*

With a slow drawl, he asked, "And how do you figure you can help us, little lady?"

Suddenly, I wished I hadn't removed my Glock back at the station. To his credit, I wasn't in uniform which made his confusion understandable.

"It's just that," I began, not sounding anywhere near as confident as I intended to, "the campground is closed right now. You can't be here."

A woman in painted-on jeans tucked into knee-high Sorel boots trimmed with faux fur at the cuff sauntered over and stood next to him. The bleached-blonde hair I'd gotten a flash of earlier hung to her waist and looked fried and frizzy up close.

"You can't force us to leave," she said with as much

vibrato as her husband. Or boyfriend. I glanced at her left hand. No ring.

One of the other couples, both somewhere in their thirties, came out of a nearby tent. These two were a striking pair, but in a kind of creepy way. Their hair color was identical, as in they probably used the same deep-auburn dye mixture at the salon. They had matching widow's peaks. Their skin tone was even the same pale ivory. They looked like they could be siblings, but by the way she held tight to his hand and hugged his arm in front of her like a protective shield, I guessed they were together. So I hoped they weren't related.

"What can we do for you?" this new man asked. "I'm Lars Sundstrom, by the way. This is my girlfriend, Didi Stieber."

I looked at the first two. "And you are?"

"Don't really feel the need to tell you that," the first man said with a pointed glare at Sundstrom. "Why don't you tell me your name, and we'll see how this goes."

Fortunately, I had my badge with me. Except, when I reached into my pocket to get it, Mr. Backwoods must've decided I was pulling a weapon. In the blink of an eye, he had unsheathed a hunting knife. He was taunting me with it, pinching it between his thumb and first two fingers, wiggling it as though wanting to make sure I knew he had it.

It wasn't a very big knife, but the striped handle was so distinctive, I couldn't miss it. The handle appeared to be made from narrow slices of different woods stacked and probably glued together. The blade had a swirly design etched into it. Even from six feet away, I could tell it was a skillfully made weapon.

The four other people traveling with these two couples had been sitting around the campfire outside the farthest tent. When the knife came out, the three men and one woman got to their feet and formed a half circle behind Sundstrom, Stieber, and the other unnamed pair.

From the back of my Cherokee, I could hear Meeka barking. She was sensing my emotions again, and right now she surely knew my heart rate was elevated and my adrenaline was pumping.

I raised a hand in a calming gesture and slowly removed my badge from my pocket. "There's no reason to get upset. Everyone, just stay calm." I held up my badge and showed it to them. "I'm out of uniform but am the sheriff of Whispering Pines. Jayne O'Shea."

The first man looked at Sundstrom as he returned the knife to the sheath at his side. Then he stared me down. "I'm Gavin Lindsey. She's Kendra, my girl."

Girl. Not girlfriend. He was older but not enough that she could be his daughter. The way she leveled a blank stare on him and sighed told me the word was a chauvinistic claiming and not a term of endearment.

I met eyes with them one by one. "Gavin. Kendra. Lars. Didi. And who are the rest of you?"

One of the men and the other woman introduced themselves as Darryl Allen and Cheryl Carpenter. The other two were Chaz Lindsey and Marcel Allen. I guessed they were brothers of Gavin and Darryl.

I returned my badge to my pocket and took a shuffle step closer to my vehicle. "Are you all passing through?"

"Eventually." Gavin was clearly the leader of this troupe. "Thought we'd hang out for a few days."

Kendra flipped her fried hair behind her shoulder and nodded in agreement.

"We're happy to have you," I told them while willing my racing heart to relax. "And if you were only staying one night, I'd probably let this go, but like I said before, the campground is closed for the season. I can't let you stay here."

"What's the problem?" Lindsey hitched his thumbs in his belt loops, his legs bowing as he shifted his stance. "Not like we're disturbing anyone."

"Rules," I said with a shrug, forcing myself to stay in full sheriff mode. "I don't make them, but I do have to enforce them. If you follow the highway east, you'll come to a hotel. It's about two miles from here, little more. There are actually four of them side by side, but only the first one is still open for business. The others have shut down for the season. I happen to know the open one has rooms available."

"What if we decide we don't want to leave? It'll get a little chilly at night, but we got ways to stay warm." Lindsey hooked Kendra around the waist and yanked her close. To each their own, but the thought of sleeping next to that man made my skin crawl.

"Gav." Sundstrom stepped in and slapped a hand on his shoulder. "We don't need to be causing any troubles, man. Let's just do as the sheriff asked." Then more quietly but still loud enough for me to hear, he added, "Remember why we're here. It doesn't really matter where we stay."

As Sundstrom spoke in calming tones with Lindsey, my own adrenaline level decreased. This wasn't a good thing, not right now. I knew only too well that, in about a minute, I'd get weak in the knees and need to sit down.

Lindsey and Sundstrom had a little discussion about whether doing as I asked was a big deal or not, Lindsey's point being he didn't want some *woman* telling him what to do.

"Especially the sheriff of this little messed up village," Lindsey hissed.

Messed up village? It took all my willpower to ignore that.

"Look," I confronted, "there's no discussion to be had. You can't stay here." This statement served two purposes. First, to exert my authority. Second, to increase my adrenaline level again. I couldn't be going all noodle-legged with the

Backwoods Boys deciding if they were going to obey me or not.

Finally, Sundstrom convinced Lindsey it was best to do as I'd asked so they didn't get kicked out of the village altogether. The others didn't seem to care one way or the other. This made my instincts regarding this group flare yet again. Why were they so focused on being in Whispering Pines? Sundstrom made it sound like they were here for a specific purpose. What could that possibly be? I asked and got the response I'd pretty much expected.

"You're a nosey one," Lindsey replied. "Ain't really none of your business why we're here."

Oh, how I wished I could arrest people for being disrespectful. The jails would be crammed full all the time.

"We're planning to do a little hunting," Sundstrom added in an attempt to ease the tension. "Probably hang out in the village for a couple days."

While the group tore down their campsite, I leaned against my vehicle and watched them. First, though, I let Meeka out of her cage because she was going ballistic back there with the need to protect me. After she was loose, I pulled my Glock out of the carrying case and slid it into my jacket pocket. Best to be prepared.

They tore down quickly and, within twenty minutes, were ready to leave the campground. Lindsey, Kendra, Didi, Sundstrom, Darryl, and Cheryl loaded into the Excursion. Chaz and Marcel got in the pickup truck with all the gear tossed in the back. Lindsey circled the Excursion around and stopped next to me. My immediate thought was that they were going the wrong way on a one-way road and I should scold them for that. Fortunately, I realized I wasn't firing on all cylinders at the moment due to reduced blood sugar and kept my mouth shut.

"Can I see that badge again?" Lindsey asked, wanting me

to prove I was who I claimed to be, I guessed. I pulled it out and flashed it in his face, close enough that he could see but far enough away that he couldn't grab my arm. "Yep, says sheriff. So, you're that lady sheriff I been hearing so much about. Sounds to me like you could use some help up here since you ain't doing much good for these people. Are you?"

Before I could respond, he stomped on his gas, spraying gravel at Chaz's pickup truck behind him. I stood at the ready with my hand clutching the gun in my pocket until both vehicles turned onto the highway and were on the way to the hotel. Then my legs went weak and I slumped hard against my truck.

Chapter 5

I COULDN'T DECIDE WHICH WAS more upsetting, that I was about to crash because the adrenaline rush was over, or the words Lindsey had said before he sped off. Who was I kidding? No question, it was Lindsey. He had just verbalized my biggest fear since taking over as sheriff, that I wasn't going to be able to serve this village properly. But where had that fear stemmed from? That I was a woman? Because I was young? Or maybe it was this place. I never doubted myself in Madison. Not before Frisky died, at least.

Fortunately, I'd left a small bag of M&Ms in the glove box from the last time I went grocery shopping with Tripp. It took a few minutes, but the sugar gave me an energy boost and I was able to get back to work. Lindsey's group had left the fire burning, and I wanted to make sure it was out before I drove away.

Once at home, I entered through the back door and heard laughter and general commotion coming from the kitchen. At first, I thought Tripp was making something for our guests, but his truck was still gone, and the laughter and voices were all female. I found Melinda, Silence, and Gloria giggling and going through the pantry and all the cupboards while talking about what to make. Well, Melinda and Gloria were giggling and talking. Silence scribbled on her whiteboard with a dry-erase pen. Tavie sat at the kitchen bar, supervising them. She turned and smiled at me after Meeka rushed in and let out some excited *yips*, joining in the fun.

"They're only looking," Tavie assured. "They love to cook, though, and want to know if they can make dinner for us tonight."

I had told them to make themselves at home. I'd meant have a seat in the great room and wait for me, not take over my kitchen, but they weren't hurting anything by looking. Since I had zero idea when Tripp and River would be home, I said, "I guess that would be all right. Do we have everything they need? We could run over to the store."

"Are you kidding?" Melinda asked with the same giddy expression Tripp sometimes got while preparing his menus. "This kitchen has everything."

Tavie pulled out the stool next to her and indicated I should sit. "Melinda makes the best sloppy joe's you'll ever taste, and Gloria can fix a salad that even the biggest vegetable hater will love. Silence is our baker and will whip up a batch of blondies that will rival anything sold in your local bakery. And yes, we stopped in there for scones and coffee when we got here."

"What's a blondie?" I asked.

Everyone looked to Silence who wrote on her whiteboard, then turned it to face me. *Vanilla brownies.*

"Sounds fantastic. Go right ahead, my kitchen is yours." Or rather, Tripp's kitchen was theirs. A little voice in my ear said, *won't he be upset to have people taking over his territory*? Possibly, but I didn't see the harm. And unless he came home for dinner, he'd never know anyone had been in there. "Why don't I get you all settled into your rooms before you start that."

"How many rooms do you have?" Gloria wanted to know.

"Five of the seven are available. Business is a little slow this weekend." Much to Tripp's conflicted delight. We needed the business, but finishing the attic was high on his to-do list.

The three stared at each other with hopeful, excited expressions and then at Tavie.

"Can we?" Gloria asked.

"Oh, please," Melinda begged. "Please say yes."

Silence folded her hands together and nodded her head eagerly, eyes wide and bright.

Tavie smiled at the trio and asked, "Is it all right for us to take four of those rooms?"

All right? I mentally shoved away the dollar signs in my eyes. "If you want to pay for them, I'm happy to rent them to you."

While Tavie and I took care of the business side of the rentals, I could hear the girls clomping around upstairs looking at the available rooms. Meeka was barking, her happy bark, and was surely chasing them from room to room. I told them that The Suite at the top of the stairs was already booked, but they could duke it out over the others. A few minutes later, they came back downstairs with their decisions made: Tavie would have The Alcove with the inviting window seat and a breathtaking view of the lake. Melinda wanted The Jack, and Gloria said she'd take The Jill next door. Silence was torn between The Treehouse and The Side but settled on The Side, which put her close to Tavie.

Once they'd taken all their bags up to their rooms, the girls got to work on dinner.

"Something's bothering you," Tavie noted as we watched them cook.

"It's nothing to worry about," I said with a dismissive shrug. "Those people at the campground were a little challenging."

I fixed two mugs of tea and tried to pry Meeka away from

Silence's side. The Westie wouldn't budge, determined to stay near the girl. Figuring I should at least keep an eye on Tripp's kitchen, Tavie and I settled down at the six-chair oval dinette set Tripp and I had recently added to the kitchen area. A guest had mentioned it would be nice to have a table where people could spread out with games or a cup of coffee and look out at the lake. We decided it was a great idea and wondered why we hadn't thought of it before.

We sipped our tea and listened to the giggling and meal-planning discussion. Breaks in the conversation meant Silence was writing on her board.

"I have to ask, is Silence really her name?"

Tavie nodded. "That's what she calls herself."

While she gazed at her boarders with a proud smile, the back of my neck prickled. I had no reason to believe this arrangement was anything but legitimate. The girls seemed happy and comfortable with Tavie and each other. The cop in me always needed to verify things, though.

"Do you mind if I ask—"

"How old she is? Do I know anything more about her?" Tavie guessed. "She's eighteen, a legal adult. She showed me her ID, so I know her legal name and where she came from. She asked me to keep that information to myself, however."

I relaxed a little. If Silence was eighteen, her life was her own. "Is she hiding from someone?"

"She is. She told me she ran away from home shortly before her eighteenth birthday because her uncle hit her and her single mother wouldn't do anything about it."

"You look skeptical about that."

Tavie lifted a shoulder. "I'm the last one to downplay any sort of physical abuse, so don't take it that way, but I think it was worse than being hit. Right before she came to me, Silence had been selling herself on the streets so she'd have a place to sleep at night. She needs help getting on her feet and seems comfortable with us. Who am I to mess with something that's working?"

"Is it that she can't talk or that she won't?"

"I believe it's the latter. Every now and again, I hear singing coming from somewhere in the house. It's always when the other two are either with me or out of the house. I'm sure it's Silence and not music from somewhere. She's a good girl and an absolute joy to have around, so I'll let her have that little secret."

With the blondies in the oven, the meat mixture simmering on the stove, and lettuce soaking in the crisper, the girls asked where we should eat. I pointed toward the dining room and told them they could use any of the dishes in the china cabinet. They went off to set the table, and I turned back to find Tavie studying me hard.

"Something's really eating at you, Madame Sheriff. What did those people at the campground say that's got you so upset?"

It went deeper than what Lindsey had said, but I wasn't about to get into all that with a stranger. There was something about this vibrant woman that made me want to open up to her, though. Since she shared a little about her life, I could share a little of mine.

"It wasn't all of them, just their apparent leader. He told me I needed help here, insinuating that a woman sheriff couldn't possibly know what she was doing."

Tavie nodded slowly, eyes still on me. "Hit a nail of some kind right on its head, did he?"

"I guess." And just that quickly, I was sharing more. "It's a long story, but something happened a year ago that kind of knocked my confidence down a few pegs."

"It's always a struggle for women," Tavie interrupted my thoughts. "Always having to prove ourselves. Even harder for someone like you in a male-dominated career."

The tone in her voice told me she understood exactly what I was experiencing. The strong women of Whispering Pines sided with me, but quite honestly, they were secluded from the "real" world up here. Also, the female villager population outnumbered the males by almost two to one. Many of them had either been born here or had lived in the village since they were young. They'd been able to live their lives on their terms without a lot of flak, from either men or society, and couldn't fully appreciate the frustration I felt when I was challenged regarding my abilities.

"Even here," I began, "in a place where I thought it would be easy to do my thing, it sometimes is a struggle. I'll feel like I'm at the top of my game for weeks, and then one sideways comment can push all those fears right back to the surface."

"How big of an issue is this thing that happened a year ago?"

I stared into my now-empty tea mug and thought, *it's huge*. At least, at the time, it was huge. My life had moved past all that darkness when I came to Whispering Pines. What I told her, though, was, "I took a good deal of harassment for it from the men at my station, but not because I'm a woman. I was expected to remain loyal to my 'brothers in blue.'"

"Have you dealt with it? This thing that happened?" Tavie asked, using the same tone I heard from Dr. Maddox, my therapist in Madison.

"I saw a therapist."

"That's not what I asked. The fact that you're somehow associating that event with the comment this man made tells me this thing is buried deep and still needs to be addressed."

"It's not that the two events are associated. They're really not. It's more that I'm feeling vulnerable right now, for various reasons, and the man's comment made that feeling worse."

She studied me again. "You haven't closed that year-old circle yet. Anniversaries can be good times to deal with old wounds."

I laughed, thinking about how much she sounded like some of the witches and fortune tellers in this village. "You could fit in very well here."

"Honey," she pushed her shoulders back, "I could fit in anywhere I go. And as I understand it, that means I can't fit here. Am I right?"

"Hit it right on the head." I winked and let the conversation go quiet for a few minutes as the girls focused on their final meal preparations. I refilled our tea mugs and asked Tavie as I sat, "You said you came here to pray for the village."

"We did."

"You know what's been going on here, then."

She sipped and sighed. "I'd never even heard of Whispering Pines until last month when that boy went missing. Then the reports surfaced about how there had been one death after another here since the start of the tourist season in May. There's something very broken in this village, isn't there?"

"I think so. It's my mission to figure out what it is exactly, but with each new bad thing that happens, I feel like I'm failing at my job."

"Which is also why that man's comment hit so hard."

Melinda stood before us with a kitchen towel draped over a bent arm like a server at a high-class restaurant. She stood tall with her shoulders back and chin high, then cleared her throat and announced importantly, "Dinner is served." She bowed low, arm still bent, and held her other arm out toward the dining room.

Thank goodness. I was saying way more to this woman than I'd intended to.

Gloria held out the chair at the head of the table closest to the hallway and indicated that seat was for me. Silence did the same at the opposite end with a chair for Tavie.

"Can you believe I rarely eat in here?" I told the group as we all settled.

"That's an absolute shame," Gloria said wistfully, looking around. "This is a nice room."

What was her story? I'd learned a bit about Silence, but what about the rest of them? Tavie as well. It felt inappropriate to ask. They were guests, not friends after all, but I'd love to know about all of them.

"Just seems to be the way it goes," I explained. "We're always so busy serving our guests that when it's time for us to eat, we just sit at the kitchen bar. Sometimes we go out on the deck, which I love. Maybe now that we're into the slower time of year, we can make a point of having dinner in here."

"Who is 'we?'" Melinda wanted to know, a mischievous grin lighting up her face.

I couldn't help but smile back. "Tripp Bennett. My partner."

Silence scribbled on her whiteboard. *He's your boyfriend, isn't he?*

"Oooo. Jayne's got a boyfriend," Gloria said in a singsong while Melinda made kissing noises. It was like suddenly inheriting three annoying little sisters.

"He is my boyfriend," I admitted.

"Duh." Melinda rolled her eyes. "First you blushed then you grinned like he's the greatest thing ever."

Silence batted her big beautiful blue eyes and held up, *Is he?*

"The greatest thing ever?" I asked. "Most days."

Where did that come from? Supposedly, the truth was revealed when you replied with the first thing that popped into your mind. Tripp was the best thing that had happened in my life in a very long time. There'd been a bit of tension between us lately, however. As exciting as it was to move in together, we had to get to know each other in a whole different way. We had to learn to sleep with someone else in the bed . . . and all that went along with that. Then there was dealing with the invasion of previously personal space, such as one of us leaving dirty clothes in a heap in the corner—me—and the other insisting they belonged in a hamper. It was just growing pains. I knew that. We'd be fine after the adjustment period. However long that took.

We piled buns with Melinda's sloppy joe meat, heaped Gloria's salad into salad bowls, and had just dug in when the front door opened.

Chapter 6

MY BACK WAS TO THE door, so my four guests saw who had entered before I did. Still, I knew who it was. I turned to see Tripp and River standing in the dining room entryway looking surprised. As I introduced everyone, I noted the girls' reactions. Gloria's mouth formed an *O*. Melinda leaned back in her chair and let her eyes travel head to toe over the two men. Silence fluffed her hair and smiled so big the dimples in her cheeks got crazy deep. Tavie stood and walked around the table, hand extended.

"Which one of you is Tripp Bennett?" she asked, her hand pivoting between the two until Tripp held his out.

"That would be me. This is our friend, River Carr. And who are all of you?"

"Tavie Smith," she announced. "Jayne found us in the Pentacle Garden and took us in like a pack of strays."

Tripp looked at me, amused, with an eyebrow cocked in question.

I laughed and explained, "It wasn't quite like that. They were in the Pentacle Garden holding a prayer session for our village, and I asked if they had a place to stay." The praying part amused him too. "Good news, we're almost fully booked. One room left."

Tripp analyzed the remainder of dinner still on the table. "I know you can grill just about anything, but I've never seen you make anything like this."

"And you still haven't. Melinda, Gloria, and Silence made dinner for us tonight." I winked at the three of them. "You've got a little competition."

"Would you like something to eat?" Gloria asked Tripp and River. "I'll get plates for you."

"It looks good," Tripp began, "but we stopped for dinner before coming home."

That little spot in me that angered easily lately, flared. Tripp didn't even call to ask if he could bring me something.

"Regretfully," River announced in his standard formal way, "I must again depart to visit my lady and her mother."

"I couldn't eat another bite." Tripp placed a hand over his stomach. "But I'll sit with you all if that's okay."

Silence nodded eagerly, her eyes sparkling, and patted the seat between her and Tavie for him to take. Interesting. The seemingly shy girl had some impressive flirting skills. Her quiet way worked like a charm and she captured Tripp in her web within seconds. I assumed that was how she used to secure her "place to sleep at night." Not that that's what she was doing now. Her actions seemed innocent enough, but perhaps like me always being prepared with my badge and weapon, it was old habits rising to the occasion?

We chatted as we continued eating and laughed our heads off over Gloria's impersonation of Mickey Mouse, which wasn't much of a stretch for her considering her naturally tiny voice. When we were done with the meal, Silence brought out the blondies. Tripp helped himself to one of those. He declared them delicious and asked her to leave the recipe.

"In the afternoon," he explained, "I leave cookies on the table in the hallway for our guests. I think they'd love these."

As they were washing and putting away the dishes, the trio convinced Tripp to let them make breakfast in the morning. Then they ran off to their rooms, excited for a night of bubble baths and privacy.

"They'll take over the house if you let them," Tavie warned. Her eyes shifted between Tripp and me, and the smallest of frowns turned her mouth. "Just say no if they're intruding."

"They're not intruding," I assured. "I'm happy to have you all here."

Happier than I could explain. Something about this woman comforted me. She felt like a beloved aunt who had come for a visit. The girls like cousins.

She pulled me to the side, away from Tripp. "Silence isn't up to anything. I saw the looks you were giving her at the table."

I was going to object but instead said, "Is she like that with all men?"

"Not always. She tends to turn it on when she's out of her comfort zone or feeling insecure. I think it's a self-protection thing, like she's keeping her skills sharp, so to speak, in case she ever needs them again."

My heart hurt for the girl. "I hate that she feels that's what she has to resort to."

"Sadly, there are far too many like her." Tavie gave my shoulder a little pat and headed for the stairs. "I noticed books in the alcove at the top of the staircase. May I borrow one?"

"Of course. We put them there for guests to use. Let us know if you need anything else. We're in this room down here. Just knock."

"I might interrupt something," she replied with a sassy grin. "At least I hope I would."

I smiled as I let Meeka out to patrol the yard and then joined Tripp on the couch. "You two were gone a long time today."

"We had a lot to do. River also wanted to pick up some things for the baby that Morgan mentioned. Then we stopped for dinner. I didn't realize we had guests. You could've called. My cell phone works outside the village, you know."

I stiffened. "That means it also makes calls. You could've called and let me know you wouldn't be home for dinner. And I'm fully capable of checking in a few guests by myself."

"That's not what I meant." He paused before adding, "Sorry I didn't call."

I crossed my arms and stared out the windows at the moonlight glinting off the lake and then over at the boathouse. From here, I could see the front edge of the deck. On some nights, like tonight, it still felt strange to not cross the yard to my little apartment at the end of the day. After six months of having space all to myself—something I hadn't had since leaving my parents' home nearly a decade ago—I couldn't really relax. I could get into bed, but sometimes I just wanted to take off my bra and sprawl on the couch. The great room was the equivalent of a hotel lobby, so I couldn't do that with guests wandering around.

"Any idea when you'll be done with the attic?" I asked.

"You keep asking me that. I told you, drywalling takes a long time. Once that's done, everything else should come together quickly."

"When will you be done with the drywalling then?"

"Soon. Would you like me to go up and work on it now?"

I didn't respond, hating that we were so short with each other lately. "What's wrong?"

"Why do you think something's wrong with *me*?"

I ignored the implication that the problem was with me. "Because until we moved in together, we never argued. It feels like that's all we're doing right now."

"It takes two to argue. What's bothering you?"

"Lack of privacy."

He laughed, a huffy little sound. "You can't be serious. You've had nothing but privacy. We haven't had guests other than River in ten days, so it's not like anyone's been bothering you. Today was the first time you left the house or gone to the station in a week. All you've done is mope around here while River and I work on the attic."

"Then maybe I should say too much privacy. I thought we were going to work on the attic together, and River would help us now and then. I haven't been allowed to do a thing. What's the problem? You don't think I'm capable of using a power tool?"

We sat in steaming silence until Meeka pawed at the door. I let her in, then headed for bed. A few minutes later, Tripp climbed in next to me. Not ready to be done being mad, I pulled the blankets up to my neck.

"Look," his voice was softer now. "I know the thing with Lupe really threw you. It threw a lot of us. I also know you don't have a lot going on right now. That's why I'm working so hard to get the attic done. So we'll have our own space."

"This room isn't enough?" Don't know why I even asked the question. It wasn't anywhere near enough. While it wasn't tiny, there was only room for the bed, a six-drawer dresser, and two chairs with a small table between them by the bay window. Those chairs were the only place we could sit and chill that wasn't in public view.

"No." He turned my face, so I was looking at him. "It's nowhere near enough. We need more than a room that we're borrowing from our guests. Someplace we can make our own."

"That's what I want too. I'd like to have a little more say in what's going on up there, though. At this rate, the apartment is going to be yours and River's, not yours and mine."

That wasn't quite fair. Tripp and I designed the space together. We chose the colors and bathroom tile together. I just felt very left out of the process now.

"Other than going to 3G to eat and watch the games tomorrow, the plan was for River and me to do nothing but work on the apartment."

"Has that plan changed?"

He flung a hand toward the second floor. "Yeah. We have guests. Now, I have to get up and make breakfast. I hadn't planned for that."

"Sorry I brought business in and messed up your day. You don't have to worry about tomorrow. You told the girls they could make breakfast."

And suddenly, we were angry again. We lay there, neither of us wanting to speak first, but Tripp finally did. "River told me he's now planning to be over at Morgan's all day tomorrow. Would you like to help me sand the final coat of drywall spackle before we go to the buffet?"

Forcing my irritation away, I said, "Sure. I'd like that."

There was a long pause before Tripp said, "So you went into the village today? Anything exciting going on?"

I rolled onto my side to face him and told him about the Flavia and Reeva debacle. "I think there might also be a little trouble brewing in the village again."

"What now?"

"There was this group trying to stay at the campground." I explained the whole incident.

Tripp pushed a lock of hair behind my ear. "Is that why you're suddenly accusing me of sexism? Because of what that guy said? If anything, I'm afraid you're more capable of using a power tool than me."

Now he was patronizing me. Or maybe I was just cranky. I inhaled deep and exhaled hard. "It might be nothing. Maybe they were just trying to be tough guys. But—"

"But your instincts are tingling. Be careful, babe, okay?" Then preemptively, "I know I don't need to tell you that. I know you know what you're doing and are great at it." He flipped onto his back. "Good thing we live where we do. I'd worry all day, every day in a place the size of Milwaukee or even Madison."

After a quick peck of a goodnight kiss, I lay there wondering if he was trying to make a point of some kind. Did he want me to step down as sheriff? He'd mentioned many times that he'd be happy if we just ran the B&B together. The thing was, being sheriff wasn't just my job, it was part of who I was. If he couldn't accept that, he couldn't accept me.

Chapter 7

I WOKE TO THE SMELL of bacon. What a fabulous way to start the day. I stretched happily and rolled to face the sunny windows, surprised to find Tripp watching me.

"You smelled bacon and thought it was me?" he asked.

"Yes. Bacon always makes me think of you."

"It's the girls. Remember?"

I stretched while saying, "We should hire teenagers to cook breakfast for us every day. That way you can lounge in bed with me longer."

"We'll have our own someday. I'll teach them young. I'm thinking three or four. Then we don't have to wait until they're teenagers."

He knew I wasn't ready to talk about having kids. I distracted him from the comment by giving him a proper good morning greeting and then slid into the shower. On one hand, I was glad that the fight from last night was done. On the other, it upset me that we just moved on rather than talking about whatever had caused the fight.

Breakfast consisted of bacon, scrambled eggs, cut up fruit, and banana-nut muffins. That would be just enough to hold me until we headed to the Thanksgiving buffet around one.

"Did you still want to help me upstairs?" Tripp asked after the girls pushed him out of the kitchen, insisting they would clean up everything and put it all back exactly where they'd found it.

"Sure," I answered. "It's been a few days since I've seen the progress."

"Don't get too excited. Not a lot has changed."

The hallway on the second floor formed what Rosalyn and I always thought of as a racetrack. We always started at Gran's bedroom door and ran in opposite directions around the "track." The first one back to Gran's room won. I was bigger and had longer legs, but Rozzie was faster.

When Tripp and I got to the top of the attic stairs, he held aside the sheet of heavy plastic hanging there to keep the drywall dust from floating down to the bedrooms.

In the back-right corner of the space was a platform elevated by two steps and tucked into an alcove. We thought that would be the perfect spot for the bed. Tucked next to the stairs in the front-right corner was a space twice as long as it was wide. That would be our walk-in closet. Straight ahead was the bathroom with a small window that let in lots of light. A small kitchenette took up the far left-hand corner and was open to what would be our living room. A row of three four-feet-tall by two-feet-wide dormer windows gave a great view of the lake.

We'd decided to go with light moody-blue walls, ivory on the ceiling, black trim, and medium-brown floors. I could already picture how cozy it would be.

"It's coming along," I said and sneezed from all the dust. "What do you want me to do?"

"Prepare to get dusty."

He showed me how to sand the spackled wall seams, not that it was a difficult task, but this was the final coat and it was important that it be as smooth as possible. I slid on a pair of goggles and a dust mask and got to work. While I couldn't say it was an enjoyable job, there was something meditative about it. My mind went from one topic to another—the recent rash of arguments with Tripp, the people at the campground, and what I was going to do with myself all winter. I'd be decorating our new apartment but hanging curtains and choosing throw pillows wouldn't take long. I really did need a hobby.

Two hours later, Tripp declared the sanding portion of the job officially complete. The dust was powder fine and got everywhere, so we spent another hour vacuuming. We hadn't finished, but it was time to head over to Grapes, Grains, and Grub.

After taking a second shower—seriously, that dust got everywhere—I slipped on my uniform shirt and paused. This was a fun community gathering. I didn't need to be Sheriff O'Shea tonight so took off the shirt and swapped it for my "87" Packers jersey instead. Then I contemplated the tools I usually carried in my cargo pockets. I would skip the cargos tonight, too, and wear jeans but couldn't go unprepared. Wearing my shoulder holster and having my Glock on display didn't feel right, but I fully expected Gavin Lindsey and his gang to show up and cause problems. I dug out my waist holster. The jersey nicely covered my weapon while still affording easy access should the need arise. Best of both worlds. And team spirit.

I grabbed my badge along with a few zip-strip cuffs to shove in the pocket of my fleece jacket and left the room to find Tavie and the girls in the great room. Like every other young adult I knew, Silence, Melinda, and Gloria were sprawled on the sofas, staring intently at their cell phones.

"They're not bored, are they?" I asked Tavie.

"Bored? Roaming this beautiful home, no chores, and that lake view? They're in heaven."

In a hushed tone, I noted, "But they're not viewing the lake."

"Yes, we are," Melinda said, eyes seemingly never leaving the phone's screen.

"They have their ways," Tavie said with a chuckle.

I was out of touch. When I lived in Madison, my cell phone was an accessory I was never without. Pulling it out to text someone or snap a quick picture had been as common as pulling out a credit card to pay for a cup of coffee. Something else I didn't have to do anymore thanks to Violet's *No family member of Lucy O'Shea's ever has to pay for coffee in my shop* generosity. Over the last six months, with cell reception in the village being nonexistent unless connected to WiFi, my phone had become a device for notes and taking the occasional picture. Old-school walkie-talkies were my go-to for communication now.

That reminded me, I'd forgotten my talkie. I grabbed it from its charger on my nightstand and came back out to find Silence sitting in the oversized reading chair in the corner outside our room. She looked up at me and smiled her megawatt smile.

"Found yourself a little nest, did you? I won't bother you."

She scribbled on her whiteboard. *You're not bothering me. I just wanted to get closer to the lake. It's so beautiful.*

"Isn't it?" I agreed. "I'm blessed to live here."

You are very blessed.

In many ways was the unwritten conclusion to that statement. I knew I was, but I forgot to remember that sometimes.

I gasped at the sudden memory of one of Gran's favorite sayings.

Whenever Rosalyn or I would proclaim we hated something, Gran would say, "Don't forget to remember how blessed you are." Or, "Don't forget to remember that somewhere a person isn't getting dinner tonight." Or, "Don't forget to remember there are little girls living on the streets."

Like Silence.

Are you okay, Sherriff?

I laughed, fighting off threatening tears. "I'm fine. I was just remembering something my grandmother used to tell me. This was her house. Funny how even though we've changed almost every room, I still feel her presence here."

She gave me a tight closed-lip smile that didn't reach her eyes.

I understood what the look meant. She thought I grew up privileged. I wouldn't say that, but I certainly didn't want for much. Except my dad. He was never around.

"Silence?" She looked up at me. "Can I ask you why you don't speak? Tavie explained your circumstances to me. I hope that's okay. I don't mean why don't you speak; I mean why do you continue to be mute?"

She scooted to the side of the big chair and patted the cushion for me to sit. She cleared her whiteboard and then started to write, the marker squeaking as it left hot-pink words behind.

No one was listening to me. My uncle abused me. Not just with his fists.

Her jaw clenched, and her beautiful face turned serious as she waited for me to nod that I understood what kind of abuse she meant. She cleared the board.

One morning I decided since my mom refused to listen, I'd stop trying to get her to. She knew.

I'd never understand how a person could know that kind of thing was happening and still do nothing. I nodded and she wrote again, the slight smell of alcohol in the ink permeating the air around us.

I left in the spring right before graduation.

"You waited until spring because it would be warm enough to sleep on the streets?" I'd heard this kind of story enough times that I could keep my voice steady. Inside, though, between this and the fact that her mother did nothing, I was raging for her and wanted to scream. The world was chock-full of scum and enablers.

Right. I stayed in parks, keeping clear of cops the best I could. I knew no one so didn't bother speaking.

Pause. Nod. Wipe. Write.

She blushed. *My not speaking became a sort of pick-up line. I learned to get what I needed using other means of communication.*

I had a pretty good idea of what that entailed.

You hear a lot more of what's going on around you when your own voice isn't getting in the way. She erased the words. *It's amazing how much bigger the world becomes if you get quiet and listen.* She cleared the board again and then tapped her forehead. *You learn more about yourself by listening to your thoughts instead of your voice.*

"That scares some people."

Listening to their own thoughts? Yes, it does.

I chuckled. "Sometimes when I'm interviewing witnesses, I'll ask a question and then sit mutely and wait for them to answer. There tends to be a lot of squirming before they finally respond. Quiet makes people uncomfortable."

That's because there's so much going on in the silence.

"The kind around us and the one sitting next to me too."

The dazzling smile returned, joined by sparkling baby blues.

"What did you hear in your thoughts?"

That I was being tested. That better things would come if I survived.

If she survived. "So far so good. You're a very strong person, Silence."

She shrugged off the compliment. *More stubborn than strong.*

"It depends on how you look at it. You found a way out of an awful situation. That's what matters. It wasn't a way anyone would choose if they thought they had another option. I'm sorry that's the only one you felt you had."

She shrugged again. This time it was a gesture of submission. *You do what you need to do.*

We both looked out at the lake then. The bright sunlight sparkled on the surface. A few puffy white clouds floated past. The trees swayed ever so slightly.

"Is it possible that along with your own thoughts you were hearing that higher power Tavie talks about?"

She considered this as she wiped the board slowly and thoughtfully but only responded with a shrug.

"I'm glad you made it through that part. I'm so grateful there are people like Tavie out there helping those in need."

Me too. She saved my life.

I didn't doubt that for one second.

I did graduate, by the way. No one was there for me. It was one of the best days of my life.

My throat clogged with emotion, and I couldn't respond. Instead, I spread my arms wide and wrapped her in a hug. Tavie was right. Silence was a joy to have around.

Tavie appeared from around the corner. "Here you are. What are you two doing?"

Silence tapped her board as I said, "Having a chat."

"If you're ready, the others want to get over to the buffet. Gloria says she's starving."

Gloria is always starving. Goes right to her cheeks.

Tavie laughed, a big happy belly laugh.

"You all can ride with us if you like," I told them.

"No need to cater to us. We know where to go." Tavie cleaned the lenses of her glasses and held them up to the light, checking for any remaining smudges. Satisfied, she put them back on and leaned in to me. "Besides, I believe you and Mr.

Tripp need all the alone time you can get."

Was our squabbling that obvious? We'd managed three hours in the attic without a single sideways word. Of course, we were both wearing dust masks. And we worked at opposite sides of the room. Still, I'd count that as a win.

~~~

There was a line outside Triple G when we got there. Not an unusual sight during the summer season, but unexpectedly thrilling today. That line meant lots of villagers were attending the buffet. We dropped Meeka off in the doggie play yard behind the pub. Standing electric heaters for the less furry pups, and therefore more easily chilled, were scattered across the yard. Meeka was thrilled to have playmates and ignored my impression of a guilty mom dropping her kid off at daycare. She was fine. What was I getting emotional about?

"Buffet is all you can eat," Maeve said, for probably the hundredth time, as she charged us for the buffet at the door and handed Tripp his change. "Soda and milk included. Beer and other alcoholic drinks are extra, and you'll have to get them at the bar. We're running on a lean staff tonight, so catching a server to get something for you will be tricky."

Inside, the pub was packed. The building itself was a cottage that used to be someone's home and had long ago been converted into the restaurant it was now. Rather than tear down all the walls to accommodate a single large dining area, they'd turned each room into a separate dining space. One long, narrow room held a twenty-foot table normally used as a community dining spot for singles, couples, or smaller groups looking to socialize with others. Today, it held the buffet. Extra seating had been shoved in wherever it would fit throughout the pub. I prayed there wouldn't be a
~~~

fire because we were well beyond the fire code tonight. A violation I'd ignore for this one occasion.

After filling our plates with turkey, mashed potatoes, stuffing, and other traditional Thanksgiving offerings, Tripp and I chose a table along the outside wall in the big main room. We discussed the attic as I dunked my turkey into my mashed potatoes with gravy, and Tripp mixed everything together into a sort of casserole.

"I was thinking," I said between bites, "it's too bad there isn't a fireplace up there."

Tripp stared at me with a look that said he was envisioning the space. "We could put a little freestanding pot belly stove in the corner next to the windows. Not quite the same as a fireplace, and we'll need to put in tile on the floor and walls to deal with the heat, but it could be done. It would keep the space nice and toasty."

"Sounds great. Add it to the list." Then I amended, "That can wait until after we're moved in."

"That will require venting to the outside which means exterior work. Not something I want to do when it's cold outside." He shoved a forkful of his casserole into his mouth and chewed happily. "So nice to have someone else make dinner now and then."

I filled my mouth with stuffing rather than saying if he wanted me to cook, all he had to do was ask. I wasn't much good in the kitchen but did know how to grill. Maybe I'd surprise him with burgers or brats one night this week.

"You know, we don't really have to buy any furniture," my frugal boyfriend said. "We've got all that stuff in the garage loft."

"True. I'm fine with antiques if you are. As long as they're comfortable. We will need to buy a mattress, though."

He waggled his eyebrows at me. "So our first purchase as a couple will be a bed?"

I grinned and heat spread from beneath my collar to the top of my head.

As we ate, numerous people stopped by to say hi and wish us a Happy Thanksgiving, most of whom I had to introduce to Tripp.

"Didn't realize you knew everyone in the village." He took a long swig of his beer, looking at me over his mug.

"I don't know everyone, but it is part of my job to get out and patrol the village as often as possible. I meet a lot of people that way."

His brow creased at that comment. I hadn't left the house lately, much less patrolled the village, but he knew what I meant. He waved at someone across the room. "Those are the guys that helped with the renovation. I haven't seen them in a while. I'm going to say hi."

He placed a quick kiss on the top of my head and walked away.

Speaking of my job, I was with the community now. I left our jackets lying at one end of our table and went on patrol. And to find some dessert. I took the long way around Triple G, stopping to greet villagers and proving my earlier point that I didn't know everyone by meeting some folks for the first time. It amazed me how people could live so close together and never see each other.

Groups filled the corners of the bigger room and gathered in tight clusters in the smaller ones. They laughed and talked nonstop, everyone keeping an eye on everyone else's kids. I suddenly had a pretty good idea of what the weekly Sunday gatherings would be like this winter. That would be the time not only for everyone to check in with each other during the cold months, it was also when Tripp could get to know more of the villagers.

Tavie and her group had taken a table almost smack in the center of the main room. They looked like they were enjoying themselves and waved when they saw me looking. I couldn't help but notice Silence. It was like watching my college roommate Taryn all over again. Taryn's eyes would start scanning the room, looking for a "date," the second we'd walk into a club. She always dressed in micro-miniskirts that barely covered her butt, filmy spaghetti-strap tank tops, and heels high enough I was sure she'd fall off them. I hated how she put herself on display that way. She didn't need to do that to get a date. And the guys who responded to her clubbing costume weren't the kinds of guys she deserved.

I was about to wander over and see how they were doing when I spotted my deputy. He was at a small table tucked all the way at the back of the main room next to the door that led to the pub's massive deck. By the dazed look in his eyes, it seemed Reed had been sitting there for a good while, pounding back beer.

"Hey there, Sheriff," he slurred. "Happy Thanksgiving."

I recognized Brady Higgins but not the two other guys sitting with him. They all greeted me in the same slurry way and gave off a vibe that said I'd interrupted a private conversation.

"Are you here all weekend?" I asked Reed. We hadn't spoken since he returned to school in Green Bay after everything with Lupe fell apart. That was three weeks ago.

"Yeah."

"Do you have time for a chat?"

"I'm busy right now." He refilled his mug from the pitcher in front of him, sloshing a bit on the table as he did. Good thing no one had to drive home tonight. "I got a lot to do on my cabin, too, so . . ."

Speaking as his boss, I said, "We really should talk soon."

In unison, the other three raised their mugs to their mouths. I suddenly felt like the parent who had shown up at the kegger and publicly humiliated her son.

"Yep, guess we should." He stared past me at the television hanging on the wall.

Even if we made a plan to get together, he wouldn't remember it tomorrow. Maybe I'd stop by his place. I hadn't seen his cottage yet.

The tension broke when I took a half step back. I got it. I wasn't welcome.

I said hi to a few more people as I wandered, then paused in the buffet room. I loaded two big slices of pumpkin cheesecake and pecan pie on a dinner plate. As I covered them in whipped cream, a voice in my head told me I was reverting to old habits of self-medicating with food.

"I am not," I whispered at the voice.

Well, maybe I was, but it was just this one time. Everyone was here with family or celebrating with friends. I had no idea what my family was doing today. Guess I could have invited them up. Mom wouldn't have come but Rosalyn might have. My boyfriend was with his friends, and I didn't see Morgan anywhere. I felt all alone in a room full of people on Thanksgiving. So what if I celebrated on my own with a bit of cheesecake?

I returned to my table with the overfilled plate in hand and froze. An envelope with "Sheriff O'Shea" typed on it, exactly like the one I'd gotten at the station, lay on the table in the spot where I'd been sitting. Was this person following me around the village?

With a steak knife from one of the flatware bundles on the table Tripp and I hadn't used, I sliced open the envelope. The card inside was also identical. Except for the message.

You know what you did.

Who the hell was leaving these? And what did they think I did? I stood and slowly scanned the room, pausing at every table and cluster of people standing around. I looked at every face, checking for any sign of responsibility. No one was paying any attention to me. If the guilty party was one of them, they were hiding it well.

I was about to check out the smaller rooms and see if anyone there seemed suspicious, but before I could, the front door opened, and Gavin Lindsey and his posse strode in like they owned the place.

Chapter 8

THE GROUP OF EIGHT STOOD together as Lindsey looked for a place to sit. Visions of lunchroom bullies flashed in my mind, and I half-expected he'd stride over to an occupied table and tell the diners they were in his spot. He settled on a table close to Tavie's, and as the group members draped their jackets over the backs of the chairs, Lindsey stood leering at Melinda, Silence, and Gloria like they were items on the menu. Darryl noticed them too. In fact, the two never took their eyes off the trio as they passed by too close on their way to the buffet table.

Melinda was unflappable, staring them down without blinking, clearly ready to take them both on if necessary. Gloria's expression was more amused than confrontational and said, *please, I've dealt with worse than you punks*. Silence, seemingly unable to turn off her flirting, gave off the opposite vibe. Her smile was practically saying, *Hey, sailor, buy me a drink?*

"Trouble?" Tripp appeared at my side, his own plate of dessert in hand.

"Not yet, but I think it's coming."

Casually, he followed my gaze to Tavie's table. "What's going on with Silence?"

He saw the obvious flirting too. Good. At least I knew my actions were that of a concerned professional and not a catty woman. I turned him to face me, so I could surveil the group over his shoulder instead of both of us staring at them, and repeated what Tavie had told me about Silence.

"Thankfully," I concluded, "she's got Melinda and Gloria ready to jump to her assistance."

Tripp agreed. "She sure is attracting attention, though. And not just from the men."

He meant the scowls Didi, Cheryl, and Kendra were fixing on Silence. Great. A cat fight/bar brawl would really put a damper on this fun community gathering.

"Anything I can do?" he offered.

That was sweet of him, but I could tell he really wanted to go back to the guys. Now that he wasn't their customer, they could hang out.

"Thanks, but not right now."

"What's that?" He tapped the envelope still in my hand.

If I told him, he'd insist we go home or would hover and distract me from focusing on the problem with Lindsey and company. I needed to be here and alert.

"Nothing. Just a card someone left on our table."

"Nice." Assuming it was a Thanksgiving card, he gave me a quick kiss, flavored by the pumpkin pie with whipped cream he'd been nibbling on, and returned to his friends.

Before tucking the card into my jacket pocket, I asked the people at nearby tables if they'd seen who left it.

"No, sorry, Sheriff."

"Is it your birthday?"

When I shook my head, they assumed like Tripp had that it was a holiday card.

My instincts were on full alert now. I sat with my back to the wall, dessert plate in hand, and kept an eye on the group. Chaz Lindsey and Marcel Allen chose a table at the far end of the room away from the others. They'd all walked in together. Was there suddenly dissension in the ranks? Had there been an argument of some kind? Or was there another reason the two didn't want to be with the rest of the group?

Gavin Lindsey and Darryl Allen stuck together at their table and other than flirting mildly with Gloria and Melinda and paying way more attention to Silence than was necessary, they weren't doing anything the sheriff should get involved with. If they didn't back off soon, however, their girlfriends would likely be stepping in to take care of things. And letting the women deal with their men seemed like a fine solution.

Gloria and Melinda hovered around Silence like her personal protection unit, but in spite of their best efforts to distract her with billiards, darts, and food, Silence couldn't stop flirting. Tavie stayed close, giving off a clear vibe that said if anyone dared mess with any of them, they'd meet Mama Bear.

I gave them credit for trying, but the more I saw Silence in action, the more upset I became for her. Really, they should just take her home. This wasn't a good environment for her.

As the afternoon slid toward evening, and more alcohol was consumed, the crowd got a little rowdier. Especially once the Packers game started, hoots and hollers and language my mother wouldn't approve of filled the pub.

Gavin, Darryl, and now Lars Sundstrom continued harassing Silence. As a woman, I was getting really uncomfortable for her. As a law enforcement officer, I had just about reached my limit. Fortunately, Melinda had too.

Loudly, so everyone in a twenty-foot radius could hear, she said, "Shut your sexist mouths, back off, and leave her alone."

I took that as my cue to see if I could help.

"They're trying to get Silence to talk," Gloria explained. "Happens every time we go out, even if it's just to the grocery store."

"Every single time," Melinda agreed. "Men seem to think not speaking is her way of playing hard to get."

Gloria batted her eyelashes and, in a voice presumably meant to be Silence, said, "I'm so shy all I can do is stand here and pretend I'm not interested. But you know all I really want to do is jump your bones."

Melinda burst out laughing. Silence swatted Gloria's shoulder then stuck a finger in her own mouth and pretended to gag.

I laughed along with them, even though the whole situation infuriated me.

"If you ask me," Tavie said, nodding past me, "it's the women around here that I'm more worried about."

She saw the same thing Tripp had earlier. The death glares from Didi, Cheryl, Kendra, and a few others not with their group, had become more intense.

"Let me know if you need me to step in," I offered. "I'll either kick them out or get the owner for you. Maeve will be happy to have them removed."

Another half hour passed, and a happy buzz settled over the pub because the Packers had caught up from a fourteen to nothing deficit. I was chatting with some of the villagers when Marcel and Chaz came up to me.

"Can we talk to you, Sheriff?" Marcel asked.

Five foot ten, medium-brown skin, short Afro shaved on the sides, bodybuilder physique.

"Is there trouble?" I asked.

Marcel's eyes darted toward Lindsey's group, and he asked, "Can we go outside?"

These two didn't look like they'd hurt anyone, but I was still a little hesitant to go outside alone with them. Instinct told me to be leery of everything anyone in this group did.

"I'll be right there. Let me grab my jacket." I tried to catch Tripp's eye, but he was busy laughing about something with the guys. Instead, I asked the people next to our table to keep an eye on Tripp's sweatshirt and purposely said, "I'm just stepping outside for a minute."

The looks they gave me indicated that wasn't something to worry about in Whispering Pines. No one would take his sweatshirt, but they humored me with a serious, "No problem, Sheriff."

Once on the red brick pathway outside Triple G, I asked Marcel, "All right, what's going on?"

Chaz remained mute, letting Marcel do the talking. "Gavin is obsessed. He's been going on and on about how messed up Whispering Pines is and how the people here need someone who knows what they're doing to take care of the problems."

Gavin's words from yesterday rang in my ears. *Sounds to me like you could use some help up here since you ain't doing much good for these people. Are you?*

"Hang on." My pulse couldn't seem to decide if it wanted to race or freeze. "Tell me you're not talking about vigilante justice of some kind. Are they planning something?"

"That's what we don't know," Marcel insisted as Chaz shrugged and shook his head. "Sincerely, we don't know what they're up to, just that it don't sound good. Darryl made it sound like we were coming up here for a guys' weekend. You know, hang out, maybe do a little deer hunting. I never met any of the others, but D said they're okay. Then once we got set up at the campground yesterday, Gavin started spouting off about keeping the people here safe." He paused, thinking. "You know, it might be like you said, some kind of vigilante thing. Everyone else was nodding like they knew exactly what he was talking about. Me and Chaz didn't want to get involved with whatever they were talking about so went for a walk around the campground. We got back just before you showed up."

As he spoke, I mentally started putting together my defense. Who could I gather for reinforcement? Reed was here, but too inebriated to be of service if something happened tonight. Tripp, obviously. The villagers came together nicely last month to search for Jacob Jackson, but some of those same people had started complaining about the troubles going on here. Still, if I put out the call, the villagers would respond. Wouldn't they?

"We don't got a clue what's going on," Marcel repeated, "but we figured you should know they might do something. Like I said, we don't want nothing to do with it. We came to get something to eat and are heading back to the hotel now. We're gonna stay the night since we already paid for the room but are cutting out of here first thing in the morning. If we knew what they were up to, trust me, we'd tell you."

We talked for another minute or two, and they promised to contact me if they thought of anything important and then went back to the hotel.

Inside the pub, I found Tavie's group sitting at their table holding hands and praying.

The villagers were so accepting of whatever people did, none of them seemed to even notice. Lindsey and his group, however, were smirking and whispering to each other. Probably working up to a different kind of harassment.

Feeling unsettled and desperate, I crossed the pub to the one person in the village who had the skills to help me formulate a plan. It was a fool's errand, I knew that. Even if Reed had miraculously sobered up and was capable of helping me, he most likely wouldn't. Still, I had to give it a try.

He was sitting by himself with a mostly full, mostly flat beer in front of him. Since the other three had left I helped myself to the chair across from him. With effort, he raised his head to look at me. It took even more effort for his eyes to focus.

"Whatever you're here to say, I'm off duty. Told you two weeks ago, I'm taking a leave of absence. I don't want anything to do with this village right now."

If that was true, why was he here in the heart of a village celebration? Easy answer, he needed the comfort and familiarity of his people around him. It seemed that Lupe may have broken more than his heart—she might have broken his spirit too. She hadn't been his first girlfriend, but she'd been the first he fell hard for.

"You're still taking classes, aren't you?" If he quit school, quitting his job might be next.

"We're on a break." He lifted his beer mug to his mouth but set it back down without taking a drink. Looked like he'd reached his limit. "School's closed, so I'm closed."

I signaled for a server to take away the pitcher and mugs. "Cut him off, okay? Make sure no one else serves him."

The twenty-something man with thick light-brown hair to his shoulders and a full beard promised to spread the word.

"Did you want something?" Reed asked. "Or did you just stop by to harass me?"

"I'm not harassing you." I considered telling him about Lindsey's vigilantes for half a second. "It doesn't matter what I want, you're too drunk to be of service anyway."

"That's right, I am." He narrowed his eyes, and I could tell he was about to ask what was going on. No matter what he said, he cared deeply about this village. "I'm just sitting here minding my own business, not bothering anyone, so I'd appreciate it if you left me alone."

"Tell me one thing. When did you get here? Does Flavia or Reeva know you're here?"

"That's two things." He held up two fingers in a *V*. "I got here this morning. And no, they don't know I'm here. I don't need to report to mommy and auntie every time I come to town. I got my own place now." He dropped his head to the table and quietly moaned, "One I was gonna share with Lupe." Then a little louder, "Leave me alone. Please."

I stood and took a few steps away.

"Heard the word." Maeve paused at my side with a tray full of dirty dishes in her hands. "He's done for the night. In fact, I'll find someone to take him home now."

"Excellent. Thanks." I found a spot where I could see almost all of the main room at once and leaned against the wall. There were plenty of familiar folks sitting at the various tables. Violet and her brother Basil sat with a group of younger villagers. The percentage of division across the age groups in Whispering Pines was fairly equal. The twenty-somethings were particularly close. Probably because few of them were married or even partnered. If I wasn't sheriff, would I fit in with them? Or would I fit even though I'm the sheriff and should just go sit with them?

Not tonight. I needed to stay alert for trouble.

As with the twenties, the high school kids hung out together. Fortune teller Lily Grace, her boyfriend Oren, and a couple dozen others had taken over one of the smaller dining rooms. They were half-watching football and half-playing some game only they understood.

Effie, Cybil, and some of the other fortune tellers had been here for a while but had already gone home. Most of the circus folks had left the village for the off-season, but those still here—Creed, Janessa, Igor, and Britta—had already gone home as well.

A group of business owners was gathered around a table. Treat Me Sweetly's owners Sugar and Honey, Laurel from The Inn, clothing shop owner Ivy, hobby shop owner Ruby, and Mr. Powell from village services looked to be having a serious discussion. Too serious considering it was Thanksgiving night. Probably an impromptu business owners' meeting. Laurel, especially, was big into meetings.

Most surprising of all the clusters was a pairing of eccentric Mallory with her tinfoil hat securely in place and wacky Sister Agnes. Where had Sister Agnes been? I hadn't seen her since Mabon Fest two months ago. They were sitting at the bar, chatting, and drinking what were probably virgin something-or-others. From the bright-pink color, I guessed Shirley Temples. What could they possibly be talking about? Mallory had a hard-enough time putting a sentence together, let alone a whole conversation.

I crossed the room to say hi and was ten feet away when Mallory looked at me through her hag stone, a rock with a naturally formed hole in it, and proclaimed, "Good one."

"Still looking for fairies, Mallory?"

She reached into her pocket and pulled out a smaller, similar stone. Where did she find these things? Morgan told me they were rare. She handed the stone to me.

"Help sheriff," she said in her broken way. "Tell truth."

"It will help me tell the truth?" I asked.

"Possibly," Sister Agnes interpreted. "She means it will give you the ability to know when others are telling the truth."

A truly helpful gift for a law enforcement officer.

"Thank you, Mallory." I put the stone in my pocket and turned to Agnes. "Where have you been? I haven't seen you around in months."

Across the room, Lindsey moved to a chair closer to the boarding home girls. It looked like his taunting had ratcheted up another notch. Just what I'd feared would happen.

"Sorry, Agnes, I need to see what's going on over there."

I closed the gap between me and the group by half, not wanting to intervene unless necessary. Hopefully, my presence would be enough to keep trouble at bay.

"What's happening?"

I turned to see Tripp standing next to me. It comforted me more than I could say that he was here. My deputy was no help, regardless of his sobriety level, so I was feeling abandoned, not to mention vulnerable. Me and my little Glock could only do so much. Maybe I should get Meeka from the play yard out back. Those little pearly whites of hers could do major damage to the back of someone's leg.

"Hopefully nothing." While keeping an eye on the crowd, I filled him in on what Marcel had said. "They're the ones I told you about from the campground. They think the reason there's so much death and chaos in the village is because I don't know what I'm doing."

"Of course you know what you're doing." He looked ready to fight the guy for that reason alone. Chivalrous, but not necessary. "Do you have a plan?"

I smiled at his confidence in me. "I'm trying to come up with one. Depending on what happens over there"—I nodded at the still-taunting Lindsey—"things could turn in a heartbeat. My deputy was practically passed out at his table in the corner, so someone took him home. All I have is my Glock."

"And me," Tripp insisted. "I won't say anything yet, but you give me the signal, and I'll rally the renovation crew. They'll help."

That was six more guys. Good, I could work with that. I nodded and gave him a quick kiss. "Hopefully I'm overreacting, but this group set off my instincts the moment I saw them."

And right now, I was twitchier than I'd been in a long time.

When the football game ended in a win for the Packers, in typical dramatic last-minute fashion, the crowd thinned by more than half. The younger villagers, and many of the older ones, weren't ready to call it a night yet and stayed to watch the next game.

While making my rounds to get a feel for how many were still in the pub, I noticed Darryl and Cheryl having a serious discussion in the small dining room at the back of the building that was reserved for couples. No children or groups larger than four were allowed in the quiet, romantic space. While Darryl hadn't been hovering around the boarding home group anywhere near as much as Lindsey and Sundstrom had, it had clearly been enough to upset Cheryl. No need for me to worry about him. Cheryl was handling the problem just fine.

As I circled back around to the main room, I found Tavie talking with Maeve. She must've finally had enough and was complaining about their harasser. Maeve signaled to the man at the front door. Jagger, the bouncer, was approximately the size of a bull and drew everyone's attention as he charged across the room.

My gaze slid from him to the vigilante table. Only Lindsey and Kendra were there. Darryl and Cheryl were still in the little dining room at the back. Sundstrom and Didi were now at a table in the back corner. He was holding her hands across the table as though trying to calm her down.

They'd split into groups. What was going on? Was the division into couples simply a matter of ticked off partners needing attention? Or was this part of the plan Marcel was worried about and they had stationed themselves around the pub to take action?

Jagger was talking to Lindsey now. Probably telling him to back off or he'd be out the door. Clearly happy with this development, Gloria and Melinda were laughing and devouring pieces of pie, cheesecake, and cookies. Tavie was drinking something from a mug, probably mulled cider. And Silence was . . . Where was Silence?

I scanned the main room. She wasn't there.

"Where is she?" I murmured out loud.

I took a few steps toward the front of the pub, planning to check the other dining rooms for her, when she appeared at the far end of the bar. She must've gone to the ladies' room.

My stress level, which had been rising and falling like a rollercoaster all night, dropped again. Maybe there was nothing going on and I was simply being paranoid.

"Sheriff?"

I turned to see Sundstrom standing next to me. "Mr. Sundstrom. What can I do for you?"

He pointed toward the door that led to the deck and had to raise his voice over the noise of pub patrons and music. "Can I talk to you for a minute?"

What could he want to talk to me about? Did he have information about Lindsey's agenda?

"I think they locked that door," I told him. "We can get out, but won't be able to get back in."

He grabbed an unoccupied chair from a nearby table. "We'll wedge it open. It's so loud in here. This will just take a minute."

I squeezed my elbow tight against my side, letting the feel of my Glock comfort me and give me confidence. Then I held a hand out toward the door for Sundstrom to take the lead. "All right."

My plan was to prop the door open with my body instead of the chair while he stood out on the deck. That way, if he was up to something, I'd simply step back inside the pub. That was my plan. But as often as not, plans had a way of going off the rails.

Chapter 9

BEFORE I COULD EVEN REGISTER what had happened, Sundstrom had grabbed me by the arm, yanked me out onto the deck, and was back inside Triple G with the door closed.

I grabbed the door handle, twisted, and pulled, but the door was locked.

"Hey! Let me in!" I yelled and pounded on the windowless door. This was a waste of time. No one would hear me. I'd have to run around to the front.

As I rounded the building, I passed the doggie play yard.

"Meeka, come!" Noting the urgent tone in my voice, she didn't hesitate and ran right over to where I stood by the fence. I reached over and snatched her up. Blue, the village cat, was the only other animal in the yard.

"Sorry," I called to Blue as we sprinted for the main entrance. "Meeka's on duty now."

With Westie in hand, I took the pub's porch steps two at a time and then tugged on the front door's handle. It was locked as well.

What was going on? A hostage situation? They weren't going to hurt people, were they? Was it some weird cult thing where Lindsey was trying to turn the village against me?

I peered through the door's window and saw what looked like a bar fight about to break out. I pounded on the door and screamed for someone to let me in, but no one heard. Where was Jagger? Why wasn't he at his post by the door? Maybe he'd gotten caught up in the fight. He'd been talking to Lindsey last I saw and that's where the crowd was gathered, near Lindsey's table. Had Lindsey been stupid enough to pick a fight with Jagger?

Even though I couldn't hear what was being said, I could tell by the hand gestures and facial expressions that people were angry. As I watched, people gathered from other areas of the pub. A few tried to get in the middle of the melee to break things up. Still others appeared to be joining the fight, making things worse by adding an additional layer to whatever was going on. Most people hung to the fringes, leaving distance between themselves and the fight. This wasn't good. I had to get in there.

"It's going to be chaos any second now," I said to Meeka as I pounded on the door, trying again to get someone's attention.

I was about to break the window pane closest to the dead bolt when I saw Tripp skirting the edge of the crowd. He was looking around, probably for me. I pounded harder on the door and screamed his name. Finally, he looked our way, his brows furrowing with confusion. I waved him over and pointed at the doorknob.

"What are you doing out there?" he asked, holding the door open as I lurched inside.

"Sundstrom locked me out on the deck."

The people clustered at the center of the main room were becoming more agitated. Bodies were pressing closer together. Voices were rising. Tempers were flaring. Finally, I spotted Jagger in the middle of it all, desperately trying to break things up.

In an attempt to get everyone's attention, I climbed on top of a table and hollered, but they couldn't hear me. Fortunately, after years of calling closing time at the end of the day, Maeve had one of the loudest whistles I'd ever heard. She got on the table with me and let loose an ear-piercing blast.

"That's enough," she shouted. She had to whistle once again before the chaos finally settled.

As she climbed down, I took over. "All of you, on the floor right now. Sit cross-legged with your hands on top of your heads and your fingers laced." Only a few people obeyed, so I added, "Don't think I could have been any clearer. That was in order. All of you, on the ground now."

Slowly, everyone sat and placed their hands on their heads as told.

From the middle of the cluster, someone cried out, "Oh God, no!"

With everyone on the ground, my line of sight was clear. Tavie was kneeling next to Silence, who lay on the ground, a knife with a striped wood handle protruding from her lower abdomen.

Gloria screamed, and Melinda dropped down next to Tavie.

"Is there a doctor?" Melinda called and then louder, "Is anyone a doctor?"

"Oh my God." I glanced at Tripp, who was equally shocked. When he stepped forward to help, I grabbed his arm, holding him back. "No, I've got this."

I handed a squirming Meeka over to him and zigzagged my way through the people sitting in a circle around the women. By the time I got to them, Jola had emerged from the crowd to assess the injury.

"Well?" I asked her after a few seconds.

"I'm not sure how long the blade is—"

"Between four and five inches. I've seen it before."

I locked eyes on Lindsey. He looked as surprised as everyone else that his knife was sticking out of this girl. He didn't do it?

"Okay, then." Jola appeared to be going through a mental anatomy book as she tended to Silence. "It's down low, so probably missed most of her major organs but could have sliced or nicked her intestine. Possibly, if it went in deep enough, it hit her spine. Either way, she needs to get to the hospital as quickly as possible."

I scanned the room, looking for Maeve or any of the other pub employees. Maeve was the first I found. "Call for an ambulance."

"No," Jola insisted. "There's no time for an ambulance. You know they'll take an hour to get here. The faster we get her treatment, the better her chances of recovery." Jola inhaled deeply, settling her nerves, and then hollered, "Drake? Are you here?"

From the line of people sitting on the ground near the front door, a man in his early thirties with buzzed blond hair leapt to his feet. "Right here."

"Get the van," Jola ordered. "Drive up as close to the pub as you can."

"On it," Drake said and darted out the door.

"Unity's van isn't the same as an ambulance," Jola explained while tending to Silence who had turned a scary shade of pale. "It doesn't have all the bells and whistles, but it's stocked with supplies and is a far better option than waiting. I need something to cover her with and something to put under her head." She glanced at me, worry etched into her face. "Let's try to make her as comfortable as possible."

Someone in the crowd produced a heavy jacket to serve as a blanket. Someone else handed over a sweater to use as a pillow. While Jola took care of Silence and talked with Tavie and the others, I pulled Tripp and Jagger off to the side.

"Jagger, you man the front door. Tripp, I want you to cover the back door."

"What exactly do you want me to do?" Tripp asked, Meeka still fidgeting in his arms. The Westie's focus was on Silence. She really wanted to go to her.

"Just make sure no one leaves the pub until I clear them."

"What about the windows?" Jagger asked. "There are a ton of them, and it's a single-story building. People can jump out without a problem. I've seen it happen many times."

He was right, we needed more than three of us to control this crowd of close to two hundred.

"Time to rally the renovation guys," I told Tripp. "You're sure they weren't involved with this?"

"Positive. We were watching the game at a table toward the back of the room when the fight broke out. I came up here when I heard the commotion."

The look in his eyes said, *to make sure you were okay.*

"All right, ask them to spread out through the pub and keep people from leaping out windows."

Tripp stared at me instead of walking away.

"What?" I asked.

"You're going to interview all of these people?"

I glanced around at the dozens of patrons, mostly villagers, sitting on the floor. They looked scared, like they wished they would've left after the Packers' game.

"What choice do I have?" I responded.

"You can let me help." When I hesitated, he said, "You've been telling me about your job for the last six months. Remember the discussions we had out on the sundeck about interview procedures? I worked a lot of different jobs before landing in Whispering Pines. Most of them were at restaurants and involved dealing with the public. I may not have formal training, but I can tell if someone's lying to me." When I still didn't jump at his offer, he sighed hard. "We're going to be here until two in the morning if you don't let me help."

"Me too," Jagger said. "Keeping an eye on a crowd is pretty much my job. I know of at least thirty people who weren't anywhere near this when it started."

My fear over letting a guilty party walk away warred with my desire to get through everyone quickly and efficiently. My gut told me it wasn't a villager. It had to be one of the vigilantes.

"Fine. You two interview people at the door. I'll deal with this cluster in the middle. If you're certain they weren't involved, let them leave but take down their names, so I know who was here and how to contact them if I need further information. If you're not sure or if they want to make a statement, have them stay and I'll talk to them when I can."

While Tripp and Jagger got to work slowly emptying the building, I hovered near Silence. Until Drake returned with the van, I kept things calm and quiet, which was a challenge with Lindsey a few feet away. He was belligerent and kept hollering about how he didn't do this and how it wouldn't have happened if a man was in uniform.

"It wouldn't have happened," I said, "if your buddy hadn't manhandled me out the door." I pointed at Sundstrom. "Prepare to be charged with assaulting an officer." To Lindsey, I said, "Sit there and be quiet or I'll cuff you and lock you in the walk-in cooler."

I wouldn't really, but oh, I was tempted.

While we waited for Drake, I asked Maeve for a plastic bag and masking tape.

"You can't pull it out," Jola blocked my hands when I reached toward the knife. "It's acting as a plug."

"I'm not going to pull it out," I told her as I placed the bag over the knife's striped handle and secured it with the tape. "I'm preserving evidence. There might be fingerprints. Make sure they don't remove the bag at the hospital. Someone will come get it."

"Someone who?"

Good question. I couldn't leave with all this going on. Reed was of no use. I really couldn't send a civilian. Deputy Atkins over at the county station popped into my mind. "Tell them Deputy Evan Atkins will be by sometime. Not sure when."

A few minutes later, Drake was back with a stretcher.

"I turned off the highway and drove behind all the cottages," he said to no one in particular. "The grounds crew will have to do a little landscaping repair. I'm parked right out front."

Moving her as though she was made of the finest, most fragile glass, Jola and Drake put a neck brace on Silence first to keep her stable. Then they slid a backboard beneath her before lifting her onto the stretcher. Moving slowly to keep the jostling to a minimum, they carried her out to the van.

"Come on, girls," Tavie said to Melinda and Gloria. "We're following."

I stopped her before they left the pub. "Are you okay to drive? I'm sure I can find someone to take you. I'd do it myself, but I need to sort through these people."

Tavie closed her eyes and inhaled slowly. When she opened her eyes again, a look of steely resolve was there. "I'll be fine. I need to be with Silence. You figure out who did this to my girl."

"I will. Are you sure you can keep it together?"

She pushed her shoulders back. "She needs me." Her nostrils flared, and her eyes glistened. "I have to keep it together at least until we get back to the bed-and-breakfast."

The look on her face showed her strength. It also showed me she'd need someone to be there for her later. "I'll be waiting whenever you get there."

Jola and Drake had already left, so I gave Tavie directions to the hospital and walked her to the front door. Before leaving the pub, she paused and turned back. To the entire room, she said, "I don't know who did this, but I want you to know that Silence is the most innocent of the innocents. You don't know her background. You don't know why she does the things she does. She's a really good kid, though. For whatever reason, you felt this was the answer to your problem, which tells me your problems run very deep. I will pray for you. Eventually, I'll forgive you. Right now, I'm far too angry."

As Tavie spoke, I kept my focus on the group of vigilantes and villagers sitting in the center of the room. One of them did this, but who? As I scanned the group, pausing on each person. Those who gave no visible signs of guilt faded away like shadows being taken over by the sun. Once I'd gone through the group once, I did it again with the remaining folks. After that, I was left with a couple of villagers I wanted to talk to along with all of Lindsey and his group.

I turned my focus back on Lindsey. It was definitely his knife, but his initial reaction to seeing it in Silence's abdomen told me a lot. Either he was innocent or a really good actor. I didn't think he stabbed Silence, but I did believe he was guilty of instigating this fight so would charge him with inciting a riot. That left me with five vigilantes, all of whom would stick up for each other.

As I watched them, Darryl caught my attention next. He appeared genuinely upset over the events of the last twenty minutes. The others in the posse sat there with looks on their faces that basically said, *Shame about the girl, but bad things happen*. And then there was Lindsey. He stared directly at me with a look that said, *Bad things happen when you got a little girl playing sheriff*. Was I too quick in assuming his innocence? It was possible he'd been putting on a good act. I mentally rescinded my earlier declaration and added him back to the suspect list.

"Who's the weak point?" Jagger asked quietly after

closing the door behind Tavie. At my surprised look, he explained, "I saw you staring down the group in the middle."

Jagger intrigued me. "What kind of training do you have?"

He lifted a massive shoulder in a shrug. "I had a job as a bodyguard during college."

This guy had layers. "No offense, but you went to college and you're working here as a bouncer?"

"Life is way more laidback here. Usually. Plus, Maeve gives me free food which makes the pay pretty decent."

Not sure I could live off pub fare, but to each their own. "See the man with the Chicago Cubs hat on the outer rim of the cluster?"

Jagger actually growled. "That hat alone means he's guilty of something."

I laughed despite the seriousness of the situation. "His name is Darryl Allen. He's the only one of his group showing any emotion. Not sure about the scrawny one with the goatee, Gavin Lindsey. My decision on him keeps flipping."

"Then you need to push the two of them hard."

I narrowed my eyes at him.

"Maybe," he said, agreeing with a question I hadn't asked.

"Maybe what?"

"Maybe I'll fill in for Reed if you need help and he's off at deputy school."

That's not what I'd been thinking. I'd been wondering how deep and dark his layers went. His offer was an excellent option, however. With a guy Jagger's size, all I'd need him to do is stand in front of people and scowl.

"I'll keep that in mind. For now, let's get through this crowd."

He got to work on his group waiting to be released, and I turned to deal with mine.

Chapter 10

THE FIGHT INSIDE GRAPES, GRAINS, and Grub had started around seven thirty. It was a little after ten by the time Tripp, Jagger, and I finished sorting through everyone. Few patrons could tell us anything; most of them had been in one of the other dining rooms, alibied by the family or friends with whom they'd been celebrating the holiday. Others reported they hadn't even noticed the vigilantes or boarding home girls until after the fight started.

I set up an interview station in the far corner where Reed had been sitting. One by one, I called over the villagers who'd been in the middle of the fight and took their statements. Those who could give me details of any kind said basically the same thing. They saw Tavie and the girls holding hands and praying. Some didn't notice Tavie's group until Lindsey went up to them and gave them a hard time, saying that religion belonged in a church or at home but not in public.

"It was almost like he was picking a fight and trying to get us to join his side," a woman said. "You know how people will look around at a crowd as they speak to make sure everyone is paying attention to their oh-so-important rants? That's what he was doing. Talking to the girls but looking at us." She shook her head. "What is this, high school?"

Everyone agreed that Lindsey started the trouble. They also agreed that Tavie stood up and got in his face when he wouldn't back down after Silence tried to ignore him.

"It wasn't like she was challenging him," another woman said of Tavie. "She told him that Whispering Pines was broken and needed help, that's what they were praying for. That guy agreed about The Pines being broken but said prayer wasn't going to do anything for the people here."

A few villagers agreed with Lindsey.

"He said we needed to adopt more of a military attitude," explained a man in a deer-hunter-orange sweatshirt. "More people patrolling the village to keep the tourists in line. That kind of thing." With a look that could only be called admiration, he looked over at Lindsey who was seated alone at a table. "He said if we really want to save the village, we needed to get a man behind the badge again."

Sitting there, listening to this guy extoll the virtues of armed villagers wandering the commons and the woods made me a little sick. "What's your name?"

"Verne Witkowski."

"And your age?"

"I'm forty-four."

That surprised me. His attitude made him seem much younger. "Do you really want martial law in Whispering Pines, Verne?"

He fidgeted and looked to the side. "I dunno."

"Do you think bandaging a problem by stopping it with force rather than figuring out what's actually causing the problem is the best option?"

Verne paused before saying, "Sometimes force is necessary."

"Like tonight when you all were getting ready to duke it out right here in the middle of the pub? Do you even know what the fight was about?" Before he could respond, I added, "What about his other suggestion? Do you agree with him?"

"The thing about how we needed a man as sheriff?" He turned red and shoved his hands in his sweatshirt pockets. "Don't know that a person's sex has anything to do with ability, but something needs to be done around here."

So he was okay with a woman wearing the badge as long as that woman wasn't me.

"I got nothing against you personally, Sheriff O'Shea," he continued, "but we didn't have these problems with Sheriff Brighton."

In other words, I was the problem. How many other villagers thought the same thing?

"How long have you been here?" I asked.

"Most of my life. My mom died in a car wreck when I was twelve, and my dad was stationed overseas in the military. I came here to live with my grandparents and never left."

"You've been here long enough to know the village well."

He thought for a second. "I think so."

"Is it possible that the problems started when my grandmother died?"

"Lucy?" Verne's face twisted in confusion.

"I don't need an answer. I'd like it if you thought about that possibility, though."

Verne contemplated my question as he left and would hopefully talk to other villagers about it.

Next across the table from me was a peace-loving, twenty-something male who'd been sitting with Violet and Basil and was clearly on Team Tavie. He'd been trying to break up the fight. "That woman, Tavie, said 'might was never right' and that we need to come together and work on creating the kind of community we want to live in."

"That Lindsey guy," a female from the same group began, "what a slime. You could just see it oozing off of him." She angrily snapped pretzel twists into pieces as she spoke. "He was trying so hard to enlighten us and make us understand that women have no value other than making babies."

"Was he saying these things before or after the fight broke out?" I asked.

"Before. The thing is, I'm not so sure he really believed what he was saying. It's more like he was just trying to get us riled up and was using Tavie to do so." She pushed on the broken pretzel pieces with her thumb, grinding them to powder on the table. "He was all over the place. First he talked about women and then about how we needed to patrol the village if we wanted to keep the tourists under control." She blushed. "Then he said something about you being part of the problem."

"Nothing I haven't heard before." I gave a dismissive wave, and she relaxed. "How did the events turn? When did it go from words about women and saving the village to a young woman being stabbed?"

"Couldn't tell you that." She looked down at the pretzel mess she'd left on the table and frowned. "I didn't see who did it, but someone shoved Tavie. Hard. She almost fell. Her girls came to her defense, and that's when things turned physical. You know how people get. Can't ever have discussions about their opinions without someone throwing a punch. Or, in this case, pulling a knife."

Another villager had stepped up to help as soon as Lindsey got in Tavie's face.

"She's a middle-aged woman," a man from the cluster reported in his own defense. "I didn't know if she could take care of herself or not. I suppose it's possible she's a judo master or something. Maybe she can take down someone like Jagger by bending back his pinkie finger. Whatever. All I knew for sure was that she was an older lady, and I wasn't going to stand back and wait for her to get hurt. Yeah, I jumped into the scrum and tried to break things up." He pulled the icepack he was holding against his face away and touched the bruise purpling beneath his eye. "This is what I get when I try to help. A sock in the eye."

"I'm sure the women appreciated your efforts."

I told him he could leave, but before he did, he asked, "Is that girl going to be okay?"

Good question. "I hope so, but I don't know. Jola thought her injury was pretty serious. Do you have any idea who did it?"

"Couldn't say. I was standing behind Silence. Her back was to me and there were people all around."

"If her back was to you, how are you certain it was Silence in front of you?"

"That blonde hair of hers is hard to miss. She was standing in front of me and all of a sudden, she went down, stabbed in the gut. My assumption is that whoever did it was standing on the other side of the group from us. You can eliminate my half of the crowd." He contemplated a thought while swinging his arm across his body, low near his hips, and then angling his hand upward as though trying to stab someone standing at his side. "I suppose it could've been one of the women next to her."

"Who was that?"

"Either the one with the short reddish hair or the one with the long brown messy hair. They kept shifting positions. The redhead would start getting worked up, and either Silence or the brunette would pull her away from that Lindsey guy." He swung his arm in that same across-and-up arc again. "That would be a really awkward angle, though. Hard to get much force behind it. No, if you ask me, whoever did it had to be in this wedge." He held his arms straight out in a *V* with his hands about three feet apart, narrowing my suspect list. "Maybe someone took pictures?"

Pictures? Damn. I was off my game. I could've been snapping pictures through the front door window while waiting to be let in. Or, if I'd thought of it before we started questioning and releasing people, we could've asked if anyone had taken any. It was a holiday. People always took pictures during holiday gatherings. Even if not specifically of the fight, someone may have inadvertently caught something helpful in the background. We had a list of everyone who'd been here. I could get a willing villager or two to check in with those people and ask anyone who had taken pictures during the fight to report to me.

"What's the plan?" Tripp asked after everyone but Lindsey's group had left.

As I'd assumed, between the three of us, we'd cleared all the villagers. That left our little band of vigilantes. Which one of them stabbed Silence?

Or . . . No, I didn't think for even a second that it was possible one of the group home women was guilty. The problem was, that guy's wedge of suspects included Silence, Gloria, and Melinda. He'd targeted the people across from Silence, but the possibility was there. I had to think like a sheriff, not the B&B owner who'd become emotionally attached to her guests over the last twenty-four hours. That meant the only one in that wedge I could safely eliminate was Silence. I really needed pictures.

"We're going to put Lindsey and Sundstrom in the cells at the station," I told Tripp, answering his question.

"On what charges?" Lindsey demanded. "I didn't stab her."

"Inciting a riot," I said without hesitation. "I have witness testimony stating you started all this." I turned to Sundstrom next. "Assaulting an officer and obstructing justice. You shoved me out the door and locked it so I couldn't reenter the premises."

"Good luck making any of that stick," Lindsey growled.

"Good luck getting the charges dropped," I responded.

"What about the others?" Tripp asked.

"Until we know what's going on with Silence," I said, pondering the answer, "I can't charge them with anything more than disorderly conduct. They were all involved with the fight. That's kind of weak, though. I need to come up with something solid quickly."

"We're bringing them all to the station, then?" Tripp asked. Jagger had joined us and was ready to act.

"Therein lies the problem. My holding cells are small. I shouldn't put more than one person in each cell and there are only two cells."

"Jail overcrowding is a serious problem in this country," Jagger said while picking at a hangnail. "But you make do with what you've got."

"Girls in one, boys in the other?" I was joking. All I needed was for someone to muddy things by claiming inhumane conditions.

"They won't be in there that long." Jagger had a wicked side I never knew about but kind of liked.

"You can hold them at The Inn," Laurel offered while putting chairs on top of table so they could sweep and mop the floor.

"I didn't realize you were still here," I told her.

"I'm helping Maeve clean up. A couple of her employees were really upset about the fight. She sent them home, so I offered to stay. Anyway, I'm pretty sure we've got rooms on the top floor that aren't being used. You can put them there, and we'll make sure they don't escape."

"I'll sit in the hall and do guard duty." Jagger cracked his knuckles, really getting into character now. I almost asked who he'd worked for as a bodyguard but wasn't sure I really wanted to know.

I observed my suspects, whom we'd spread out around the room. I hadn't interviewed them yet and didn't want them talking to each other before I did.

"Any chance you've got four empty rooms?" I asked Laurel.

She stared off into a corner of the ceiling, doing a mental head count. "I think so. Let me call over to Emery."

I pulled my walkie-talkie out from beneath my jersey and handed it to her. Thirty seconds later, we had confirmation that the third floor was free. Only three parties were staying at The Inn, and to make things easier on the housekeeping staff, Emery put all three guests on the second floor.

"Okay," I said, "this works. I'll stay at the station—" I groaned and dropped my head back.

"What's wrong?" Tripp asked.

"I promised Tavie I'd be there for her when she got back to the B&B. And I need to speak with her, Gloria, and Melinda and get their versions of the events."

"I'll stay at the station," he offered.

"I'm not sure that's a good idea."

He couldn't have looked more insulted. "I'm more than capable of babysitting a couple of thugs."

"There's a reason cops have partners," I said.

"I'll be his partner." A man named Gino stepped forward. He and Tripp had become friends when Gino entered the Mabon cooking competition. He had an outdoor pizza oven Tripp had been drooling over. He was determined to install one on our back patio.

"Where'd you come from?" I thought it was only us, the vigilantes, and Triple G employees still here.

Gino pointed at the front door. "I was outside talking to some people and came in to use the bathroom."

"Can I babysit if Gino partners with me?" Tripp asked with attitude.

"You may," I replied, ignoring the attitude. "Thank you, Gino."

While Tripp, Gino, and Meeka waited at Grapes, Grains, and Grub with Lindsey and Sundstrom, I walked with Jagger, Laurel, and the rest of our merry band of suspects over to The Inn. After removing the telephones and televisions—they were on lockdown, not vacation—we put the four into separate rooms.

"I'm not crazy about you being here alone." I gave Jagger the same speech I'd just given Tripp. "I know you're like The Hulk's son, but still."

"I'll hang out with him," Emery said from behind us in the third-floor hallway.

It took all my effort not to laugh at this. Emery was five foot eleven and about a hundred twenty pounds.

"I know what you're thinking," he said, his voice cracking and his hands held up in a let-me-explain pose. "I've been studying *kyusho-jitsu* for years."

As Laurel and I looked at each other, confused, Jagger asked, "Black belt?"

"Got it two months ago." Emery stood tall and proud.

"Cool." Jagger nodded. "You can be on my team anytime."

"What's *kyusho-jitsu*?" I asked.

"It's like a martial arts secret society," Jagger explained. "They teach pressure point techniques."

Laurel shook her head. "I had no idea . . . Wait. Is that what you were doing here that night?"

"Practicing my forms," Emery explained, blushing.

"Looked like you were dancing with a ghost," she teased.

He shrugged. "I need something to keep busy while working the night shift. It gets a little boring here sometimes."

She pointed at Emery. "Show us."

Emery turned to Jagger. "Want to be my victim?"

Jagger swallowed then agreed. "Just don't knock me out."

"Are you serious?" I asked, laughing. Emery was a couple inches taller, but Jagger weighed at least three times as much.

Jagger moved into position and grabbed Emery by the shirt with both hands as though attempting to attack him. In a flash, Emery had him by both wrists, pressed on some secret spot, and Jagger dropped to his knees.

"Uncle!" Jagger wheezed, begging for release, genuine pain on his face.

"Works for me." I might have more deputy candidates in this village than I realized.

We dragged two overstuffed recliners into the hallway outside the rooms and left the men to happily discuss the various kinds of martial arts.

Meeka and I ran back to Grapes, Grains, and Grub, and found Tripp and Gino loading takeout bags.

Tripp grinned. "Leftover Thanksgiving food for midnight snacks."

Seemed all four of my guards were set to have good nights. Tripp rushed up to the west side parking lot to get his truck while Gino, Meeka, and I walked the two remaining vigilantes through the village. Once Lindsey and Sundstrom had used the restroom and were locked in their cells, Tripp walked me out the station's back door. I handed him the station keys, and he gave me the set for his truck.

"You're sure you're okay staying here?"

"I'm sure." He looked a little sheepish as he added, "This will sound stupid, but it's something different."

"Different from tending to guests' needs all day, going to bed, and getting up to do it all over again?" When he nodded, I said, "It doesn't sound stupid. You're not bored with B&B life already, are you?"

He ruffled Meeka's ears after depositing her in the passenger's seat, grabbed something from the glovebox, and then closed the door. "No, I'm not even a little bored. This is kind of like a field trip, though. Those are always fun."

"Not always." I thought back to elementary and middle school. "Do you know how many times we took class trips to Old World Wisconsin? Fun the first time. A little fun the second. Total snooze fest the next two."

"Since I have no idea what Old World Wisconsin is, I'll take your word for it." He pulled me in for a hug. "If anything goes even remotely sideways, I'll call you." He held up the deck of playing cards he'd taken from the glovebox. "Me and Gino are going to play poker."

"Tavie and I will probably drink tea and talk about what happened at Triple G tonight."

"Fun," he said half-heartedly.

"I'd rather play poker."

He waggled his eyebrows. "Strip poker?"

"Sure, but that might be a little awkward with Gino."

He kissed me deep and then tucked me into the driver's seat. "Go take care of Tavie."

~~~

Tavie's car wasn't in the driveway when I got there. I debated about calling the hospital and asking for an update on Silence. They'd been gone a long time. Surely, they'd be back soon, though.

Meeka looked up at me when she came in from yard patrol, confused to find me in the kitchen making tea instead of getting ready for bed.

"I promised Tavie I'd be here when she got here. I intend to keep that promise."

I sat in the great room and stared out at the moonbeams sparkling off the lake while reviewing the events of the night. The village council needed to know what was going on. I'd
~~~

seen a few of the council members at the pub, but was pretty sure Jola, Laurel, and Maeve were the only ones there when the trouble started. I called Violet first and then Morgan, the two at the top of our call tree, and asked them to spread the word for an emergency meeting the next morning.

"What happened?" Morgan asked. "River just left, by the way. He's on his way there."

I told her about the fight and the stabbing and how I now had six people in custody.

"Oh my Goddess," she gasped, "how awful. That poor girl."

She grew quiet almost as quickly as she'd become upset. I imagined her floating around her cottage, gathering herbs and amulets to cast a healing spell of some sort for Silence.

"I wish Tavie would get back soon. I'm dying to know what's happening with her."

"And what to charge your detainees with?"

"That too. Right now, I'm charging four with disorderly conduct, one with inciting a riot, and another with assaulting an officer and obstruction of justice. The charges for those last two will stick, but I still need to figure out who did the actual stabbing. Unfortunately, I had to issue fines to a few villagers involved too."

"Is anyone standing out to you?"

"The easy guess would be a man named Gavin Lindsey. He seems to be their leader. Also, the knife Silence was stabbed with happens to be the one he was waving around at the campground while trying to intimidate me."

"You don't sound sure."

"It's his knife, I'm sure of that. The easy answer isn't always the right one, though. There are three women with this group—Kendra, Didi, and Cheryl. They were obviously unhappy with Silence tonight."

I explained the reason behind Silence's flirting.

"That can be upsetting to a woman," Morgan said, "but upsetting enough to stab someone?"

"Possibly. You know how women can be."

Morgan laughed, a throaty sound. "If a man said that, you'd be all over him."

"I would be." I laughed with her.

"You are right, however. Women are quick to anger and can hold on to even the most minor of grudges. It's very unhealthy for the psyche. Not to mention their karma."

"But that doesn't mean one of them stabbed Silence. I really should be over at The Inn and the station questioning them all. I'm tired, though, and want to be fresh and clear when I do."

"One of the benefits to running your own station is that you can occasionally bend the rules to suit your needs."

Something I'd get raked over the coals for down in Madison. And something that was playing right into Lindsey's claim that I wasn't the right one for the job.

There was nothing wrong with letting them sit and stew for the night. They'd all be ready to talk come morning. I could only do so much as a force of one.

When I tuned back in to our conversation, Morgan was saying, "I'll call the council members on my list. I agree with you. They should know about this."

"Thanks. See you in the morning."

I was sitting at the dinette, meditating as Morgan and Briar had taught me, hoping something important about tonight would rise to the surface, when the front door opened. I jumped to my feet, expecting Tavie, and was disappointed to find River entering the great room.

"Good evening, Proprietress." He frowned and looked around. "You appear distraught. Where is Tripp? Has something happened?"

He removed his duster, draped it over a chair, and sat

across from me. Despite my earlier complaints about how much time they spent together, it comforted me to know how close he and Tripp had become. It also unexpectedly comforted me to know he would be in the house with me and our guests tonight. Even though I'd never seen River be anything but mild-mannered, he looked like a demon slayer. His appearance alone was enough to scare people off.

"Tripp is fine. Something has happened, though." I gave him the short version of events and explained that Tripp was spending the night at the station. "It's good that you, Morgan, and Briar didn't come tonight."

"Indeed. They requested that I extend their apologies. Morgan and I planned to join you, but during dinner, we began discussing my suitability to become a more permanent fixture in my lady's life. This turned into quite an inquisition. Lady Briar has a need to poke and prod at every detail of my past and present. If possible, she'd go into my future as well."

We both paused, knowing that with Briar looking into the future might be possible.

"You are the father of her granddaughter. And you are attempting to steal Morgan from her."

"I have no intention of stealing her daughter. I'm happy to give them their time together. I do have a business to run, after all." He stood and strode into the kitchen while saying, "Lucy, tea kettle on."

I'd completely forgotten about the voice commands. It turned out that River made his literal billions from his family-owned tech company. His father started it just as home computers became the rage in the late seventies. Now, they developed computer security and smart home software. River had set up a satellite office in his room upstairs, and boxes of prototypes arrived via private courier multiple times per week. We were currently testing voice-activated household appliances that were connected to a local network instead of the internet. We named our system Lucy after my grandmother. I liked that we had fun toys like this that didn't involve possible monitoring by Big Brother.

"How is the young lady who was stabbed?" River asked while waiting for his water to heat up. "Have you heard anything?"

I shook my head as I sipped the last of my tea. "That's why I'm sitting here caffeinating myself at almost eleven o'clock at night. I told Tavie I'd be here if she needed to talk when they got back."

He returned to the table with his mug, refilled mine with hot water and a fresh tea bag, and we discussed the option of Briar casting spells to reveal River's true self.

"I'm not concealing anything," he insisted. "What you see is what you get."

I gave him a squinty-eyed look. "Yeah, but you've got to admit, what we see is sort of dark and mysterious."

He laughed, a baritone sound from deep in his chest, but didn't deny my accusation.

A few minutes later, the door opened again, and three shell-shocked-looking women walked in.

Melinda spoke first, sounding robotic. "The blade nicked her intestine. They operated and were able to repair it. They're worried about infection now."

"She's in the ICU," Gloria added, "on antibiotics. Since we're not relatives, they won't let us in. They told us there was no reason to stay at the hospital and promised to call if anything changed."

Melinda crossed her arms angrily. "We just have to wait."

"Go on to bed, girls." Tavie gave them both big hugs.

"You should come too," Gloria insisted. "You're exhausted."

"I'll be up shortly," Tavie promised. "I need to talk with Jayne first."

River took that as a signal to leave as well. He kissed my cheek and then placed a comforting hand on Tavie's shoulder before heading to his room at the top of the stairs. As soon as she heard his door *click-clack* into place, Tavie collapsed into my arms.

Chapter 11

I HELD TAVIE AS SHE cried for Silence until her tears dried up. Then, following the example Morgan had taught me, I settled her onto one of the two great room sofas beneath a blanket, turned on the fireplace, and made her some herbal tea. Meeka lay on the couch between us, leaning against Tavie and letting her stroke her fur. First Silence and now Tavie. When had my dog become so sensitive to others?

I told Tavie what happened at the pub after they'd left and that I'd be interviewing all the detainees in the morning.

"I'll clear Silence's things out of her room upstairs before we head back to the hospital." She blotted her eyes with tissues and drank from her mug. "I hope you've got space for us for a few more days. We'll merge into one room if we need to, but we'd like to stay until Silence is through this."

"We've got a couple bookings scheduled but not until late next week. You're fine where you are. Those rooms are yours for as long as you need them."

She gave me a grateful smile.

"Are you ready for bed?" I asked.

"Not yet. Let's talk."

"All right. What would you like to talk about?"

"Anything. Pick a topic."

My tired mind spun for something that would make her happy and landed on her other boarders. "You told me about Silence's background, what about Melinda and Gloria? What are their stories? If you don't mind telling me."

"I'll tell you, but for it to make the most sense, we need to go back a little further first. This whole boarding home venture started about five years ago with my niece Stephanie. Her mama, my sister, got herself into a bad situation. She got hooked on drugs and couldn't keep a job. After a nasty marriage, followed by a nastier divorce, I'd been happily single for nearly thirty years. The last thing I ever expected at age fifty was to be the mother figure for a teenage girl. There was no way I could let the state put her into foster care, though, so I asked to adopt her. That decision changed my life, literally, in so many ways. Stephanie has become the light in my world."

"How did that lead to you taking in the others?"

"Stephanie." She'd said the girl's name as though it explained everything. "She went out wandering one day, probably looking for her mother, and came across Gloria."

I cringed. "I'm assuming this wasn't a good area for her to be wandering in?"

"Not good, no, but you can't tell my iron-willed Stephanie anything. No one can." A proud smile brightened her face. "Gloria was eighteen at the time, she's twenty now. Her parents had kicked her out of the house for no better reason than they couldn't afford to feed three people. They figured at eighteen she could make her own way in the world."

"I hate to ask, because I think I know the answer, but how exactly did she make her way?"

"Same way Silence did, walking the streets."

I was quick to anger lately, and it was rising in me now. "Some people have no right to procreate."

"Amen to that, child." She raised a hand in the air as though appealing to her higher force.

"Where is Stephanie now?"

"My darling niece got herself a big scholarship and is off at college. She wants to be a nurse. Gloria just got her GED and has no idea what she wants to do. She's going to start classes at the community college at the start of the next session. Something will click with her before long."

"Who came next?" I asked and held out my hand. "No, let me guess. Melinda."

She touched the tip of her nose. "Right you are. Stephanie found her on the streets, too, and begged me to bring her in."

"Is that a thing for her?" I turned toward Tavie and pulled my legs up onto the sofa to sit crisscross. "Wandering the streets looking for girls in need of help, I mean."

Tavie nodded her head. "I nicknamed her Mercy, because she calls them her Mercy Missions. Not every girl is open to receiving help. It's mostly that they don't trust people, not that they're happy with their situations. Stephanie talks with them for a bit but doesn't pressure. Those who come via pressure are likely to run, so she moves on until she finds someone who jumps at the chance." Tavie beamed with pride, but I could see the weariness and worry beneath the surface. "What made you guess Melinda came next?"

"Because she seems so comfortable with you, like you've been together for a long time."

"Melinda showed a big personality the day I met her." Tavie chuckled. "I'm guessing she's been that way since birth."

I chuckled. "I'd believe that."

"Her story is a little different in that she has no one else. Her parents died in a car crash when they were overseas on vacation. She literally has no one except for a ninety-year-old aunt in Bavaria she's never met. She received a nice inheritance from her parents and is expected to inherit her aunt's estate as well, so wasn't walking the streets to support herself. She got messed up with all kinds of illegal substances."

"Is that why she's so thin?"

"Partly. She's recovering from anorexia too. It's amazing the girl is alive. The anorexia started before her parents died. She says they demanded a lot of her, and not eating was her way of having control over herself. Did you notice how she ate at dinner last night?"

"I did. She took tons of salad and just a small spoonful of meat. No bun. I figured it was one of those trendy diets."

Tavie shook her head. "She pushes the food all around the plate to make it look like there isn't so much of it. That's something she used to do to try and trick me into thinking she'd eaten more than she had. She still does the pushing thing but now clears her plate, as long as that plate holds mostly vegetables." A sad smile turned her mouth. "She said she was real angry at her parents before they died. The drugs happened because of her grief and guilt."

"Guilt? Let me guess, she was supposed to be in the car with them?"

She touched the tip of her nose again, the signal that I got it right. "She told them she hated them and just wanted to go home."

I blew out a breath of empathy. "Guess she got her wish."

"Just not the way she wanted it. We're getting there. One day at a time."

"Well, this seems like a natural fit for you. You're really good with them. Respect and love flow between all of you."

Tavie pointed at me. "Respect. That's what we all need." She sipped from her tea. "They're all young and not always so easy to have around. They treat each other like sisters, which means they fight a lot. There are tears to counter the laughter.

Way too many hormones. But beneath it all, we love each other. I wouldn't change my life for anything."

We grew quiet then, and in that quiet, I realized how tired I was. So did Tavie.

"You look tired, Miss Jayne. Why don't you go on to bed?"

I rubbed my eyes, yawned, and shrugged. "Doesn't seem to matter lately. I won't sleep anyway."

"That almost always means something's weighing on you."

She didn't ask what that might be, but the question was hanging out there between us.

"Do you think," I ventured, "that a person has to take care of their own demons before they can be responsible for others?"

She didn't answer me right away. I'd turned my attention to the fireplace and when I looked back, her eyes were squarely on me, head tilted, eyebrow arched as though wondering if that was a serious question.

"Child, I'm living proof that you do."

"Demons? You? You're so together. You drive a nice car and wear nice clothes. You didn't even ask how much it would cost to rent four rooms in my B&B for a few nights."

"Everyone deals with a demon at some point in their life," she said without hesitation. "It was Stephanie that forced me to take care of mine. No one was more shocked than I was when the court said they would give me custody of her. The stipulation was, I needed to get myself together first." A faraway look filled her eyes for a flash. Sadness? Shame? Whatever it was, it was quickly replaced by a look of pride. "My life had been nothing worth talking about to that point. I'd been living on scraps. I never let anyone come into my awful little apartment because I was too embarrassed by it. I'd pick up whatever odd job I could find to pay my rent and buy a little food. As dissatisfying as it was, I had no ambition and no direction to do more than I was doing."

She seemed to grow taller before my eyes.

"Turned out what I did have was a deep love for my niece. For her sake, I decided it was time to get myself together. I finished the degree I'd been two classes from completing for ten years. Time had run out on some of my credits, so I needed to take a full semester. During that time, I joined a community church so I'd have people behind me pushing me to stay on track for this girl. That degree let me get a psychiatric nursing job at a hospital in Milwaukee."

I smiled, feeling proud for her. "Is that why Stephanie chose nursing?"

"I think so. She'd hang out in the hospital cafeteria every day and do her homework until I was done with my shift." She chuckled and shook her head. "That girl hated being alone. Anyway, after busting my butt for a year to fix my life, the courts decided I had proven I was serious about caring for this girl. After a few paychecks, I found a better apartment, one with two bedrooms, so Stephanie could have her own space."

Little cheers went off in my head. "Good for you."

"Best day of my life was the day I was awarded custody of that girl." She wiped her eyes with the sleeve of her tunic. "And as the powers that be tend to do, they rained down blessings on me all at once. Turned out I had an uncle that I'd met when I was little and saw maybe half a dozen times in my life. Honestly, I'd forgotten all about him. He hadn't forgotten about me, though. The man was a miser and had a nest egg the size of your car. He left everything to me. As grateful as I was for what that money could do for me and Stephanie, my life was already golden. I decided to use it to make life better for others as well."

I was in awe of this woman, as I was of anyone who did

whatever they had to do to build themself up after a fall. "Tell me you used some of that money for yourself."

"You said it yourself, honey. I drive a nice car." She stood and did a slow turn, showing off her deep-teal silk tunic and flowing black silk pants outfit. "I wear beautiful clothes. And I now live somewhere I'm proud of."

This woman was confident and comfortable with herself and her life. What more could a person need than that?

"That's when you opened the boarding house?" I asked.

"That's when. I take in no more than four girls at a time, despite Stephanie's insistence that we could fit more. I don't want them crammed in like sardines in a can. Those already living with me get a say in who joins us. Any new girl needs to fit in with our vibe. Anyone can fall on hard times, but that doesn't mean you need to let your life spiral or turn into a thug, so anyone new also needs to meet our standards. My house has three large bedrooms. The girls use one for sleeping. It's long and narrow and comfortably fits four beds. They've got portable screens set up between the beds to give the illusion of privacy. The second bedroom is set up for them to do their schoolwork or just hang out. The third bedroom is mine."

We grew quiet again and sat in companionable silence, watching the trees swaying slowly against the star-filled sky.

"You've got a beautiful place here," Tavie commented.

"Thank you. I just hope I get to keep it."

"Why wouldn't you?"

Since I'd unintentionally opened the topic, and because she'd shared so much about her own life with me, I told her about how my grandparents left the land and the house to my dad and how he wanted nothing to do with any of it.

"In the three months we've been open, Tripp and I have done better than we had anticipated with this B&B. Which is great because we did a ton of renovations before we opened.

My parents have given us one year to make back the money we spent on renovations. They said that will prove if we can be profitable or not. If we are, my parents will let us keep Pine Time open. If not, they're going to sell it all."

"Define 'all.'" Tavie angled her body to face me squarely.

"The house, of course." I blew out a shaky breath. "And the two thousand acres that Whispering Pines occupies." I paused as my voice threatened to break. "If that happens and the person who buys it doesn't want a village on their property, all eight hundred plus villagers will have to leave." A tear trailed down my cheek.

"The villagers are who you feel responsible for? They're the reason you need to slay your demons?"

"I can't fail these people. They need this place. For many reasons, this is where they belong."

"That's quite a burden for such a young woman to carry." Tavie took my mug and set it on the coffee table. Then she clasped both of my hands in hers. "Do you trust that what you want will happen?"

Unable to speak, I nodded, then shrugged.

"You need trust. Unfailing, unbreakable trust. What's your motivation?"

"To succeed?" I inhaled, pushing my emotions back down deep where they belonged. "I love this place. I honestly can't imagine myself anywhere else."

"That's a good start, but that's about you. If you want to succeed for these people, so they won't lose their homes, you need a motivator that's big enough for all of them. Think about it a minute. What or who motivates you? What does Jayne O'Shea stand for? That's where you'll find your success."

What motivated me? The people here. Truth and justice. Helping good conquer evil. I laughed.

"What's funny?" Tavie asked, smiling.

"Conquering evil." I pulled my hands free from hers and propped them on my hips, elbows to the side. "I'm Superman. Well, Superwoman."

"That you are." She winked at me. "You asked about taking care of your own demons first. This is a big goal you've set for yourself, and it's going to take a lot of stamina to succeed. If you're not as strong as you can possibly be, you'll run out of steam. If you have demons, you absolutely must exorcise them first. You can only serve one master at a time."

I considered her words. "Put on my own oxygen mask first?"

"Exactly. So now the question is, do you know what your demons are?"

"I do. I made a list last month." Morgan and Briar had encouraged me to work on my unresolved issues during Samhain. I crossed off the first item last month when I repaired my relationship with Rosalyn. It looked like, since I was being plagued by a dream, the next one was dealing with the Frisky situation.

"Very good." She yawned. The poor woman was exhausted.

"You need to go to bed."

"I do. Pray for Silence with me first."

My gut squirmed at that request. "I'm not really one for prayer, Tavie. Not that I have a problem with you doing it. I just—"

"Wasn't raised that way?"

"Right. Ours was an agnostic house."

"Then sit here with me, hold my hands, and think good thoughts for her."

"That I can do."

Chapter 12

MY FIVE O'CLOCK CHIRPING BIRDS alarm came way too quickly. I'd hoped we could push the start time of the council meeting to eight o'clock since it was the off season. Today was Black Friday, though, and people were coming to the village to shop. That meant a six o'clock meeting.

I opened my room door and immediately smelled coffee. Then I saw Melinda sitting at the dinette.

"What are you doing up?" I asked softly as I opened the patio door to let Meeka out.

She looked at me with red-rimmed eyes. "Couldn't sleep."

A quick glance at the clock told me I still had forty minutes before the meeting started. I had time so took the seat next to her. "She's still alive, so you need to remain positive. Don't mourn her while she's still with us."

I felt like Morgan had just taken over my body. Wherever the words had come from, they were true.

"It's not just that." Melinda's hands were wrapped tightly around the coffee mug sitting in front of her. "It's death in general. The people I love, they tend to die."

"Tavie told me about your parents." Melinda nodded, indicating it was okay that I knew. "I understand how it feels to lose someone close to you. This was my grandparents' home. Living here makes it hard sometimes because I think of them every day. All the villagers knew them, too, so I've got to talk about Gran and Gramps all the time with them." I was focusing on death, exactly what I didn't want her to do. "What I've learned is that when you least expect it, and usually when you most need them, new people will come to you. Tavie, for example, and Gloria. Silence is still here too."

She contemplated this while taking a drink and made a face. "Coffee's cold."

I refilled her mug while getting a travel mug for myself. She made good coffee.

"You will find who did this, right?" She took the fresh mug from me.

"That's my focus for today. I've got people in custody, and I'm positive one of them is guilty."

"Is there anything I can do to help? Not like with the investigation, but I've got money. Lots of it that I don't do anything with. Tavie won't let me pay her for rent or anything, so I buy groceries. Anyway . . ."

I understood. She needed to do something for Silence, and this was the only thing she could think of.

"I'm going to say no, only because money won't help with what I need to do. Save your money for when Silence gets better. There will surely be a ton of things she'll need during her recovery. Cozy socks and a cuddly bathrobe, for example. Put all sorts of positive energy out there surrounding her. It's got to help."

Once again, I'd opened my mouth and Morgan came out.

Melinda brightened a little behind her sadness and anger. "Silence likes to read. I could get her one of those pillows with arms that help you sit up in bed."

"There you go. Great idea."

I gave her a hug, which was honestly like hugging a bag

of sticks. The girl was so skinny. I told her I needed to leave for a meeting but that they could do whatever they wanted in the kitchen. Then I gave her directions for getting to Sundry if they wanted something we didn't have and wrote down the phone numbers for Ye Olde Bean Grinder and The Inn.

"You've probably figured out that cell phones don't work here."

She scowled. "Just with WiFi. Kinda sucks."

"It does sometimes. If you hear from the hospital or need me for anything, call one of these places. They have walkie-talkies and can get word to me right away." I glanced at the clock again. Twenty minutes. "I've got to go."

I filled two more travel mugs for Tripp and Gino before I left. I wanted to check in with them before going to the meeting, and Melinda's coffee was way better than the stuff the pod maker at the station brewed.

Meeka wasn't at all happy about her morning routine being disrupted. I filled her travel bowl with kibble and promised she could eat her breakfast at the meeting. She turned her back on me as soon as she was in her cage in the back of the Cherokee.

"It's not like I'm not feeding you at all."

She responded by dropping to the floor of her cage, too weak from hunger to continue standing. Drama queen.

We dashed over to the station and had about two minutes to check in with Tripp and Gino.

"No problems," Tripp reported, gladly taking the coffee I'd brought for them. "We played cards and ate. We set up that cot in your office. Gino's catching a few *z*'s right now."

"Where's *our* coffee?" Lindsey demanded for himself and Sundstrom. "And we want breakfast."

"We gave you food before," Tripp told him.

"Leftover leftovers at one in the morning," Lindsey complained. "It was all cold."

"The more you grumble," I said, "the less compelled I am to feed you." I pointed at the coffee maker in the corner and told Tripp, "You can make them some. Just be sure it's not too hot. Don't want them complaining that we burned them."

I gave Tripp a kiss and hurried off to the meeting. Before going into the boardroom behind The Inn's registration desk, I ran up to the top floor to see how Jagger and Emery were doing with our other detainees.

"Where's Emery?" I laid a hand on the empty chair next to Jagger's.

"Ran to the bathroom and is ordering breakfast." One corner of Jagger's mouth turned in a grin. "He's one cool little dude. Wicked pressure point skills. He's going to teach me. I'm thinking about taking classes."

They'd lived in the village together for years. Funny how a new friend can be so close and still so far away.

"Where is his school?" I asked. No one in the village taught martial arts.

"Somewhere near Superior. It's an hour drive but worth it to learn that stuff."

"And how about our prisoners?"

"They're driving me crazy," Jagger said with a blank stare.

"Why? What are they doing?"

"Kendra keeps demanding that someone has to go over to the hotel and get her makeup bag and clean underwear. She wants to fix her hair. I'm a little worried Didi might actually be losing her freakin' mind or die from separation anxiety or something. She's so upset about being away from Lars, I swear, she's like an addict going through withdrawal."

"What about Darryl and Cheryl?" I asked when Jagger didn't supply info on them right away.

"Dude's going crazy in there. I can hear him pacing back and forth and mumbling to himself. Cheryl's been fairly quiet but keeps insisting she and Darryl didn't do anything and that she can prove it."

"Excellent. I'm pretty sure he's our weak link. Maybe we've got another with her." I gestured toward the stairs. "I called an emergency village council meeting. We gather in the conference room downstairs. Are you okay hanging out here a little longer?"

He sat straight in his chair. "I am a professional. Or used to be. When Emery's here, I walk the stairs a few times once an hour or so to keep the blood flowing. I'm good."

I added "compensate all four guards for their time" to my mental meeting itinerary.

Downstairs, Gardenia, one of Laurel's housekeepers, was stationed at the front desk.

"Do you work this position often?" I asked. "I've never seen you here before."

"No, not often," replied the tiny woman with Asian features and straight jet-black hair pulled into a high ponytail. "I'd rather be moving around, not sitting here, but Emery can't work all the time. At least, that's what we try to tell him."

I crossed behind the desk, went through the door there, and found all twelve council members waiting for me. Flavia immediately spoke up.

"If you're going to call an emergency meeting, the least you can do is be on time."

"Sorry to keep you all waiting"—I checked my watch—"for two minutes. I had guards and detainees to check on. This shouldn't take long."

"Did you say guards?" Creed asked.

"Detainees?" Reeva asked. "Maeve told us there was an incident at Triple G last night. How many people are you holding?"

I explained about our vigilante tourists upstairs and at the station. "I noticed them two days ago driving along the highway and assumed they were simply passing through the village. Then I saw them again later that afternoon at the campground with tents pitched. I explained the campground was closed, sent them over to the hotel, and hoped that was the end of it. But they showed up at the pub for the buffet last night and now we've got problems."

Maeve, Jola, and Laurel nodded and murmured agreements, backing me up about the problems. Those who left the pub before the fight started were shocked to learn about what had happened.

"I'm not sure what their plan was exactly, but two of the eight told me the group's leader seems to be on a vigilante mission to save the village."

"Save the village from what?" Sugar asked.

"Like I said, I'm not sure exactly. This guy has a clear bias against women and said numerous times he doesn't think a woman can be sheriff."

This, as I'd hoped it would, brought immediate outrage from the women in the group. Being gender fluid, circus ringmaster Creed joined the protests. Mr. Powell, the only man on the council, was also upset but in a quiet, supportive way.

"That's absurd," Morgan stated.

"How could he say such a thing?" fortune teller Effie grumbled.

Violet controlled herself by saying only, "He doesn't know what he's talking about. There's no one better for this position."

Flavia, tickled pink by anything negative about me, sat back in her chair looking like she might self-combust from joy. She mumbled something about those closest to a situation sometimes couldn't see the truth. Reeva, sitting next to her, looked ready to attack, but I wasn't sure that had anything to do with her insulting me.

"The problem runs deeper than vigilantes trying to run me out, or whatever they're up to." For the next ten minutes, I explained about Tavie and the girls and what had happened to Silence at the pub.

"Why are we having a meeting about this?" elder Original and chief crabby pants Cybil asked. "You're the sheriff, taking care of incidents like this is your job, right? You could've given us a report at the next regular meeting."

"Gee, I don't know, Cybil." I sighed and signaled for Violet to pass one of the carafes of coffee she brought from Ye Old Bean Grinder over to me. "I thought vigilantes starting bar brawls, stabbing innocent citizens, and trying to rally militia troops to patrol our village might be something the council would want to know about."

Cybil clamped her lips shut and sank back in her chair.

I motioned at the box of scones Sugar brought from Treat Me Sweetly next, and Violet slid it my way. Brown sugar with pecans. Simple and delicious. Just what I needed this morning. Simple.

"Of course we want to know," Reeva said with a slight scowl at Cybil.

"Do you have a plan for dealing with this?" Jola asked.

"That's the other reason I called a meeting. I need help. I don't have room to lock up six people."

"I thought you said there were eight of them," Flavia said as though catching me in a lie.

Reeva swatted her arm. "Don't be so petty."

Flavia swatted back. "Don't hit me."

"Oh, that's rich." Reeva removed the scarf at her neck, exposing the finger marks Flavia had left there. "Shall we talk about who's responsible for physical abuse?"

"That's it." Laurel went to the sisters at the head of the table and pushed their chairs three feet apart. "You've been at each other from the second you got here. Behave or I'll push you to opposite sides of the room next."

Maeve gave her a thumbs up.

"There were eight," I continued, addressing Flavia's objection, "but the two who told me about the leader's plans left town when they realized they were up to something potentially nasty. I've got Jagger and Emery watching four of them upstairs here. Tripp and Gino are over at the station with the other two. I need four more people to rotate in so they can leave."

"If Martin was here," Flavia said offhandedly, "he would help you."

The room went silent as half of the council members looked at each other.

"What?" Flavia glanced around the table. "Why do you all look like that?"

"Martin is in the village, Flavia," Violet said.

"He's been here since Wednesday afternoon," Maeve agreed.

Spots on both of Flavia's cheeks flamed bright red, and she spun to face her sister.

Reeva held up her hands in defense. "I didn't know either."

"He's living on your property," Flavia objected.

"Technically, that half is no longer mine," Reeva reminded her. "Either way, I didn't know he was in the village. There's a tree line between the two cottages, so I can't see when he's there."

"Holy cats," Violet whispered, which meant when Reed dug himself a grave, he dug deep.

As though all of this was my fault, Flavia asked, "Why isn't he helping you? Did you ask him?"

"I asked. He's only interested in drowning his sorrows right now."

"That's a lie." Flavia crossed her arms and turned away.

Maeve fielded this one. "Not according to the bar tab he ran up last night."

Before a discussion about a pub owner's responsibility to monitor people's alcohol consumption started, I turned us back to the reason for the meeting. "As I said, I'm looking for some assistance for a day or two. I'd also like to compensate these folks for their time."

"You mean with village funds?" Morgan clarified. "I find that perfectly acceptable."

"I can send over some of my crew," Mr. Powell volunteered, missing his cup and pouring coffee all over the conference table. Maeve, used to this type of behavior from her clientele, started tossing napkins at him a heartbeat later. He nodded his thanks at her and continued, "There's not much for them to do this time of year. Haven't had any storms except for that one last month. Soon as the snow comes, they'll have plenty to do shoveling the walks."

Literally shoveling. No motorized vehicles in the village applied to snow throwers as well. I told him about Drake messing up some of the landscaping with Unity's van.

He watched while Maeve filled his coffee cup for him. "I'll get a crew on that too."

Flavia called for a vote and thirteen hands went into the air. A rare unanimous vote. With nothing else on the agenda, we separated.

"Mr. Powell," I caught up with the klutzy village services owner. "Would you ask your people to meet me at the station in an hour? I've got something to take care of first."

"Will do." He raised a hand in a salute, caught the brim of his ball cap, and sent it flying.

Shaking my head and biting back a giggle, I bolted out of The Inn and made a beeline for the station. I needed to get the Cherokee and head over to Reed's cottage before Flavia got to him first.

Chapter 13

LESS THAN FIVE MINUTES AFTER picking up the SUV, I pulled onto the parallel dirt trails slowly being carved out by vehicle tires. The trails started just before Reeva's cottage, ran northeast toward the tree line she'd mentioned, and ended behind the trees at a charming little stone cottage in progress.

Reed's new home was V-shaped with the entrance tucked into the deepest part of the *V*. A fireplace chimney made of coordinating brownish-red stones stood to the left of the door. A one-foot-tall deck stained the same rich brown as the rounded-off front door was tucked into the *V*. Cute, cozy, and very Whispering Pines.

I got out of the vehicle, let Meeka out of the back, and headed for the door. Through the trees, far in the distance, I saw another cottage. There was no rhyme or reason to where homes were placed in this area of the village. Wherever the occupant felt was a good spot, that's where their home was planted. For a second, I thought this one in question was Reeva's, but her cottage was the opposite direction and barn red while this one looked to be tree trunk brown. It also gave off a bad vibe. I shivered. It felt like someone was watching me. I quickly shrugged off the feeling. If I freaked out every time I got a weird vibe around this place, I'd have a constant eye twitch by now.

Reed opened his door and sighed, not exactly happy to see me. He left the door open, indicating I could come in, but walked away before I entered, muttering, "I knew you'd show up here eventually."

Meeka was more interested in exploring the woods than seeing her coworker, so I let her do her thing while I stepped inside and took in the wide-open space. Plenty of windows let in lots of natural light. "I'm impressed, Reed. Give me the tour?"

He sighed again but moved to the center of the space. Facing the front door, he pointed left. "The bedroom will be on that side. I'll use the loft area above for an office."

"No stairway?"

"Ladder. Stairs get in the way." He pointed to the right branch of the *V*. "That will be the living room. The kitchen and bathroom will be in the center here where we're standing."

Practical layout. It kept all the water lines in the same section. I learned that little tip from Tripp.

I wandered into his living room and placed a hand on the large stone fireplace with a fire crackling cozily in the box. "This will be nice."

"I think so." He returned to the task he must've been working on when I knocked. He drilled an approximate one-inch hole into a wall stud, fed electrical wire through it, then moved on to the next stud.

"You know how to do electrical work?"

"Used to work part-time for Mr. Powell. He'll inspect my work after I'm done."

"Mr. Powell? You trust him to not knock the place down?"

Reed laughed a little at that. "He does all right with inspections. All he's got to do is look at stuff. He'll check my plumbing too."

"I had no idea you could do all this. I'm impressed."

"I also do drywalling."

I thought of the work Tripp and River were doing on our attic. "If you need help with anything, I know some guys."

Reed nodded but didn't respond verbally.

I watched him drill two more holes. "You left before the fireworks last night. How are you feeling?"

"I've got one wicked hangover. Seems I abused myself good." He glanced over his shoulder. "I assume you don't mean literal fireworks."

He let me explain the incident, and when I started to ask for his help, he stopped me.

"I'm sorry this happened, I really am, but you know I requested a leave of absence. I need to focus on getting past this Lupe thing."

He winced as though it hurt him to say her name out loud.

"It's been three weeks, Reed."

"And I'm three weeks better, but I'm still not ready to care about anyone but myself. I know how selfish that sounds, but there it is."

"You won't even come to the station and just sit in your chair? You don't even have to put on your uniform. I just need someone in the building with the detainees while I'm not there."

He returned to drilling holes. "Sorry."

This wouldn't last much longer, at least I hoped it wouldn't. Reed and I had developed a good partnership over the past four months. I liked working with him, but Jagger was in the picture now too. He appeared to have tons of potential. And there was Emery with his secret ninja skills.

"Deputy?" At the tone in my voice, he stood to face me. Sometimes attitude held more power than a whole dictionary of words. "I understand what you're going through. I had a similar experience not too long ago. I'll be patient for a little while longer, but you need to move past this and keep living." I didn't mention that my breakup had come after a seven-year relationship and a proposal of marriage, as opposed to his two months of dating.

I didn't say anything more, just held his gaze until he looked away, and then turned and left his house. I was waiting by the SUV for Meeka when Reed came out and stood on his small square front deck.

"I heard what you said, Sheriff."

I nodded but said nothing more on the subject. Instead, I pointed at the house I'd seen through the trees earlier. "Do you know who lives over there?"

"Feels like someone's watching you, doesn't it?" Reed asked. "That's Sister Agnes' un-church."

This is where she lived? She had invited me to stop by earlier this summer but never told me where the place was. I needed to get back to the station to meet Mr. Powell's men, but an overwhelming need to go to church, or un-church in this case, overtook me. I whistled for Meeka again, and she finally emerged from the woods . . . covered in burrs. Great.

Assuming I was headed for Agnes', Reed said, "Go back past the Barlow place and take a right on the main gravel road. After about a quarter mile, take a right, and it'll lead you right to her."

"Thanks. See you around, Reed." I stuck Meeka in her crate, giving her a frown over the burrs. "Really nice job on the cottage, by the way." I opened the driver's side door and added, "Oh, your mother and aunt know you're here. Be prepared."

His shoulders dropped, and he gave a half wave as we left. I slowed as we passed by Morgan and Briar's cottage. It was dark. At first, I thought Briar must still be sleeping, which would be unheard of for the early riser, then remembered that she had planned to help with the Yule crowd at Shoppe Mystique this weekend.

One more right sent us down a path just wide enough for the Cherokee. Tree branches scraped against the sides as we bounced slowly over ruts and bumps. When we finally got to the end, I found myself sitting in front of the weirdest house I'd ever seen. And I lived in Whispering Pines.

I got out of the vehicle and let Meeka out. At this stop, she had no interest in roaming the woods. In fact, she stayed close, staring up at the structure with me.

The chestnut-brown un-church looked like a cluster of small boxes all stuck together, rather than one large building. It must've been built in phases. The outside of the entire structure was sided with rough-cut pine planks. Some of the planks were shorter in height and narrower in width than the others and were placed randomly about so the siding looked wavy. The crooked siding gave the illusion that the whole thing was leaning when really everything was square and plumb. Windows were scattered haphazardly. On the front corner to my left stood a three-story tall tower covered in shake-style shingles.

I was staring up at a narrow window at the very top of the tower, sure I'd just seen a figure with white hair peering out at me, when someone came up behind me.

"Sheriff O'Shea. Blessed be."

I jumped and turned to find Sister Agnes Plunkett dressed in full nun's habit with a basket of pine cones clutched in her hands.

"You've finally come to un-church." Agnes looked thrilled at this prospect.

"I didn't know where it was until now. It's quite a unique building."

"Isn't it?" She stood smiling at her un-church as though it was the most beautiful thing ever created. Then she clapped her hands once. "You must be ready to receive the answer to that question."

"Which question?"

She tilted her head. "The question for which you've been seeking an answer, of course."

Speaking with Agnes was a lot like a game of telephone. You were sure you'd heard what she said, but then she repeated something entirely different.

"I was visiting Martin Reed." I pointed through the trees in the general direction of Reed's cottage. That creepy feeling of being watched hit me again. I glanced back up at the tower window, which was empty this time, and was suddenly very glad Reed knew I'd come here. "I saw your, um, un-church from over there. Thought I'd just stop by and say hi. Did you have a good time at Grapes, Grains, and Grub last night?"

"Oh, yes." She clasped her hands in front of her heart, the basket sliding to her elbow. "Mallory and I were having the most delightful conversation."

A delightful conversation with Mallory? If she said so, but my guess was they were both talking about different things.

"We didn't get much of a chance to talk last night. What have you been up to?"

"Oh, I've been quite busy with a special project here."

Meeka started growling then, a sound I rarely heard. I followed her gaze to a different window and saw a shock of white again.

"Agnes, is someone in your home?"

"Yes." She nodded.

"A parishioner?" She wasn't technically a nun, she said she'd been kicked out of the church. Maybe un-parishioner would be the right term.

"A parishioner," she repeated and considered the label. "You could say that. They're my project." Then, as she'd done when I'd spoken with her in the past, she changed, as though slipping on a different, darker personality. "Why don't you come inside? I'll introduce you."

I glanced up again. Whoever was up there, they were watching us. I couldn't see a face, I couldn't even see the white hair anymore, but I could just make out the person's outline standing a few feet away from the window.

"No, thanks." I'd rather hang out with Flavia and do mani-pedis than go inside that building without backup. "I'm supposed to meet someone at the station."

"But you won't have the answer to your question."

"Guess I'll have to come back."

As Agnes contemplated that, I scooped up Meeka and got in the SUV. She didn't object to me not putting her in her cage this time. She wanted away from Agnes, the un-church, and the mysterious tower person as badly as I did.

Chapter 14

WE GOT TO THE STATION to find out Mr. Powell had sent his crew to The Inn. Naturally. It seemed that's just how this day was going to go.

"Laurel?" I said into my walkie-talkie. "This is Sheriff O'Shea."

"Let me guess," she said a few seconds later, "you want me to send two people to the station?"

"Please. I'll wait for them."

Gino had left the second I walked in.

"His wife called with a 9-1-1 about forty-five minutes ago," Tripp explained. "The toddler won't go down for a nap and is into that hyper-tired state where he's tearing around the house and knocking things off every surface he can reach."

"Why don't they put things where he can't reach them?" I asked.

This earned me a blank stare. "I don't know. But the baby is teething and had a diaper blowout. She managed to deal with the baby, but the toddler is still on the loose."

"On the loose?"

"Inside the house. She can't catch him."

My turn to issue the blank stare. "You still want kids after horror stories like that?"

He nodded enthusiastically.

"Your eyes are glazing over with exhaustion," I told him and thought the lack of mental acuity was why he was still open to children. "You should go home and get some sleep. Are you safe to drive?"

"It takes five minutes to get home. I'm fine."

He followed me into my office to give me the rundown on what had happened overnight, but when I got to my desk, I froze.

"Where did that come from?"

Another envelope sat front and center on my desk, waiting for me to sit down and open it.

"Some guy dropped it off. Gino took it from him and set it in here."

"A guy? What did he look like? Describe him."

"Whoa, slow down." He narrowed his eyes. "What's going on? You had one of these at the pub last night. You said it was nothing, but clearly, you were lying."

"I wasn't lying," I snapped and then forced myself to relax. "That wasn't my intent. I just didn't want to get into anything right there in the middle of the pub."

His mind was spinning as he analyzed the situation. "You got other cards before last night, didn't you? Otherwise you would've shown me the one at the pub last night. What's going on? Why didn't you tell me about this?"

"You'd make a good detective." He wasn't amused. "One. I got one other before last night."

"What do they say?"

He was getting angry, as would I. I had to tell him. I went to the evidence locker and pulled out the card I'd put in a plastic bag.

"'I know what you did'?" Tripp read.

I put on latex gloves before pulling the one from last night out of my jacket pocket, slid it into an evidence bag, and then handed it to him.

"'You know what you did'?" His eyes darted to mine. "What does this mean?"

"I honestly have no clue." I retrieved my letter opener from the top middle drawer and sliced the new envelope open, taking care again to only touch it by its corners and not smudge any prints that might be on it.

You ruined my life.

"Babe, this sounds like a threat." Tripp's anger turned into worry.

"Could be," I half-heartedly agreed. "Or maybe it was village kids playing around. I yelled at a group of them messing around by the negativity well one day a week or ten days ago. They were threatening to toss this little kid down the well, so I threatened to fine them with community service."

Tripp shook his head. "It wasn't a kid who dropped this off."

"What did he look like?" I repeated my earlier question. "Help me out."

He sat in one of my two guest chairs, rested his head against the back so he was staring up at the ceiling, and draped his arm over his eyes.

"A few inches taller than me," he began.

"So, six feet?"

"Little taller. Gino is taller than me and this guy was taller than Gino. I'd say six two or three."

"Okay. What else? Hair color?"

He shook his head. "He had on a stocking cap that covered his hair."

"What color was the hat?"

He paused before saying, "White. It was a team hat. Not Packers, not Brewers. Might've been Vikings. No pompom, just a logo on the forehead."

A white stocking cap. Why was that familiar? "So short hair or long hair pulled up into the hat. What about his eyebrows? What color were they?"

Tripp shook his head again. "I wasn't close enough to see them. Wait. He was wearing aviator sunglasses."

"What about a jacket?"

"It was like a suit coat. Brown, I think. Maybe black."

"A brown or black suitcoat, aviator glasses, and a stocking cap?"

Tripp opened his eyes and looked at me, blinking at the sudden light. "Sounds like a disguise."

"Not sure about that, but it does sound like he was covering himself up."

Tripp jumped to his feet and stood directly in front of me. "I don't want you wandering around alone."

"I'm not alone. I've got a K-9." I glanced across my office at Meeka. She had jumped up onto the cot Tripp and Gino used last night and had worked her way down to the bottom of the sleeping bag. Now, the dog-shaped lump was rotating one way then the other. "Are you stuck, girl?"

A muffled semi-urgent bark came from beneath the quilted fabric.

"You know what I mean by alone," Tripp pressed as I unzipped the bag.

Meeka shook herself, trotted halfway out into the main room, and stopped dead when she saw both cells were full. She snorted and then returned to my office to snuggle onto her cushion in the corner.

"Look," I told Tripp, "I understand why you're concerned. I'm a little freaked out too. All this person has done is leave cards, though. In the meantime, I have an actual crime to investigate."

"I don't like—"

Before he could finish the statement, two of Mr. Powell's employees walked in. A man in a John Deere work jacket with a pink and orange scarf around his neck called Schmitty, and Elsa, a woman with shoulders broader than her partner's and wearing heavy-duty overalls. I couldn't help staring at Schmitty's scarf.

"My little girl is learning how to knit," he said, offering no further explanation.

"What do you need us to do?" Elsa asked.

"Nothing, really," I said. "I just need someone to be in the building with these two. In case a fire breaks out or they need to use the restroom. Stuff like that."

"Fire?" Lindsey called from his cell, a note of panic in his voice.

"You're going to pay us for this?" Elsa asked, ignoring Lindsey. When I nodded, she dropped into Reed's desk chair, crossed her arms like she was here for the long haul, and stared at the two detainees in the cells.

I gave them Reed's set of keys, went over a few instructions, and showed them where everything was. I pointed at Reed's walkie-talkie sitting in the charger on his desk. "The unit is set to channel six. Leave it there, please. Use it to call me for any reason. Laurel says she'll send food over when you're ready. Just give a call over to The Inn."

Tripp handed them the deck of playing cards he and Gino used last night and walked with me and Meeka out the front door. "What I was about to say, before Schmitty and Elsa walked in, was I don't want you wandering around alone."

I didn't care for his directive and couldn't worry about his fears right now. I had Silence's attacker to catch. "Then maybe say it in a way that doesn't sound like you're trying to tell me what to do."

"That's not what I'm doing." His tone hadn't changed, though. "I'm worried about you, is that okay?"

"It is. As long as you're not trying to interfere with my job. I'll be interviewing the people at The Inn. I won't be alone."

"Except for walking back to the station later."

"I'll be fine." I took my keys from my pocket. "Do you want to use the Cherokee?"

"No. I'll walk home."

Now, he was pouting. I didn't have time for that so turned to walk away.

"Jayne." He held a hand out to me, which I grudgingly took. "Please be careful."

I squeezed his hand and held on to it. "I'm always careful. And I'm always fine unless someone starts putting the thought in my head that I might not be. Go home, get some sleep, and call me if you hear any news about Silence."

I could feel him watching me as I walked away. First the mysterious someone inside the un-church, and now Tripp. I was getting a little tired of being watched today.

At The Inn, I went through the instructions for what I wanted Jagger's and Emery's replacements to do. I thanked the guys for their time, sent them on their way, and went to Kendra's room first.

"This is unacceptable," she hissed the second I walked in. "I need a change of clothes and my makeup. I had to use body lotion from that tiny bottle in the bathroom on my face. Do you know what that will do to my pores?"

"You'll be fine for one night," I told her as thoughts of my sister Rosalyn entered my head. "In case you've forgotten, you are being held on public disturbance charges. Possibly aggravated assault. If Silence doesn't make it, murder charges. If you cooperate with me and help me figure out what happened, you can be out of here this morning." Maybe into a jail cell, but out of here. To ensure her cooperation, I needed to endear myself to her. "I think you look good without the makeup, by the way."

She placed the tips of her fingers to her face. "You think so?"

I nodded and watched as Meeka began investigating beneath all the furniture and in every corner of the room. "What's your natural hair color?"

Her hands went to her fried, unnaturally blonde hair next. "What makes you think—"

My arched, knowing eyebrow silenced her. "Consider going natural. I think it would look a lot better on you." Time to move on to who stabbed Silence. I pulled out my voice recorder and hit start. "What happened at the pub last night? How did it go from everyone having fun and celebrating Thanksgiving to this?"

Kendra inspected the ends of her hair frowning as though she'd never noticed all the splits before. "I have no idea how that woman ended up stabbed. I mean, obviously, I know *how* she got stabbed, I just don't know who did it."

"You don't sound surprised, though."

"That she got stabbed?" She tossed her hair behind her shoulder. "Well, she was flirting with every guy in the place. You're going to do that, you're going to upset a jealous girlfriend at some point."

"Did she upset you?"

"Not really." Kendra stared out the window at the Pentacle Garden.

Jagger had told me this morning that Kendra kept demanding someone get her things from the hotel. If it was Tripp and me being held, I'd ask about him. She seemed to have forgotten about her boyfriend.

"Why are you all here, Kendra?"

"In this hotel? You put us here."

I blinked at her and sighed. "No. In Whispering Pines. Before he and Chaz left, Marcel told me that Gavin had plans of some kind. It seems he doesn't think I know what I'm doing."

"Yeah, Gavin never thinks women can do anything."

"Marcel thought he might be planning some sort of vigilante takeover of the village to get me booted out?"

"That's what he kept saying, but I think it's more that he was bored. He lost his job at the foundry in Oshkosh."

Beneath the desk, Meeka started sneezing. She backed out, pawed at her nose, and moved on. Hopefully it was just dust irritating her. "That's where you live? Oshkosh?"

She nodded as I wrote that in my notebook. "Why did he get fired?"

"What makes you think he got fired? Maybe they cut jobs."

"Did they cut jobs?"

"No, they fired him. Something about him trying to get their union rep kicked out and himself voted in."

"Sounds like Gavin has a problem with authority."

She shrugged and inspected her hair ends again, this time grasping the two sides of a split and pulling them apart. I could see my mother's hand curling into a claw over that.

"How long ago did he lose his job?"

"Couple months, but he's been jumping from job to job for a year or so. He can't seem to find a good fit." She pulled apart another split. "I guess he tried to get into the police academy a couple years ago, but he couldn't pass the physical. And they said he had a combative personality. I guess that really threw him for a loop. He says he always wanted to be a cop."

"You sound unsure of all these events." When she tilted her head to the side, like Meeka did when she was confused by something, I tried a different route. "How long have you been with Gavin?"

"Oh, not that long. Two months, twelve days. I'm

thinking this isn't really working for me. Might just ghost him."

"Ghost him?"

"Yeah, take off and never see him again."

"I know what ghosting is. Don't you think that's kind of rude? Everyone deserves to know why a relationship isn't working anymore."

Would it have been easier for me to walk away from Jonah without a word? Maybe. But in our situation, the relationship ended when I turned down his marriage proposal in Paris. Talk about your never-ending plane ride home.

I pulled us back to the reason I was here. "Gavin claims he didn't stab Silence."

"Silence? Is that the woman's name?" Kendra's eyes sparkled with amusement.

With little emotion and never taking my eyes from Kendra's, I said, "I won't go into detail, but I will say there is a legitimate reason for why she is the way she is. She only communicates through writing."

"Dang, that's rough." The sparkle left her eyes, and a faraway look took over Kendra's face. "That's true of all of us, isn't it? That we are the way we are for a reason?"

I didn't respond. Instead, I took Silence's words of advice and waited for Kendra to fill the quiet. While I waited, Meeka pulled a sock from between the bed and the nightstand.

"Eww." Kendra made a face. "That's not mine. Anyway, Gavin didn't stab her. It was his knife, I saw that, but he didn't do it. I know because I was right by his side trying to calm him down."

"What was he upset about?"

"I couldn't even say. He had a few beers; that never helps. He was trying to attract an audience. He wanted to preach to the people here—that's what he said, preach to the people—about how they needed help. That black woman—"

"Tavie Smith?"

Kendra shrugged. "I don't know her name. The one who was praying with those younger women. She told Gavin that the village needed help from a higher power, whatever that means, not a mob. A lot of the villagers agreed with her, and that kind of set him off."

Sundstrom's job was to hustle me out the door so Lindsey could "preach to the people." When they didn't want to hear his sermon, he picked a fight with the woman who was stealing his audience.

"How did Silence end up stabbed then?" I asked more to myself than Kendra. "Maybe Tavie was the intended victim."

"Don't think so. She was behind the other three." Kendra squinted, remembering the scene. "It's like they were protecting her. Then each other. They kept shifting positions, it was weird. Either way, Gavin didn't do it. I was holding his right hand in my left. Sometimes the skin-on-skin contact calms him down."

Bile rose in my throat at the visuals that statement presented.

Kendra continued, "He keeps his knife on his right hip. He never let go of my hand."

"Was anyone standing in front of you?"

She closed one eye as she thought this time. "Nope. Just Silence and her friends."

"Then whoever took the knife from Gavin had to be standing behind you."

"That makes sense."

"Do you know who was behind you?"

"I didn't look. I was focusing on that girl with the super-short hair. She was feisty. I thought she was going to take a swing at Gavin."

She had to mean Melinda. "Too bad I don't have pictures."

"Ask Cheryl," Kendra suggested absently, inspecting her hair again. "She's always taking pictures. Always. My cheeks were getting sore from all the smiling."

I stood and softly whistled for Meeka to quit investigating the corner of the room that had so intrigued her. The crew generally did a good job cleaning these rooms, Laurel didn't stand for anything being done halfway, but I made a note to tell her they should do an extra thorough job on this one when Kendra checked out. I didn't want to know what had been in that corner or under the desk.

"Thanks for your time, Kendra. I'll need your contact information in case I have any more questions."

She gave me her cell phone number and an address in Oshkosh. "Best to call me. I'm not going to be at this address much longer."

"You're moving?"

She shrugged and pointed at the address I'd written in my notebook. "That's Gavin's place. My mom has been begging me to come home. I think I might do that."

"Where does your mom live?"

"Madison. She works for the school district. She might be able to get me a job there."

I scribbled down the address and phone number of Melt Your Cares. "This is my mother's day spa in Madison. She can help you with your hair."

Which would likely mean cutting off a good ten inches.

Kendra clasped a hank of her hair protectively in both hands. "It is a little dry. A good deep conditioning would probably perk it right back up."

I gave her the arched eyebrow again.

Her hands dropped to her side. "I know. It's fried." She took the paper from me. "Thanks."

Next stop, Cheryl. I needed to see those pictures.

Chapter 15

CHERYL'S ROOM WAS DIRECTLY ACROSS the hall from Kendra's. I checked that my rent-a-guards had all they needed—they were working their way through generous breakfast trays Laurel sent up from downstairs so were in good shape—and then knocked on Cheryl's door and announced myself. From the other side, I heard, "Hang on. Gotta put some clothes on."

What did that mean? Considering these four were brought here directly from Grapes, Grains, and Grub last night, I wasn't sure I wanted to know.

"It's hot in this room," she complained as she opened the door. "No, I wasn't naked, if that's what you were wondering."

The thought had occurred to me.

The room was a disaster. The sheets were in a tangle at the foot of the bed. Extra pillows had been tossed on the floor. Towels were draped over nearly every surface in the bathroom. I was afraid to think what it would look like if she had luggage.

I crossed the room to the window. "These do open, you know."

"Really? I didn't even check. Every hotel I've ever stayed

in, the windows are bolted shut." She watched as I cracked the window open an inch. Thirty-some degree lake-scented air immediately started cooling the room. "Well, how stupid do I feel?"

I pointed at the thermostat on the wall. "That's adjustable too."

Her eyes shifted from me to the thermostat and back. "Alrighty. Now that we've established I'm an idiot, what can I do for you, Sheriff?"

She made it sound like I was there for a social call. "I thought we'd have a chat about what happened at the pub last night."

"You mean the stabbing?"

"Unless something else happened you wanted to tell me about."

She shook her head. "Nothing I know of. How is that girl? The one who got stabbed?"

"The last I heard, not good. Her intestine was nicked, which they repaired, but they're very worried about infection." To her credit, Cheryl looked genuinely sad about this. "I noticed that you and Darryl separated from the group at one point last night."

"Yeah, we were having a discussion, if you know what I mean." She put emphasis on the word discussion. "Seems rude to keep calling her that girl. What's her name?"

"Silence." Then, before she could ask, "Yes, her name is Silence."

"She's really pretty. Darryl has a weakness for pretty girls. He doesn't actually do anything, far as I know, but he seems to forget I'm around when a pretty girl gives him attention for more than two seconds."

"And Silence was definitely giving him attention."

"Weirdest way of flirting I've ever seen. Her name also describes her personality?"

"Long story, not mine to tell, but she doesn't speak. That's all you and Darryl were talking about? Anything else going on that was upsetting you?"

She dropped onto the unmade bed and lay on her stomach. After wedging a pillow beneath her ample bosom, she swung her feet crisscross in the air and explained, "I thought this was going to be a getaway weekend. I'd heard from some friends that Whispering Pines is a pretty great place to hang out, so when Darryl told me this is where we were coming, I got real excited. Then he tells me three other couples are coming too." She rolled her eyes. "No big deal. Couples weekends can be fun. Then he says we were going hunting."

Her feet dropped to the mattress, and she buried her face in the pillow and screamed.

"I take it hunting isn't your thing."

"I'm vegetarian. Darryl knows how anti-hunting I am. Anyway, I didn't find this out until I saw him at the storage unit grabbing our tent and sleeping bags. Camping in the cold while hunting. About as far from a romantic couple's weekend as we could possibly get."

"It was more than that, though, wasn't it? Gavin is the leader?"

"He is, and yes, this was all his plan. He wanted to go hunting, I guess. Darryl doesn't really know Gavin, but Marcel does. I think Darryl mostly wanted to hang out with his brother and get to know his new boyfriend."

"Chaz?"

She nodded happily. "I really like him."

"Hunting was Gavin's way to get the guys here. If it was supposed to be a guys' hunting weekend, why did you, Kendra, and Didi come?"

"Lars is Gavin's best friend. Honestly, the two of them are worse than girls. They talk every day, multiple times per day, and don't do anything without each other. Didi is super jealous of all the time they spend together and wouldn't let Lars come this weekend without her. So I guess Kendra and I are here to keep Didi busy. Except, she can't stand being away from Lars. As in, she gets weird when he's away for more than two minutes—pacing, wringing her hands, repeatedly asking when we think he'll be back, that kind of thing." She stared blankly as though witnessing that scene in her mind. After a second, she shook her head and rejoined our conversation. "Kendra tells me Gavin isn't happy, because his plan for the weekend wasn't coming together the way he wanted it to."

"His plan? What exactly is his plan?"

Across the room, Meeka had pushed all of the pillows into a pile. Then she burrowed beneath them and poked her nose out. It seemed housekeeping did a good job with this room. There was nothing for her to investigate.

"I have no idea what Gavin's plan was." Cheryl lifted a foot and let it drop to the mattress over and over. "Like I said, Darryl doesn't actually know him. I guess Gavin insisted Chaz had to come along, even though Chaz's idea of a fun night is an intense game of chess. So Chaz tells Marcel they have to come. Then Marcel tells Darryl he should come since Darryl has hunted before and Marcel has never even fired a gun." She held her hands palms in the air. "I guess friendships have to start somewhere, but this is a really convoluted group. You know?"

"I hear you. You're saying that Darryl had no idea what Gavin's plan was?"

"Darryl didn't know there even was a plan. Other than to camp and go hunting. Which they never even did. That's what we were talking about when we went off by ourselves at the pub last night. After you told us we had to leave the campground, thank you for that by the way, we went to the hotel. Gavin started ranting about how this was exactly what he'd been talking about. That there was some 'woman sheriff' up here making life difficult for people and they needed to help. Or something like that." She considered this. "You don't seem to be making life difficult to me."

I bowed my head in thanks.

"Anyhoo, I told Darryl this weekend sucked and that I wanted to go home. Since we rode up here with Gavin, we were going to ask Chaz and Marcel if they wanted to leave, but they already left. What a mess." She let her head drop to the pillow again. "Next time I go anywhere with the group, I'm driving myself."

A bit of information here, a bit there, and soon I'd have a whole story. In this instance, I still needed more bits.

"I was talking with Kendra before I came over here. She says you might have taken pictures at the pub?"

Cheryl shot up into a sitting position. "I did. I took a ton of pictures."

"Did you take any during the fight?"

"Of course. When a crowd gathers like that and tempers start getting short, you can be sure that something is going to happen that could go viral."

My heart dropped to my feet. "Tell me you didn't post anything on social media."

"Well I was going to, but my phone died."

"I really need to see those pictures. They could be very helpful."

"Sure, no problem. I'll share with you. You took my phone from me last night, though."

"I did. My guards have your things. Is it in your purse?"

"Yep, outside pocket. My charger is over at the hotel."

"I think they've got charging cables downstairs. If you're okay with it, I'll bring it down to the front desk and ask them to charge it. Then you can share the pictures with me."

"Groovy. Be prepared, my phone is ancient, so it'll take

like an hour to charge. Can I go after that? I didn't do anything."

"Will the pictures show me that?"

She tapped an index finger to her chin as she thought and then said, "I think so. You'll be able to see that I was standing at the back of the group next to Darryl. I was holding him back so he wouldn't dive in there and try and help. You know how guys get. He stayed by me, and I took pictures."

"In case there was something that could go viral."

"Right."

"Okie doke. I'll be back in an hour. If the pictures prove what you say, I'll be comfortable releasing you."

Chapter 16

WITH THE GUARDS' EMPTY BREAKFAST trays in hand and Cheryl's retrieved cell phone in my pocket, I made my way down the creaking, popping, narrow staircase to the lobby. I was concentrating on dropping off the cell phone with Gardenia at the front desk and nearly collided with a man coming out of the dining room.

"Sorry," I mumbled.

He waved off the apology and continued to the front door.

"Let me take that." Laurel took my bundle and handed it off to a busboy.

"Thanks. Do you have—"

I spun toward the door. That man. He either had white hair or was wearing a white stocking cap. I ran outside, Meeka barking as she chased me, and stopped in the middle of the red brick pathway. I scanned the area slowly, searching the shadows between the cottages as I spun. He was gone already.

"Jayne?" Laurel stood in The Inn's doorway. "Is everything all right?"

I made one last scan of the area and walked over to her. "Did you see that man? The one with the white hat?"

She shook her head. "Sorry, no."

"I think he came out of the dining room. I'll check with the waitstaff." As we reentered the lobby, I asked, "You have phone chargers, don't you?"

Laurel nodded at Gardenia who retrieved a plastic bin from beneath the desk.

"What kind do you need?" Gardenia frowned at the tangle of cords that emerged from the bin when she pulled on one. She glanced at Laurel. "I'll organize this."

I handed her the phone, which had a crack running through the middle of the screen, and she promised to not only charge it but to not let it out of her sight for even a second.

"How's it going upstairs?" Laurel asked.

"Nothing condemning yet," I reported. "But it sounds like the pictures on that phone might be helpful. I'll probably be letting a couple of them go soon."

"Good," Laurel mumbled through the hairclip clamped between her teeth as she twisted her long mostly gray hair into a chignon. "A few people asked about vacancies."

"I'll clear them out as soon as possible and ship the guilty party over to county." I paused and my mouth twitched with a smirk. "We've got a couple rooms available at Pine Time as well."

"I'll send you my overflow." She grinned and winked a gray-blue eye. We had a friendly competition going to see which of us could get to full vacancy fastest each week. She usually won. For now. Pine Time was gaining in popularity.

"Different topic," she said while guiding me to the dining room. "We might have a little trouble brewing."

I sighed and stretched my neck side to side. "What now?"

Laurel took me by the elbow and guided me to the dining room's double door entrance. It was packed, but the group she was concerned about was gathered around the table in the far righthand corner.

"Is that Flavia?" I straightened in surprise. "With a group of people? Flavia doesn't like being with people individually let alone in a group."

"It's Flavia." Laurel placed a hand on my forearm, a gesture that could either be comforting or preparatory. In this case, it was the latter. "I think they're discussing the rash of deaths and other negative tourist incidents."

I squinted across the room at the group which appeared to consist of only villagers. Some I'd seen before but didn't know by name. Others I knew such as Brady Higgins and Sister Agnes. I couldn't fathom even a single scenario that teamed up Agnes and Flavia.

My gaze continued around the table and froze. Sugar too?

Since the day I arrived here, Sugar had been warm to me one day and cold the next. She was the one who first told me some of the villagers thought I brought these troubles with me. Or woke them up. Or whatever they thought I'd done. After the death of her ex-best friend and culinary rival Gin Wakefield, I thought Sugar and I had come to an understanding. Apparently, I was wrong. Who was the ringleader of this little group? Flavia or Sugar?

"Sugar and Flavia?" I mumbled.

"You know Sugar likes to stir the pot." Laurel's voice was maternal, soothing.

"I do, but she also has a way of convincing people to believe things that aren't necessarily true."

"The villagers know you, Jayne, and we know how much you love this place."

"I know." That didn't mean they thought I was doing my job well. "But Sugar and Flavia teaming up? I'm not sure if that hurts or scares me more."

Laurel moved in front of me and put her hands on my shoulders but didn't speak until I looked her in the eye. "Stay the course. Trust yourself."

Laughing at something one of her tablemates had just said, Sugar looked our way. Wounded more than I thought I could be by something like this, all I could do was stare at her. Her smile faded when she registered that it was me standing with Laurel, and she quickly turned away.

Standing behind me now, Laurel murmured in my ear like she was my conscience. "Ignore her. You've done nothing wrong. You're in this village for a reason."

I nodded and blew out a breath. "Thanks, Laurel."

She patted my back and then returned to work.

I glanced at the group once more. What about Sister Agnes? It couldn't have been a coincidence to find her here moments after I'd nearly run into the man with the white hat. He must have been the person I'd seen in the un-church's window. It was a person with a white hat, not white hair. He also must've been the one who delivered the envelope to the station. He and Agnes were linked. But how? And how were the two of them linked to Flavia and Sugar?

The aromas wafting around the dining room hit my stomach then. I hadn't had more than coffee and a small scone since the council meeting this morning and it was nearly eleven o'clock. Every table was full, but one option presented. Lily Grace was sitting by the windows, sun shining down on her, as she studied something on her laptop.

"Mind if I sit here?" I asked, indicating the empty chair across from her.

She blinked, coming out of the focus fog she'd been in. "Hey, hi. Yeah, go for it."

Sylvie, one of the servers, arrived as I was sitting and Meeka was settling into position beneath my chair.

"Coffee, please, Sylvie. And a skillet breakfast with ham and cheddar."

"Toast or muffin?"

I looked up at the blonde in the black peasant dress and

knee-high black boots. "You look rested."

"That surprises you?"

"A little. You work yourself ragged here, Sylvie. You've either caked on the undereye concealer or . . ."

"I have not had work done, if that's what you're thinking." She placed a hand to her cheek. "All natural, baby. We were closed yesterday. I slept for fourteen hours and never got out of my pajamas. Didn't feel like cooking a turkey, so the hubs and I had ice cream for dinner and watched movies. It was great."

"Good for you, sounds like a good day." Did Tripp and I have a free day coming soon where we could do that? Not that I needed downtime. Some time alone with Tripp would be nice, though. "I'll have a muffin. Poppyseed if you've got one. Second choice is peanut butter."

She jotted down my order, stuck her order pad in her apron pocket, and filled my coffee cup from the carafe she'd set on the table.

"Homework?" I asked Lily Grace as I tapped her open laptop.

She shook her head, her partly curly, partly straight hair bouncing as she did. "Researching veterinary schools in the tri-state area."

"You decided?" I nearly choked on my swig of coffee. I'd never seen anyone have a harder time deciding between sticking with the family business, so to speak, and going to college. "You're going to vet school?"

"I haven't decided yet, but I realized I can't make that kind of decision without knowing all my options." She chewed on her bottom lip and sighed at the screen. "I got my ACT and SAT scores. Both are really good. Not to brag."

"By all means, brag it up, sister." I held my mug up to her in a toast. "I took the tests once each, managed to get the lowest possible acceptable score on both, and called it good.

My mother was sure that wouldn't be enough so schmoozed the selection committee at UW Madison and promised free facials and body wraps."

She stared blankly at me. "You went to college on bribes?"

I frowned and heat spread over my face as I realized how that sounded. "I was joking about the spa treatments. My GPA was really good. As far as I was concerned, that showed I was a good student and didn't see why I had to take a separate test to prove it."

"Glad we had this conversation after I took my tests."

I grinned at her. "Has your research helped with your decision?"

"Not really. All I know now is that veterinary school is stupid expensive. Although, my grandmothers have a fund set aside for me." She tapped a spoon rhythmically against her teacup. "The village could use a vet. But we already have Igor up at the circus. He knows enough to take care of all our animals."

Everything about Lily Grace was fifty-fifty. She was mixed race. She loved being able to help people by telling their fortunes but hated her "gift." She wanted to stay in the village she loved but yearned to see more of the world.

"You'll figure it out." I did my best to stay middle of the road because while she loved the attention she got when she asked for people's advice, she hated when folks offered it freely.

Sylvie arrived with my skillet and a bag of biscuits for Meeka in record time. "Figured you've got more important things to do today than hang out here. I put your order at the top of the stack."

"Thanks." I remembered my creepy secret admirer. "Hey, did you serve a guy wearing a brown jacket and white stocking cap earlier? Might have had aviator sunglasses?"

"Doesn't sound like anyone I served. We're always

packed on the weekends between Thanksgiving and Yule. When we're this busy, I barely even remember the people sitting at my tables let alone the others."

While I ate, thankfully with my back to Sugar and Flavia, and slipped biscuits to my K-9, Lily Grace continued with her research. She started a list of positives and negatives to staying and leaving, stating each one to me as she wrote. I wished I could help, but this was a decision only she could make.

After Sylvie had taken away my empty plate and given me one last refill on coffee, Lily Grace asked, "What's wrong, Sheriff?"

"What makes you think something's wrong?"

"I can feel stress coming off you in waves. It's starting to bum me out. It's Sugar, isn't it?"

"Sugar?"

"She's at that table in the corner, which I'm sure you know, and has been staring at you for the last five minutes."

"That explains why I feel like I'm being watched. For the third time today." I shook my head at her look of confusion. "It's not just Sugar. It's also the woman who got stabbed last night and other things going on around the village." And the fact that Tripp and I were arguing all the time. And that I was having nightmares.

Lily Grace closed her laptop and held out her hands to me.

"Really? Right here?" She wanted to read me. At this point, I'd take all the guidance I could get so placed my hands over hers.

"What do you want to know?"

I wanted to know who the stabber was. Why I was having these dreams. When Tripp and I would get back to normal. "Tell me something that can help with . . . anything."

"That's not very specific."

I shrugged. "I've got a lot going on."

Usually, she wanted a bit of space between her hands and

her customer's. She said her visions formed in that little energy gap. This time, though, she grabbed my hands as she closed her eyes and almost immediately got a response for me.

"I see two pink cylinders side by side." After a few seconds, "I see a jagged scar running across a smooth plane."

When she opened her eyes, I was staring at her, as were the people around us.

"Anything?" she asked.

"Two pink cylinders and a jagged scar. Guess I won't know if that's helpful until it is." Which was true of most of the readings she did for me. "Does it mean anything to you?"

"I'm not an interpreter, just the messenger." She turned to the diners nearby who were still staring. "She's a friend. I'm not giving freebies."

Disappointed, they turned back to their meals.

"This vision came on fast."

"Told you. You're oozing."

"Pleasant. Now I want to go take a shower." I tossed back the rest of my coffee. "Thanks for letting me share your table. Good luck with your decision."

She swatted at me like she didn't want to talk about it anymore but had already returned to her pluses and minuses list before I walked away.

In the lobby, I stopped by the front desk. "How's the phone charge coming?"

Gardenia picked it up and shook her head. "Almost at fifty percent."

Not enough yet. "You'll still keep an eye on it?"

"I'll treat it like a baby and take it with me wherever I go," she promised.

I thanked her and headed back upstairs. Time to talk with Didi.

Chapter 17

MEEKA DARTED UP THE STAIRS ahead of me, easily beating me to the third floor. Then she stood at the top, like the queen of the mountain, gloating as though she'd accomplished something massive.

"It's hardly a fair race," I told her. "You're much faster and have four legs. Besides, I wasn't racing anyway."

Sometimes, it felt more like we were siblings rather than owner and pet. Of course the question was, who was the owner and who was the pet?

She turned away from me, head held high, and trotted over to the guards. Or rather, guard. Jagger was back.

"What are you doing here?" I asked. "Where did the other two go?"

"I sent them home," he said. "It's in my training; I need to finish the job. I ran home, literally, got in a quick workout, took a shower, and grabbed something to eat. Now I'm back."

"Let me out of here," came a pleading wail from Didi's room. "I need to see Lars."

"Someone's finally awake." Jagger jerked a thumb over his shoulder at her room. "She was doing that off and on all night."

"You're sure she's okay?" I asked as a loud thud sounded against her door. She must've thrown herself against it. "She isn't hurting herself, is she?"

"I checked on her a couple times," Jagger informed. "She's fine."

"She realizes the door locks from inside, right?"

"She knows. I think she's doing that to make sure we hear her. She tried to bolt a few times. I caught her and carried her back in there. The last time, Emery put one of his Spock moves on her and threatened to cuff her if she did it again. If she sticks to her pattern, she'll start sobbing hysterically soon. I think that's how she fell asleep last night, wore herself out."

"Just like little kids," I mused. "Run around like crazy people, pitch a fit, then sob until they pass out. Or so I've been told. All right, I might as well end some of her suffering."

I'd barely tapped on the door when she screamed, "Let me out. Let me out of here right now, I need to see Lars."

"Didi?" She didn't respond right away. "Didi, are you listening?"

"Yes, let me go." Then in a long, plaintive wail, "Please."

I tried the knob, it was locked. Probably to keep Emery from coming in and pinching her. "It's Sheriff O'Shea. Let me in."

A soft *click* sounded as she turned the lock and then opened the door a few inches. An instant later, she flung the door open wide and darted past me . . . and straight into Jagger's arms.

"Warned you, didn't I?" He cinched an arm around her waist. With her arms and legs flailing, he carried her back into the room and set her on the bed. "Stay."

I gave him a nod of thanks and stood in front of her. "Are you going to try and run again? Because I can cuff you if necessary." I pulled a pair of zip cuffs from my pocket as proof.

"What did you do with Lars?"

"Lars and Gavin are safe and sound at my station. I've got them locked in my jail cells with two very competent people watching them. Lars is fine."

I'd never seen anyone as fidgety as Didi. She played with her fingers. Her legs bounced up and down. She adjusted positions on the bed every few seconds. She looked out the window and then at me. If her head wasn't swiveling, her eyes were darting about. No wonder she was so tiny. She burned calories at a constant, high rate.

Meeka was uncomfortable around all this motion. She positioned herself near the door rather than exploring the room as she had the others.

"The sooner you settle down and talk to me, the sooner you'll be able to see Lars."

"I *need* to see him." She stood, then sat when I held out the cuffs. "You took my phone away; I can't even text him."

"I took his phone away, too, so even if you could text him, he couldn't respond. Here's the thing, I don't know who stabbed Silence yet. I can't let any of you go until I've figured that out. Is there anything you can tell me about that event?"

Her expression of desperation turned to one of fury. "Silence is that woman? That skanky one who was all over my Lars?"

She'd gone from antsy to practically seething with anger, going on and on about how Silence was flirting with all the men and especially with Lars. She was getting herself more and more worked up, and nothing I could have said would have convinced her Silence wasn't trying to steal Lars from her. If I was going to get anything useful out of her, I needed to change tactics and stay away from the topic of Silence.

"I was talking with Kendra and Cheryl earlier," I began.

"Where are they?" She perched on the edge of her bed as though ready to take off again. "What did you do with them?"

"I didn't do anything with them. They're across the hall in their own rooms. Didi, you've really got to calm down." Jagger had made the comment earlier that Didi was like an addict when it came to Lars. She did seem addicted but not just to Lars. It was like she was coming down off something. "Tell me why you came here this weekend."

"I'm here with Lars."

Oh geez. "Yes, I know that. You came here with three other couples, though. Whose idea was that?"

"Gavin's. Gavin is Lars' best friend. They wanted to go hunting."

Good. She'd settled by a degree or two.

"Did they go hunting?" I asked.

"No. Gavin said your village needs help. So we're doing that instead."

I asked a few more questions but didn't learn anything more than what Kendra and Cheryl had already told me. I couldn't tell if it was that she didn't know anything else, or if she was simply too distracted about her boyfriend. She reminded me of girls I'd seen, mostly those at college parties, who'd had too much to drink and were obsessing over a guy they liked. They'd go on for hours, sucking other girls into their drama vortex to commiserate with them. I'd never seen anyone as desperate to be with a person as Didi was to be with Lars. Honestly, that level of dependency was a little scary.

"Thank you for talking with me, Didi."

She sprang to her feet. "Do I get to see Lars now?"

Maybe she was suffering from a disorder of some kind. I thought briefly of Helen and David Zaleski, an oddly amusing couple who had spent a few days with us last month. Helen had told me that David suffered from a disorder and became agitated when he wasn't with her because she was his normal, his happy place. It was possible Didi suffered from something similar. She could be on medication of some kind and had missed a dose because I locked her up. And here I was judging her. If it was meds, we'd take care of that as quickly as possible.

"I told you that I needed to figure out what happened to Silence before you could see Lars again. Remember?"

She nodded and frowned a little. "I didn't tell you?"

"No, you didn't, but I still need to talk with Darryl. Maybe he can tell me what happened. Why don't you take a little nap? Hopefully by the time you wake up, I'll have my answer."

"I'm not sleepy."

"Okay, but I'm a little worried about you. You seem really upset. Is there something I can get for you that would help you calm down?" I held up a hand to stop the request I knew was coming. "I can't get Lars for you. Not yet."

I hoped she'd say, "my medication over at the hotel," but instead she sat and looked around the room. "It would be nice to watch TV."

"Sounds good. I'll have Jagger bring one in for you. Okay?"

She made a little nest of pillows near the head of the bed to settle into and watch television. Watching her place the pillows was almost like watching an artist create. She'd arrange them, stand back, fix the corner of one, smooth the case on another. While she did that, I looked around her room. It was spotless. If I didn't know she'd spent the night in here, I'd swear housekeeping had just finished with it. Everything was perfectly in its place. I hadn't taken the time to watch Didi and Lars together, but he very well could be her rock, her Helen, the person who centered her and kept her together. Or he was her obsession.

"That was quick," Jagger said when I stepped out of the door.

"We may have misjudged Didi. Would you bring a

television back in there for her? She needs something to occupy her while we're working through this."

An expression of understanding crossed his face and he pushed himself up from his comfy chair. "Right away. Is there anything else she needs?"

"You can ask her. No, she can't see Lars."

Jagger smiled. "I figured that."

Once he had everything set up for her, I approached the last occupied room on the third floor and knocked. "Darryl? This is Sheriff O'Shea, I'd like to come in."

The door flung open before I'd finished speaking. "Thank God. I've been waiting to talk with you. Please, come in."

He stood back and held out an arm welcoming me into his room as though I'd come for dinner.

"How is she?" he asked.

I wasn't sure if he was referring to Silence or Cheryl, so I chose Silence. "The blade nicked her intestine, and now they're monitoring her for infection. It's not good. She could die."

"The poor woman. Okay, ask me anything you want," he said, and before I could do so, he started right in. "Marcel is my brother, you knew that, right? He asked me to come up with him this weekend. He wanted me to bring Cheryl, too, so we could meet his new boyfriend."

I held out both hands to get him to stop speaking. "Darryl, we're going to get to all of that. I need you to slow down and go through this in a more organized fashion." I pulled my voice recorder out of its pocket, as I had with the other three, and pressed the red button. "I'm recording this conversation."

"Okay." He inhaled deeply and blew it out in a hiss. "What can I tell you?"

"Tell me how you decided to come here this weekend."

As Kendra, Cheryl, and Didi had, he explained about the

plans to come camping and hunting but that, somewhere along the line, those plans changed.

"Why did they change?" I asked.

"I don't know all of the details. I wasn't in on any of this but was able to pick up on some of the plans. It's kind of amazing what you can learn by sitting quietly and listening."

Silence's face flashed in front of my eyes, and a surge of emotion for her came over me.

I cleared my throat and blinked. "What did you hear? Whose conversation were you listening to?"

He sprang to his feet and started pacing. "I hope this is okay, I can't sit still and talk."

I positioned myself closer to the door, just in case. Meeka sat between me and Darryl, eyes fixed on Darryl, ready to attack his ankles. My little protector.

"It's fine," I agreed. "Keep your pacing to that half of the room, though, all right?"

He nodded. "Okay, so it was that first night after you told us we couldn't stay at the campground. We rented four rooms at that hotel, and Cheryl, Kendra, and Didi stayed up in one of the rooms while Gavin summoned the rest of us to the bar downstairs."

"The rest of you being yourself, Lars, Marcel, and Chaz?"

"Right. All the men. I'm sure you can imagine why Gavin didn't want the women with us."

"I have a good idea." The sexist jerk.

"Anyway, Marcel and I were feeling really uncomfortable because we didn't know any of them. I think Marcel might have met Gavin before, since he's Chaz's brother, but he didn't hang out with him or anything. Gavin ordered a couple pitchers of beer and then he and Lars started going over their plan."

"I've heard a lot about this plan," I said, "but no one has been able to give me specifics."

"It wasn't anything complicated. Gavin wanted to prove he had the skills to take care of a town in turmoil."

"Is that what he called Whispering Pines? A town in turmoil?"

"His words exactly. Chaz told Marcel that it's been Gavin's dream for years to be a police officer."

I nodded in agreement. "Kendra told me they wouldn't accept him at the academy."

"Right, that's what Chaz said too. I guess Gavin has been scanning the news in papers and online."

"What was he looking for?"

"Towns in turmoil. He read something online about a boy who went missing last month. After that, Gavin started reading everything he could find about Whispering Pines. He learned that not only was there the trouble with the boy but that there's also been a bunch of deaths over the last six months. Then he found out that you're the sheriff. We already know what he thinks about women, so learning about you was like the match that lit his fuse. The plan was to come up here, cause a commotion, and then he would be the hero who fixed problems in seconds whereas you haven't been able to handle things for months." He paused, then added, "His words, not mine."

"Are you telling me that he purposely set up the fight just so he could stop it?"

"That's what Chaz said, and that's what I was hearing in the bar that night."

"He recruited you all, without your knowledge, so he'd have a gang, so to speak, who would be involved in a fight? And then, what, he'd give the signal and you all would stop fighting?"

"Basically, yes. You ever hear about how someone will start a wildfire and then get hired to be on the firefighting squad? And then they find out the person was an unemployed firefighter looking for a job?"

I took a second to work through that one. "Can't say as I've ever heard of that exact scenario, but I understand what you're saying. This was Gavin's way to try and get into the police academy. He'd be praised as the hero here, and the academy would realize their error and let him in."

He nodded and, in a voice apparently meant to be Gavin's, said, "See what a hero I am? You should let me be a cop."

"Kendra told me the reason he couldn't get into the academy was because he couldn't pass the physical."

Darryl pressed his knuckles to his mouth to hold in a laugh and looked at me as though I'd just said the funniest thing ever. "What a moron. He still wouldn't be able to pass the physical. The guy slams back whiskey like it's water and smokes at least a pack a day."

My turn to laugh. "He's got to really be enjoying his time in my jail cell, then. No booze, no smokes."

"Won't he accuse you of denying him his legal rights?"

"Maybe. Don't care. So how did we get from staging a fight to a young woman being stabbed?"

Darryl shook his head. "That, I can't answer."

Of course he couldn't. That was the one answer no one could give me. However, Cheryl's cell phone had to be charged by now.

"Where were you when the fight broke out?"

"In another dining room talking to Cheryl. She wasn't happy and wanted to leave. Then we found out that Marcel and Chaz split on us."

"They only went to the hotel. I talked to them before they left the pub."

"Are you serious? We thought they left town. We would've gone with them." He propped his hands on his hips and shook his head. "I mean, the only reason we came here was because Marcel asked us to, and then he leaves without even telling us? Dude's going to have a lot of explaining to do when I get home." Then he paused, like he'd said something wrong. "You believe me, don't you? You are going to let me go, aren't you? I didn't do anything. I for sure didn't stab that woman."

"Tell me first, during the fight, when the stabbing occurred, where were you?"

"At the back of the crowd. Like I said, we were in that little dining room, and by the time we got out to the big room, things were already heated. I figured his signal was coming at any second 'cause it was intense. People were getting hot."

"What was the signal?"

"He was going to take off his baseball cap and scratch his head. After a minute, he still didn't do it, and I was going to break things up on my own. I figured someone was going to get hurt." He shook his head. "I thought some punches would fly, stuff like that. Sure didn't think someone would get stabbed. Cheryl wouldn't let me do anything. She held me back, told me not to get any more involved than we already were."

"Smart woman. She tells me she was taking pictures during the altercation."

Darryl laughed. "I'd only be surprised if she wasn't taking pictures. Honest to God, how many selfies of us does that woman need to post? I mean, you name it, she takes a picture of us doing it." He paused, realizing what he might have implied. "Not that. I wouldn't let her take a picture of us doing that."

I held in my laughter. "I believe you, Darryl. Cheryl's cell phone has been charging down at the front desk. I'm going to go get it and then you two can go through the pictures with me. If it shows what you claim, that the two of you were at the back of the group, I'll let you go."

He slumped with relief. "Never thought I'd hear myself say this, but if that's what gets us out of this, she can take all the selfies she wants. I might start taking some too."

Chapter 18

CHERYL'S PHONE HAD REACHED EIGHTY-SEVEN percent charged, enough to send pictures to my station email. I thanked Gardenia for tending to it, turned to go back upstairs, and found myself face to face with Flavia. Sugar gave me a long look over her shoulder as she left through the front door.

"I have to thank you," Flavia said with a sniff.

"*There's* a reason for concern," I replied, knowing this would be backhanded. "You never thank anyone for anything. What did I do?"

"At the council meeting this morning, you confirmed my suspicion that you are not the right person for this job."

I wasn't even a little surprised by this. "I respect your right to have an opinion, Flavia." I turned to angle past her, but she wanted to chat.

"There are plenty of others who feel the same way."

Memories of the day the council voted me in as sheriff played in my mind. Flavia, Donovan, Maeve, Mr. Powell, and Sugar had all voted against me. Maeve had since apologized, we hadn't known each other very well at that point, and told me she wished she could go back and change her vote to a yes.

But Flavia wasn't talking about only council members.

"Villagers aren't happy with what you've done to Whispering Pines."

She was poking at the sore spot inside me, the one that also wasn't happy with my performance and kept scabbing over only to split open again. Fortunately, the lobby was empty except for Gardenia, who purposely avoided looking at us as she popped on a pair of headphones and began bopping to whatever music she was listening to.

Meeka, ever my protector, sat like a little furry gargoyle in front of me.

"What exactly did I do to the village?" I pushed insecure Regular Jayne to the side before she could make things worse and let confident Sheriff Jayne take the lead. "It's not like I sent out invitations to murderers to come visit us." I waited for her to respond. When she didn't, I continued with my defense. "The only thing I'm guilty of is stumbling upon and uncovering one secret after another. Honestly, I don't think there's anyone in this village who doesn't have one." I was about to walk away but turned back. "And for the record, I did not bring Martin and Lupe together. You need to quit acting like it's my fault or anyone else's that your son is pulling away from you. That's one hundred percent your doing."

She hissed at me, not with surprise but as though casting a spell. The look on her face sent a chill through me. It was the same one I'd seen a few days after I arrived here. Morgan had invited me to observe her coven's gathering at the Meditation Circle so I could better understand Wicca. During their ceremony, each member read from their list of intents for the upcoming tourist season. Basically, it was a prayer session for the village. After reading their list, the person either buried the paper in the ground or tore it into pieces and let the wind take it. A few saved their list to toss into the lake or creek where it would dissolve. Flavia threw hers into the fire pit. Some of the pieces drifted up with the hot air currents from the flames. Other burning pieces flew sideways toward me. I still didn't know how she did it, but somehow, she directed those bits at me. That's how she looked now, like she wanted to light me on fire.

I burst out laughing and wiggled my fingers in front of her mouth. "What's that? Are you hexing me?" A small voice inside me urged me to run home and get the protection charms Morgan had given me shortly after that coven gathering. *Why aren't you wearing the amulet or carrying the charm bag? That's why she gave them to you.* I silenced the voice. "Cute as you and your little group of warriors are, I know there are more people on my side than yours."

Meeka leaned against my leg as the little voice said, *Meeting aggression with aggression rarely works.*

Little voice was right this time. "Flavia, please don't cause problems. We all want harmony around here. If people aren't happy with the job I'm doing—"

"There's no 'if' about it. There are plenty who aren't happy with you. Enough that you should pay attention. We never had problems like this when Karl wore the badge."

Little voice tried to stop me again, but this time I mentally shoved a gag in her mouth.

"Maybe there didn't appear to be any problems, but that was on the surface." I stared straight into Flavia's intense blue eyes. "Something was going on that the villagers didn't see. Something bad enough to make him eat a cyanide capsule in front of me. Problems like we're having now don't just happen. They start bubbling far beneath the ground and slowly ooze their way to the surface. I didn't cause any of these problems, and you know it. Those buried things started happening forty years ago."

Her only reaction was a slight twitching of her pursed lips.

"Look, I'd be happy to sit down with your group and discuss it like adults." I flung a hand toward the dining room. "Gathering in corners and getting each other worked up about things will only lead to more problems."

She pushed her shoulders back. "We were simply sharing thoughts. There's nothing wrong with that."

"And I'm open to hearing those thoughts." Cheryl's phone vibrated in my hand. Someone was texting her. "Right now, I need to take care of this other problem we've got going on."

I didn't give her the opportunity to respond further. It's not that I wasn't taking villager concerns seriously. Of course I wanted to believe I was doing my job perfectly, or at least better than my predecessor had. If I was being true to my word, though, that I loved this village and its villagers and wanted only the best for them, I needed to listen and learn from those who felt I could do better.

I knocked on Darryl's door and when he opened it, I asked him to come with me to Cheryl's room. However, Cheryl's room was still trashed.

"Is she like this at home?" I asked him.

"Actually, no. Our apartment is spotless. It's like this other side of her comes out when we stay in hotels. She tends to trash them. She doesn't break anything, but she tosses stuff everywhere. If I don't clean up before we leave, we end up getting an extra charge for cleaning services."

The three of us crossed back to Darryl's room to look at the pictures.

Cheryl unlocked the phone and brought the pictures up, flipping through three or four dozen to get to the start of their weekend. "Okay, here's the first one."

I took the cell phone from her. The crack in the screen obscured the images a little but not enough that I couldn't tell what I was looking at. I started scrolling slowly, then flipped a little faster because the first twenty were of their road trip from Oshkosh to Whispering Pines. Another couple dozen taken at the campsite showed Lindsey, the distinctive handle of the knife in question sticking out of the sheath on his right hip. Finally, after a collection of Cheryl, Kendra, and Didi in a hotel room doing each other's hair and makeup and drinking what looked to be cosmos, I came to pictures at the pub.

The first few were of the group, minus Marcel and Chaz, gathered at their table with plates full of Thanksgiving dinner in front of them. Then there came some of the guys talking with Silence, Melinda, and Gloria. It was immediately obvious there was a lot of flirting going on between the six of them. A few were closeups of Darryl talking to Silence. Cheryl was right about the effect a pretty girl had on him. He looked like a lovesick schoolboy with an aw-shucks grin on his face.

I paused on this one for Cheryl's sake.

"See what I mean?" Cheryl asked him. She reached over my shoulder and pointed at his face on the screen. "See that? That's the look you get whenever you talk to a beautiful woman."

Darryl took her hand and kissed it. "Then I must have that look all the time when I'm at home."

Smooth talker. Cheryl blushed a rosy-pink and swatted his arm.

A few screen swipes later, I finally got to the pictures I'd been waiting for. Cheryl had taken dozens of shots of the group gathered at the center of the pub's main room. Just as she and Darryl had said, the images showed Lindsey, Kendra, Sundstrom, and Didi front and center facing Silence, Melinda, and Gloria. There were two villagers on the vigilante side. I had spoken with them that night, and they claimed that they hadn't done anything other than stand there and, sickeningly, encourage Lindsey. That had been all the motivation I needed to issue disturbing the peace fines.

As a few of the detainees had also mentioned, Silence, Melinda, and Gloria kept shifting positions. In one, Silence was upfront with the other two behind her. Then Gloria was upfront with Silence and Melinda in back. In still another, Melinda was upfront with Silence in between her and Gloria.

I counted the images, so I knew how many to expect, and handed the phone back to Cheryl. Not only did I need the pictures for evidence, I wanted to study them on a bigger, uncracked screen.

I paused, realizing this had to be Lily Grace's vision. A "jagged scar across a smooth plane." Her record continued.

"Send all of these to me at the station, all right?" I gave Cheryl my email address. Once she had completed the task, I said, "I told you that if these pictures proved you weren't involved, I'd let you go. It's safe for me to assume that Cheryl was at the back of the group taking pictures since this is her phone."

A panicked look came over Darryl. "I was standing right next to her."

"I didn't actually see you in any of the pictures," I told him. "Can you prove that you were next to her?"

As he stood there running his hand over his close-cropped hair, Cheryl blurted, "There is!" She scrolled rapid-fire through the images until she came to one that she wanted me to see. "Look. Here's his tattoo."

I took the phone back and enlarged the image on the screen. It showed the arm of someone on her right with a distinctive tattoo. I looked from it to the one Darryl was holding in front of my face. It looked at first like a weirdly shaped letter M. Or, "Is that the top half of a heart?"

"Mm-hmm," Cheryl hummed through pursed lips. "His ex-girlfriend has the bottom half with his name next to it." She placed her own forearms side by side. "Put them together and they form a whole heart. Isn't that cute?"

I squinted at the image and then at the word on his arm. "What does that say?"

"It says Charity," Darryl explained. "I keep telling Cheryl we could complete the heart and tell people I believed in donations to the Heart Association."

"There's no way you're keeping her name on your arm."

With the right font and some creativity, a good tattoo artist could probably turn "Charity" into "Cheryl." I kept that thought to myself, though.

"All right, you're both free to go."

"How are we going to get home?" Cheryl asked. "We don't have a car."

"We're making Marcel come back and get us," Darryl said. "The little twerp owes us for leaving us here."

They gathered their things and walked down the hall, making plans to go shopping and for a hike until Marcel returned.

"Two down, two left," Jagger said.

"Two?" I asked.

"Didi and Kendra."

"Oh, yeah. I forgot about Kendra."

"They've been really quiet. You could leave them here for a while. I'll stay."

I considered that option, but Laurel wanted to rent the rooms to guests. Then again, Pine Time had a couple rooms available.

"That's a tough one," I replied. "I hate to disturb Didi when she's so calm, but I think I'll bring them over to the station and let them be with their men."

As though it weighed nothing, Jagger picked up his lounge chair to return it to the room he'd borrowed it from. "Thanks for letting me help. I forgot how much I like this work."

"Really? All you've done is sit here."

"That's how it looks." He tapped his temple. "I'm mentally composing poetry at the same time."

How many layers could one guy have? "You write poetry?"

"It's more like narrative poetry. I make up stories in verse form about the people I guard."

"I have no idea what you just said, but I trust that it's awesome. Thanks for your help. Can I call you if I need assistance again?"

"Around here? I'll expect to hear from you next week."

He was joking, but only a little.

I knocked on Didi's door and poked my head inside. "How are you doing in here?"

"Okay, but I've already seen this movie three times."

"Why didn't you change the channel?"

"I can't find the remote."

"There are buttons on the television." I pushed one to demonstrate an alternate way to change the channels.

She shook her head, impressed. "I think I could learn a lot from you."

She was really very sweet when she was calm. "Would you like to go see Lars now?"

Instantly, she climbed out of her little pillow nest and put on her shoes. "Yes, please."

We stopped and retrieved Kendra, who claimed she'd rather stay in the hotel room. As though she was on vacation.

"Except you're still a suspect," I reminded her. "I just eliminated Darryl and Cheryl. If you can tell me who stabbed Silence, I'll let the innocent parties go."

"Wish I could." Kendra retrieved her coat from the room's closet. "I have no idea what happened. It was chaos in the pub."

It was. Good thing I had pictures to clear it all up.

Chapter 19

USING HER NEWFOUND INSTINCTS AS a support dog, Meeka walked closer to Didi than Kendra and me on our way to the station. When we passed by Treat Me Sweetly, Sugar rushed outside to talk to me.

"I'm escorting these women to the station, Sugar. I don't have time to talk." I was also mad at her and didn't care what she had to say.

"Two minutes," Sugar begged.

I sighed and pointed to the bench on the sweet shop's deck. "Ladies, would you have a seat up there, please?"

Once they were out of earshot, I turned to Sugar. "Yes, I saw you with Flavia. Are you going to say it wasn't what it seemed?"

Sugar shook her head. "No, it's pretty much exactly what it looked like. Flavia is rounding up villagers who want to take back the village. Just thought you might want to know what they were talking about."

"You mean what *we* were talking about. You're one of them."

"In a way. I'm not looking to kick you out of Whispering Pines—"

"Good," I interrupted. "Seems like a few people around here have forgotten that I own the village."

"Well, technically your father does."

She just couldn't stop herself from aggravating me. "And the only reason he hasn't put this place up for sale to the highest bidder is because I asked him not to. It's in everyone's best interest to work with me on this, because all of you will be looking for a new place to live if I walk away. Next time you have your little gathering of vigilante villagers, tell them that."

"You don't need to get so defensive."

"Don't I?"

"No." Sugar's voice rose and then dropped again. "I told you before, there are some here who believe you woke up this darkness by uncovering the truth of how Yasmine Long died. Then you went deeper with Priscilla Page's death."

"None of this has anything to do with me. I didn't create your *darkness*. All I did was expose the truth."

"I also told you," Sugar continued, ignoring my statement, "I believe you're the one who will free us from whatever is going on."

I leaned back and studied her. "Your involvement with Flavia's group is what exactly? Are you trying to tell me you're a double agent?"

Wouldn't be the first time. When they were young, Sugar and her sister Honey used to spy on the bigger kids. Apparently, Honey was so little that the group of kids my dad used to hang out with, nicknamed The Pack, didn't notice when she was hanging around. She'd gather information and bring it back to Sugar. Little kid stuff then, but they committed their acts of espionage so often, doing this kind of thing was firmly implanted in their personalities now. I didn't trust Sugar. I didn't trust anyone who played both sides that way.

"Double agent," Sugar repeated with a glint in her eye. "I

guess you could say that. Believe me or not, I am trying to make the group see exactly what you just said. That this bad vibe is due to things that happened a long time ago. You know how people can be. If it's new in their world, it must be new altogether."

"I agree with you on that, but honestly I'm not sure I can trust you."

She looked wounded. Tough, she brought it on herself. "Guess I have to prove that I love this village as much as you do."

"I don't doubt that, Sugar, but you seem to think you have rights here that I don't."

"I have been here longer."

Honestly. If she kept poking the bear, she'd end up getting bit. "Which means nothing when I'm holding the deed."

Startled at my response, Sugar flinched. "Is that a threat?"

"I don't need to threaten you. I just told you, if I go down, you all go down with me."

The truth was if I wanted to do away with the village council and rule Whispering Pines as the monarch, there wasn't a thing any of them could do about it. Always a businessman, Gramps insisted that stipulation be written into the fine print. None of us wanted that to happen, though. Everyone having a say was always better. Well, usually better.

I turned to find Didi and Kendra now enjoying ice cream cones. Honey, standing in the shop window with a big smile on her face, waved at me with both hands. How long had I been talking to Sugar?

"Let's go, ladies."

"Thought we were going to have to break up a fight," Kendra said when we were twenty yards down the Fairy Path.

"What do you mean?" I asked.

"You don't like that woman," Didi noted.

It was that obvious? "Not right now, I don't."

Didi licked a drip making its way down her cone and said with childlike innocence, "Maybe you will the next time you see her."

And right there was the definition of my relationship with Sugar. "Maybe I will."

Didi squealed with delight when we entered the station. She ran straight over to Sundstrom's cell. "Let me in there, Sheriff. Lock me up."

"Nothing at all weird about that," Elsa noted to Schmitty as I opened the cell door and let Didi in.

"She really missed her boyfriend," I told them as we watched him wrap her in his arms. Kendra, however, wasn't as thrilled to see her guy.

She leaned in close to me. "Remember what I told you in the hotel room? I'm ending things with him."

"I appreciate and encourage that. I have nowhere else to put you, though. Unless you want to have it out with him right here, you're going to have to play nice until I identify the stabber."

"Great." She rolled her eyes, put on a facsimile of a lovesick smile, and turned to Lindsey. "Hey, baby."

"Where's everyone else?" Lindsey demanded.

"Marcel and Chaz left the pub before the fight started," I explained. "Cheryl cleared herself and Darryl with pictures she took with her phone at the pub."

Lindsey grumbled something about not being able to trust people as I put Kendra in the cell with him. Then I turned to my guards, "Thanks for helping. I'm going to be here for a while, so you can leave."

"Do you want us to come back?" Schmitty asked.

I checked my watch; it was one thirty. Unless I wrapped this up in the next couple hours, I would need someone to stay here tonight. I used to be able to stay alert and awake for two days straight if necessary. I was out of practice. I couldn't remember my last multi-day marathon.

"Give me a call at four thirty. I'll know by then if I need your help." They agreed and left the building.

In my office, I found my K-9 sitting on her cushion. I knelt next to her and scratched her ears. "What's going on with you? Why are you so attached to people lately?"

She leaned into the scratch and then blew out a breath and dropped onto the cushion as though to say she couldn't help herself. People generally paid attention to little kids' and animals' responses when it came to trusting people. Meeka was usually so spot on I almost went and released Didi on her approval alone. Instead, I settled into my desk chair and pulled up the images Cheryl sent me. There were so many, I separated them into two folders, "Helpful" and "Unhelpful." Finally, I got to the pictures of the fight.

Silence, Melinda, and Gloria were easy to spot as they were facing the camera. Kendra Grossman's long bleached hair made her easy to ID too. The man on her left was Gavin Lindsey. She'd told me she was holding his right hand in her left. I couldn't see anyone standing in front of them. That also matched her statement that whoever stabbed Silence had to be behind them.

Marcel Allen and Chaz Lindsey were gone by this time. Cheryl Carpenter was taking the pictures, and Darryl Allen had been standing on her right. That left only Didi Stieber and Lars Sundstrom. I zoomed in on one of the pictures and spotted two heads with identical hair color. They were standing directly behind Lindsey and Kendra. Lars or Didi was likely my stabber. But which of them did it? And why?

And that's when I remembered, I never called Deputy Atkins about picking up the knife. Talk about being out of practice.

"You like having a direct line to me, don't you?" he teased

when he heard my voice.

"They always send me to you anyway. This just eliminates a step."

He chuckled, a pleasing sound. "What do you need me to do?"

I explained the events at the pub and how Silence was now at the hospital. "Deputy Reed is on personal leave right now, so I'm pretty much on my own."

"Still working through that stuff about his ex-girlfriend?"

"Yep. Sure hope he gets himself together soon. Anyway, I can't leave here and need someone to go to the hospital, retrieve the knife, and check it for prints. The hospital folks should know you're coming."

"Will do. I can head over there now, but by the time I get the knife and get it back to the station, I won't likely be able to get it processed until tomorrow."

"Any chance it can be early tomorrow? I've got four people in my cells and need to charge them with something more than disturbing the peace soon."

"I'll put a rush on it. It'll go faster if I have prints to compare to."

"I'll get sets from all four and send them right over."

"Perfect. I'm going to pass this off to someone more skilled than me. Lifting prints isn't exactly my forte, and I don't want to mess it up."

"I appreciate that. I'll send you what I've got on these four. In the meantime, I'll keep pushing them for more answers. Maybe one of them wants out worse than they want to keep quiet."

Out in the main room, I took the guest chair from in front of Reed's desk, turned it to face the jail cells, and had a seat. Meeka sat at my side.

"Is it tough cop time?" Lindsey sneered at me.

I shrugged. "Interpret it however you want. Thought I'd

give you all a chance to speed this up. A deputy from the county station is heading over to the hospital to retrieve your knife, Mr. Lindsey. We're going to dust it for prints."

"How long will that take?" Kendra asked.

"He'll get the knife tonight, but they won't be able to process it until tomorrow. That's where I figured you all could help.

"You mean we have to stay in here all night?" Kendra asked. "I told you it wasn't me."

"You did say that." I jerked a thumb over my shoulder at my desk. "I have pictures that Ms. Carpenter took of the fight in the pub. Those pictures show that you four were the closest to Silence during the fight. Unfortunately, they don't show me who actually did the stabbing."

"You think one of us did it?" Sundstrom asked.

Didi had gone quiet again. Like she had been when I first saw her at the campground, she was holding onto one of Lars' arms, clutching it in front of her like a shield.

"Silence was stabbed in the abdomen. You four were closest, so yes, I believe one of you is the guilty party."

Lindsey and Kendra looked at each other and then simultaneously turned to Lars and Didi, indicating they thought it was one of them. I remembered the look on Lindsey's face when the crowd sat and Silence became visible with his knife in her abdomen. The shock was instant. His hand had gone to his side, confirming that it was indeed his knife. He incited a riot, but I didn't think he stabbed Silence.

My instincts were telling me it wasn't Kendra either. According to the pictures, she would've had to lean in front of Lindsey to reach Silence with the knife. I couldn't imagine Lindsey risking taking the fall for her if she'd done it. He'd turn her in. No, either Lars or Didi was my stabber.

"All four of you were right there, front and center. One of you must've seen something."

"Wasn't me," Lindsey insisted. "See, if it was, I would've taken my knife back. It's custom made. Cost me five hundred bucks. No way I would've left it behind."

Twisted as that was, I believed him.

"I already gave you my statement," Kendra said. "I'm sticking to exactly what I said before."

I turned to Lars and Didi. They remained mute.

"All right." I stood and returned to my office. I had a little less than two hours before Schmitty and Elsa called. While I waited, I cleaned my office. Something I hadn't done in months. It was satisfying, mindless work that kept me busy until the phone rang at precisely four thirty. I made a show of wandering out to the main room to answer on Reed's extension.

"It's Elsa. Do you want us to come back?" She sounded hopeful that I did.

"I'm not sure. Hang on." I turned to the cells. "My guards are ready to return for the night. Unless one of you has something to tell me." No one said a thing. "Come on back, Elsa. Soon as you're ready."

When they walked into the station twenty minutes later, I handed the keys to Elsa.

"You know the drill. Call me if there's an emergency. I should be at Pine Time all night." I felt like a parent going over instructions with the babysitter. "Feel free to order food from The Inn. Grapes, Grains, and Grub is closed today."

I said good night to my suspects and headed home to find out the latest on Silence.

Chapter 20

I ENTERED MY HOUSE TO find Tavie, Melinda, and Gloria in the kitchen. They were a much more subdued group than Wednesday night but seemed in slightly better spirits than last night.

"What's going on in here?" I asked.

"Tripp is up in the attic," Gloria said. "He really wants to get that space done for you."

I laughed. "For us, you mean."

Melinda shook her head. "Yeah, but mostly for you. He's worried about you."

Tripp was talking to our guests about me? Not sure I liked that.

Gloria agreed with her. "He said that when you come home from a long day, he wants you to have your own place to go to. He said you used to live in the boathouse."

"That place looks so cool with that big deck and all," Melinda said. "Why don't you two live there?"

"It's not the whole building, only the top floor," I explained. "The bottom is the boat garage. The upper area was perfect for me and Meeka, but it's way too small for three of us. Tripp and I would be in each other's way all the time."

They'd done it again. These three had a way of making us talk about personal things. I didn't like Tripp talking about me, and I didn't like that I was talking about him.

Tavie must have sensed my frustration. She left her post, the dishwashing station, and took me out into the great room.

"They get a little nosey," she said. "You left early this morning. You must be exhausted after such a late night last night."

"I am starting to run down. I was able to eliminate two more people, though. We should have fingerprints off that knife tomorrow."

She clasped her hands. "Does that mean you'll know who did it?"

"I hope so. Unless I'm way off base, I'm down to two suspects. I don't want to promise anything, though."

Her head bobbed up and down in agreement. "I understand. I won't say anything to the girls."

"You went to the hospital today. Do you have any news on Silence?"

"No change from yesterday, which I guess is okay in this case. They're continuing the antibiotics and watching for sepsis." Her voice broke, and she waved me off when I attempted to comfort her. "I'm not a patient person. After working so hard to get my life going in a good direction, I have little tolerance for anything that deviates from that. I just want to know she's going to be okay."

"Maybe they can move her," I suggested. "They're a good hospital, so it's not that, but you'd probably be more comfortable at home." I groaned and slouched back on the couch. My words weren't coming out right. "Not that I'm trying to kick you out. You're welcome to stay as long as you want."

Tavie patted my hand. "I understand what you're saying, and you're right. Once they know she's on the mend, and I firmly believe she will pull through, I'll ask that she be transferred." She paused before saying, "Why don't you go see Tripp. You spent all day on our issue. Go see your man."

I went to change clothes first, pulling on leggings and a big sweatshirt, then climbed the stairs to the attic. At the top, I stopped and looked around my soon-to-be attic home with surprise.

"It's clean."

Startled, Tripp spun to face me with a large sponge in his hand. "Hey. Did you just get home?"

"Couple minutes ago. The dust is gone."

"Yeah, that's what I worked on today." Two folding yard chairs sat in the middle of the space. He pointed to one, indicating I should sit, and took the other. "I re-vacuumed every square inch of this place, walls and ceiling included. Now, I'm wiping down the walls with a damp sponge to get any last bits off."

"Then you'll start painting?"

"We'll be putting the texture coat on tomorrow. That will need to dry before we can paint but shouldn't take long."

"So we can actually move in soon?"

He went through the to-do list. "The primer and paint shouldn't take more than two days. Another two or three days for the flooring then kitchen and bathroom fixtures. I'm guessing ten days. Two weeks at most."

This made me ridiculously happy. A place to be away from the guests. I loved our guests, I loved owning a B&B, but on those days when I'd dealt with tourists for eight or ten straight hours, it didn't matter how much I loved them. I just wanted my own space to slip away to.

With Tripp. My own space with Tripp.

"Too bad we're not going to have a deck," I mused. Regardless of how nice this would be, there were things I'd miss about my boathouse apartment.

He frowned and returned to the wall he'd been working on. "How did it go today? Any confessions?"

"No, but I've narrowed the suspects down to two. Atkins got the knife from the hospital, and I should have prints in the morning." I watched him wash away the last of the spackle dust. The next time I came up here, paint, or at least primer, would be covering all evidence that spackling had even happened. We'd know it was there, of course, but when entering a home that someone else had built, you had no idea what lay beneath the completed surface.

"What are you thinking?" he asked. "Narrowing down two criminals to one?"

"No. I was actually thinking about how important all this prep work is that you've done. If you don't lay a good foundation, the final results won't look like what you'd envisioned." I paused then quickly amended, "You as in the universal you. Not *you* you."

"I understood what you meant. No matter how long I took on this part, it wouldn't be perfect. There would still be imperfections. That's what the texture coat is for. It will cover up any less than perfect spots."

As he crouched down to rinse out his sponge in the big bucket of water, I said, "But once you start putting the pretty stuff on, you don't want to have to go back and try to fix things. It's important to do all that hard work up front."

He looked at me with eyes narrowed, hands frozen in a squeeze around the sponge. "You're not talking about the walls anymore, are you?"

I blinked. "I'm not?"

He shook his head, then dropped the sponge into the bucket. He crossed the room and positioned his chair to sit in front of me. "The walls are a metaphor for something else. What are you thinking about?"

I stared into his light-hazel eyes, and my heart seized. But with fear, not love. Not that I didn't love him. I did very much. That's partly what scared me. "I—"

"Tripp? Jayne?" A small voice called from the bottom of the stairs. A second later, Gloria appeared. Her eyes went wide when she saw us. "Sorry, I'm interrupting something."

"No, nothing," Tripp answered too quickly.

"Okay." She looked like she didn't believe him. "Dinner's ready."

"Great." I stood. "I'm starving."

Tripp took one of my hands. "Jayne—"

"Dinner's ready." I pointed down the stairs. "We can talk about metaphorical walls later."

This was the exact wrong time to talk about us. Mostly because nothing was coming out the way I meant it today. I was so tired. Honestly, I could have crawled into bed right then and slept until morning.

The dining room table was set for the five of us. River was with Morgan and Briar again. A platter of pork chops sat at the center flanked by a casserole dish of scalloped potatoes and a bowl of homemade applesauce on one side, a big bowl with a mixed lettuce salad on the other.

"This looks great," I said, taking my assigned seat closest to the hallway.

"It does," Tripp agreed, taking his seat across from me at the opposite end. "I'd better stay on my toes. I might be out of a job soon."

"Your job is safe," Tavie assured him. "As soon as Silence is strong enough to move, we'll leave you two to get back to normal life."

"Unfortunately," I began as I filled my salad bowl, "events like this *are* normal around here."

The pork chops and potatoes were very good, but dinner was nowhere near as laid-back and fun as it had been two nights ago. That was partly because there was this unshakable tension between Tripp and me that everyone felt. Mostly, though, it was because everyone was worried about Silence. We chatted about nothing in particular while we ate. As soon as we were done, Tripp went right back up to the attic, leaving me with our guests.

"You may run things differently in your B&B," Tavie said, "but I'm pretty sure it's not your job to entertain us. Owners of a hotel certainly wouldn't." She flicked her fingers at me in a shoeing motion. "Go do your own thing."

"I don't mind sitting with you."

"You're exhausted, Jayne. Your eyes look ready to slam shut. It's still early. I think the girls and I will go for a short walk."

"It's chilly outside," I told her. "Make sure you bundle up. I'd suggest you walk along the lake, but there are large stones that make it tricky at night, and there's an almost full moon which means the tide is in."

"I was thinking we'd just go up the driveway. I love walking at night with all the different sounds. It even smells different. Have you noticed that?"

There was an instant tugging at my heart. How long had it been since I'd sat outside at night and listened to my whispering trees? How long had it been since Tripp and I had done that together?

I cleared the emotion from my throat. "I have noticed that. The campground should be empty right now. It's closed, but you can wander along the road that runs past all the sites. It loops around and will bring you back to the drive and home again."

"That sounds like a good plan," Tavie said. "We'll see you in the morning, Sheriff."

Fifteen minutes later, the kitchen was spotless, and the three women had gone off on their walk. Other than the sound of Meeka's claws clicking on the hardwood floor as she trotted over to the back door, the house was silent.

"You want to go out?" I asked her.

She wagged her tail in response.

I shoved my feet into my extra-warm, heavy-soled slippers, grabbed my jacket and a blanket, and went outside with her. I took in a deep breath and the chilly lake-scented air replaced the warm cozy feeling I'd had after eating dinner. Invigorated, I stared across the yard at the boathouse sundeck and thought for a minute about sitting up there. After moving my things out of the apartment, we pushed all the furniture to the far side of the deck and covered it for the winter. If I went up there now, I'd have to stand at the railing. We'd also pulled the dock in for the winter, so sitting there wasn't an option for me either. I could just sit here on the covered back patio; we hadn't done anything with that furniture yet. I wanted a little more solitude than that, though, so standing at the boathouse railing sounded like a better option.

As I climbed the stairs to the sundeck, a puff of wind blew across the lake and made the trees sway. It almost felt like a greeting. *Where have you been? We've missed you.*

I pulled the blanket tighter around me and leaned against the railing. Even though the bit of snow we'd gotten a few days ago had melted, the temperature consistently dropped below freezing at night now. Meeka had discovered that the shallow edges of the lake had started to freeze. Thinking herself a brave explorer, she tried to step on the ice one day last week. It held her for approximately a second before she broke through. It took hours before she stopped shivering but at least she learned her lesson and stayed away from the lake now.

"What's going on with me?" I asked the nearly full moon. "I was so excited to move into the house with Tripp. I really do love him, but lately all I want is space to myself."

I stood there as though expecting the trees, the lake, or the moon to actually answer me. The only thing I heard was Meeka barking. She was standing by the back doors of the house, barking for someone to let her in. I whistled for her and burst out laughing when she leapt into the air with a surprised *ruff*. She raced across the yard to the boathouse and stood staring up at the deck but didn't climb the stairs. Funny that she didn't think to come look for me up here. That used to be automatic at the end of the night. It seemed she considered the house to be home now.

She still hadn't seen me. Maybe, if I stayed very quiet, this could be my alone spot. Until summer, at least, when we rented out the apartment to guests.

Finally, she did see me and gave a tired little grunt before climbing the stairs to stand next to me.

"Don't tell anyone we come up here. It'll be like our secret clubhouse. Just us girls."

But I had to wonder, why was I excluding Tripp?

Chapter 21

I HAD NO IDEA HOW long I stayed out on the deck last night, but my nose and toes were freezing by the time I went in, and Tripp was already in bed. When I woke the next morning, he was lying there looking at me.

"Where'd you go last night?" His voice was gruff with sleep. He must have woken only a minute before I did.

"I was out on the sundeck." I yawned and stretched. "The moon is going to be full tomorrow."

"You should have told me. I would've gone out there with you."

"You were working on the attic. It's okay if we don't do everything together."

He rolled away from me and threw off the covers. "It would be nice if we did something together, though. Other than eat. Don't you think?"

Maybe that was it. I'd been in a funk for weeks, and he'd been working like a crazy man on that attic. Maybe it wasn't that I needed space, but that we hadn't done enough together lately.

"That would be nice. I miss you."

He looked over his shoulder and robotically said, "Miss you too."

I was about to suggest watching a movie together tonight or coming to bed early to have a little fun. But Tripp had already pulled on the work clothes lying on the floor next to the bed and left the room before I could ask him.

The smell of bacon being fried permeated the room the second he opened the door. It didn't help that Gloria and Melinda kept taking over the kitchen. Even though he really wanted to finish the attic, the kitchen was Tripp's domain, and I knew he felt bad about not taking care of our guests the way he normally did. I'd have to have a talk with Tavie about that. Of course, I should probably ask Tripp what he wanted first. My instincts hadn't been serving me all that well lately. Maybe he didn't care about the girls using his kitchen.

After showering, I dressed in my cargo pants and the black T-shirt I wore beneath my uniform shirt. Breakfast this morning was a much simpler affair than yesterday. Gloria was at the dinette table with a plate of bacon and a glass of orange juice in front of her. Tavie sat beside her with a cup of tea, toast, and fruit.

"Good morning, ladies," I greeted. "You're up early."

"We're going over to the hospital in a little while," Tavie explained. "I had paperwork proving my relationship with Silence sent over there yesterday. They're going to let us into the ICU today."

"That's great," I said. "I'm sure it will ease your mind to see her."

I poured myself a mug of coffee and grabbed a banana nut muffin. Melinda was in the great room munching on grapes and studying something on her phone with great interest.

"Mind if I join you?" I asked.

"It's your house," she snapped and then softened. "Sorry. Yes, please, have a seat."

I chose the chair next to the sofa she was sprawled on.

"What are you looking at?"

She turned the phone, showing me a mostly dark screen. "There was something scurrying around in the tree line, following us as we walked last night. I took a video and am trying to see if it ever made an appearance. All I see is darkness and an occasional tree branch moving."

I thought of Cheryl and all the pictures she took with her phone. "Do you take a lot of pictures?"

She shrugged. "Some. I do more videos than pictures. I mean, pictures are great, but capturing more than a freeze frame of a moment is way better." A shadow crossed her face. "I've got tons of pictures of my parents. I can't remember their voices, though."

The comment stabbed at me. "I understand what you mean. I didn't get to see my grandparents very often when I was younger, but I felt really close to them. Even though we did a lot of remodeling to this place before we opened, and it looks very different, I still get hit with memories of them in every room. I swear, sometimes I can smell Gran's lavender bath salts, but I can't quite remember her voice or the exact way she used to dance around the house." I laughed. "Gran loved to dance."

We grew quiet again while I picked at my muffin and sipped my coffee. I thought again of Cheryl's pictures, and one, in particular, came to mind. I set down my breakfast, ran to my office, and signed on to the cloud-based storage where we kept all the station files. This system was so much easier, especially during times, like now, when I wanted to access something but hadn't thought to lug the laptop home and didn't want to run all the way over to the station.

I drummed my fingers on my desk. It was taking forever for the photos to open. When they finally did, I opened the "helpful" folder and then specifically the shots of the group fight.

I gasped when the one I'd been thinking of filled the screen. In all the other pictures of Melinda, her hands were hidden behind other people. This image very clearly showed her phone in her hand. I ran back out to the great room.

"Melinda, did you take pictures or movies at the pub that night?"

"Yeah." She paled, her freckles standing out against her ivory skin. "Holy crap. The video can help you, can't it?" She swiped her finger across her screen and tapped multiple buttons. "I've been so worried about Silence I didn't even think about that."

I dismissed her concern. "Don't worry about it. Will you forward a copy of that video to me?"

Her fingers were flying across her keyboard. "Already on it. What's your address?"

She followed me down the hall to my office and watched as the video loaded onto my screen. Curious about what we were up to, Tavie and Gloria joined us.

"Sorry about all the jumping around," Melinda said. "I have a tendency to speak with my hands and get really animated when I'm upset."

Gloria snorted a laugh. "No doubt. She was ticked off at some guy who took her spot in the parking lot one time and backhanded me right in the face."

As Cheryl's pictures had shown, Melinda, Gloria, and Silence changed positions often during the altercation. Fortunately, when Melinda stepped to the back, she remembered to be still and quiet and to record the action going on in front of her. As I'd seen in Cheryl's pictures, Lindsey and Kendra were standing directly in front of Silence. Behind them, Sundstrom remained mostly quiet, occasionally adding a word or two to backup Lindsey. Didi stood glued to Sundstrom's side, saying nothing, only moving in tandem with him. Except for one instance.

Once again, my instincts were off. I'd been sure Sundstrom was the guilty one.

"Oh my God," Tavie whispered.

"Play it again," Gloria begged in a whisper, not because she wanted to see the outcome, but because she was as shocked as the rest of us.

I backed up the action and replayed it at half speed. We watched in horror as tiny Didi reached between Lindsey and Kendra, his knife in her left hand, and plunged it into Silence's stomach. In real time, it had taken no more than two seconds.

We couldn't determine what had been said just before the stabbing, there was too much crowd noise, but whatever it was, it spurred the people behind Lars and Didi to action. They surged forward, pushing the pair into Lindsey and toward Silence. That's when Didi made her move and snatched the knife from Lindsey's side. If Melinda had pointed the phone even two inches to the side, the act wouldn't have been caught on video.

"You've got her." Melinda's voice was deep with emotion and triumphant.

"I do." I agreed. "You all, go to the hospital. News like this will surely give Silence a boost." I looked at Melinda. "Good job. If you can learn to keep your hands still, you might have a future as a videographer."

I saved the video to the station's cloud then picked up the phone and dialed Deputy Atkins.

"You're wondering about the prints, aren't you?" he asked.

"Tell me you were able to lift some."

"They're doing that right now. Looks like they've got a few partials."

"A few as in multiple partials from one person, or partials from multiple people?"

He laughed. "Couldn't tell you that."

"Tell them to check against the prints I sent you for Didi Stieber first. I've got video evidence of her stabbing the victim. Her prints on that knife will make this rock solid. I'm heading over to the station. Call me there when you've got something."

I finished getting dressed—uniform shirt, essentials loaded into my cargo pockets, shoulder holster with Glock—then got my K-9 suited up in her harness.

We were halfway to the station when I realized I hadn't told Tripp I was leaving or asked him about a movie tonight. I made a mental note to give him a call later.

At the station, I thanked Schmitty and Elsa for their help and dismissed them.

"Will you need us to come back again?" Schmitty asked.

I locked eyes with Didi in the cell across the room. "No, I'll be wrapping things up this morning. Thanks, though."

Even though I'd purposely spoken loud enough for Didi to hear me, she didn't flinch. She sat shoulder-to-shoulder with Sundstrom, one of his hands clasped in both of hers, her head resting on his shoulder. Sundstrom, however, was trying to send me a message of some kind via a pointed stare and a wrinkled brow.

After Schmitty and Elsa left, I went to the cell to get Didi, but he met me at the bars.

"Can I talk to you?"

"Sundstrom," Lindsey said in a warning tone.

"This isn't about you," he snapped.

"What is it about?" I asked

He glanced past me at the interview room. "In private. Please?"

I should've asked either Elsa or Schmitty to stay. Sundstrom wasn't big, but he was muscular, and I wasn't comfortable being alone with him. It would take Atkins thirty or forty-five minutes to get here.

"Hang on," I told him.

I silently cursed Reed for not being here with me as I picked up the extension on his desk and called Grapes, Grains, and Grub. Even though it was early, Maeve answered.

"Is Jagger there by any chance?" I asked.

"Not yet. Are you still having problems?"

"I am. I need someone here with me while I interview one of my suspects."

Maeve hummed, as though making a decision, then said, "I'll give him a call. Since we were closed yesterday, he might be up by now."

Not even five minutes later, Jagger called, informing me he was on his way. As I waited, the phone rang again.

"We've got a clear print for Gavin Lindsey," Atkins said.

"That makes sense. It's his knife."

"We checked the system and found plenty of public disturbance charges for him. No prints on the knife for Kendra Grossman, but she came up with a shoplifting charge about five years ago. Lifted a box of tampons. Nothing in the system for Didi Stieber or Lars Sundstrom."

"Okay, let's get to the punchline. You said you had multiple partials. All Lindsey's or did any of them match Stieber?"

"We got one really clear partial that came up as a match for her."

I slumped with relief. That plus the video evidence meant this case was done. "Excellent."

"I already sent the report to your email. I'm on my way to pick her up."

"Bring a second squad or a van. I've got minor charges for Lindsey and Sundstrom as well. Lindsey is sure to do some time since he's a repeat. Plus, I'm charging him with inciting a riot."

By the time I'd reviewed the report from county and queued up Melinda's video to play on the screen in the interview room, Jagger was standing in my doorway.

"What do you need me to do?" he asked before I could say a word.

"Be my bodyguard," I said with a laugh. I explained the situation and the bouncer positioned himself in the corner of the interview room while I brought in Sundstrom. I placed him with his back to the door. I turned on the voice recorder as I sat across from him and asked, "What did you want to talk with me about, Mr. Sundstrom?"

"She did it," he said.

Chapter 22

HAD SUNDSTROM REALLY JUST TURNED in his girlfriend?

"She who?" I asked for clarification. "What did she do?"

After blurting out the first part, he appeared to be struggling to say more. As I waited for him to speak, I thought back to interviewing her at The Inn.

I told you that I needed to figure out what happened to Silence before you could see Lars again. Remember?

I didn't tell you?

That she stabbed Silence? Was that what "I didn't tell you" meant?

Sundstrom moaned with his eyes closed as if in pain and said, "Didi stabbed that woman."

I glanced at Jagger, who took a wider stance. "How do you know this?"

"We were standing there behind Gav and Kendra, Didi had her right arm looped around my left arm. For like two seconds, she pulled away, which was the first sign 'cause she never lets go of me. She leaned forward and then she was right back in place. I knew she did something but had no idea what until you had us all sit on the floor."

"You didn't think to mention anything to me at that point?"

"I didn't have proof. I figured it was her, but it's not like I was going to turn in my girlfriend on a hunch. You wouldn't let us talk at the pub, and then you put us in separate buildings. I didn't get to talk to her until last night after Gav and Kendra fell asleep and the guards were in your office. That's when she told me she did it."

"Why? Any idea?"

"She's manic."

It took me a second to realize he meant she had a disorder. As I'd suspected. "Bipolar?"

He shook his head. "Manic isn't really the right word. She's got something like OCD where she fixates on things."

"Let me guess, she fixates on you? Is this why her hair color matches yours?"

"Yeah." He dropped his head back and sighed. "She made me go to her stylist with her a couple years ago so they could match it. People think it's cute, so I don't care."

"Not all people."

He lifted his head again and looked at me. "She gets this way about stuff too. Like reorganizing the house. Everything has to be in the right spot. Everything has to look a certain way." He put his hands over his face and rubbed his eyes. "She's been steady for so long. I thought it was under control. She goes to therapy and takes antidepressants, but I guess she could've stopped her meds. She says they make her feel funny."

"You don't monitor that?"

"If she takes her pills? No. I can't be there all the time. I mean, I could stand there and watch her put a pill in her mouth, but there's nothing stopping her from spitting it out after I walk away. She probably figured she was better and stopped taking them even though her doctor said she'd need the pills forever. I don't know." He paused, becoming emotional. "What are they going to do with her?"

"Some of that will depend on what happens to Silence."

He sat forward, elbows on his knees. "She can't go to prison."

I agreed with him there. Unfortunately, that was beyond my control. "Didi clearly has mental health issues. Psychiatric hospitalization would be best for her. I'm sure they'll take that into consideration."

At least I hoped they would.

He shook his head. "I can't deal with this again. Last time she got this way, like two years ago, she kept arranging and rearranging the house. I'd come home from work and everything, every single thing, from the kitchen would be laid out in the family room. For two weeks, I couldn't touch anything until she decided where it belonged. Then she'd start on the bedrooms. Then back to the kitchen." He put his hands to his face. "I can't do this anymore. I've got a job and kids to support from my first marriage."

"That's your choice to make, although you've got troubles of a different kind coming your way." I paused, waiting for a response from him.

He stared at a spot on the floor. "I know."

"What was the point of you all coming here this weekend? Was the plan to cause trouble?"

He looked away, embarrassed. "I lost a bet."

"I'm sorry?"

"I've been friends with Gav since high school. We made this bet graduation night about which of us could pick up a girl faster at a bar. I lost and wouldn't accept the punishment." He held a hand up at me. "Don't ask, it's too embarrassing. Gav agreed to let it slide only if I agreed to let him collect later. He agreed but the conditions were whatever he said, whenever he said it, no questions asked, I had to do it. This was, what, fifteen years ago? I figured he forgot about it. Then a couple weeks back he tells me he got fired from the foundry but that was okay because he had this idea for how he could get into the police academy."

He told me almost word for word what Kendra and Darryl had said yesterday about how Lindsey didn't make it in. Sundstrom's account was so similar, in fact, I assumed this was a rant Lindsey had gone on more than once and they were repeating his words.

It took all my willpower to not tell him what a moron I thought he was. "Coming here and causing problems in my village was a better idea than dealing with whatever punishment Lindsey wanted to dish out?"

He stared down at his feet. "Sorry."

"Hope it was worth it because you could do jail time for this."

"I understand."

I glanced out into the main room. "I need to talk with Didi now. One more question, can you confirm that the others had nothing to do with this idea of Lindsey's?"

"No one else knew anything. It was just going to be me and Gav. I'd do this and satisfy the bet, but Didi was pitching a fit about me leaving for a weekend. Guess I should've seen that as a sign, but like I said, she'd been good for so long. Anyway, because she was coming, Kendra had to come. The original plan was for me to start a fight with someone and Gav would be the hero and break it up. No big deal. Since the other guys were here with us, Gav decided to make it bigger. He told me to harass those girls, figuring other dudes would come to their defense. Then, once it turned into this big fight, Gav would step in and take off his hat. That was the sign for us to stop fighting."

"He didn't count on Silence and her friends not needing help from anyone, did he?"

Sundstrom shook his head. "No, he didn't."

But why did he choose them? Because they were alone without a man to defend them? No, couldn't go there. Tripp had warned me about trying to figure out the criminal mind. Ultimately, it didn't matter to me why they did what they did as long as I got the cuffs on the right people in the end. Sundstrom confirmed I could let Kendra go. She was completely innocent. Good. I hoped she ran far away.

I brought him back to the cell and asked Didi to come with me.

"Not without Lars," she said evenly and with absolute conviction.

Knowing what I now knew about her, if I pulled her away from him, she might turn back into the hysterical woman I'd seen in the hotel room earlier. Sundstrom agreed, so I brought them both into the interview room, where Jagger was still at the ready should his services be needed, and positioned a second chair next to the one Sundstrom had been sitting in.

Didi sat mute and motionless as I played the video. Sundstrom winced and turned green. Then, as I had at home, I backed it up and played the pertinent part again.

"It's obvious you did it," I told her. "Not only do I have a video of you committing the crime, I have your prints on the weapon, and Lars said you confessed to him. You'll be charged with aggravated assault, second-degree murder if Silence dies. Do you have anything to say in your own defense?"

She still said nothing, so I appealed to Sundstrom to get her to talk.

"Didi, baby, go ahead and tell her what happened."

Her eyes locked onto the voice recorder sitting on my knee. After a very long thirty seconds, she said, "She was upsetting everyone."

"Who was?" I asked gently.

"That woman. The one who wouldn't talk. Even when the knife went in, she didn't make a sound."

I winced internally, staying externally steady. "Is that why you stabbed her? To get her to speak?"

Didi laughed. "No. I told you, I stabbed her because she was upsetting everyone. She was wooing the men with her big blue eyes and shiny white smile. They couldn't help themselves. That's what Cheryl said. 'Darryl can't help himself when he gets around a pretty woman like that.'"

That was exactly what Cheryl said. She just didn't mean it in that context.

"I'm pretty sure she cast a spell on them." Didi finally looked at me. "I know you got witches up here. Witches cast spells. Silence must be one of them."

I wasn't sure if this was delusional thinking from the disorder or if she really believed it. Plenty of tourists stopped here believing the Whispering Pines witches wore pointy black hats or could fly or whatever other crazy thoughts they had in their heads.

"Silence was just a visitor here like you," I told Didi. "She wasn't trying to cast a spell."

"You didn't see her," Didi insisted, anger turning the previously child-like woman into a Fury.

Motion in the doorway caught my attention. I glanced up to see Deputy Atkins and a female deputy I didn't recognize standing there. I acknowledged them with a half nod.

"She was trying to steal our men," Didi continued. "She was taunting them with her quiet ways and pretty face."

"You thought she was trying to steal Lars, so you stabbed her?"

She sat tall. "It worked, didn't it?"

There was no point in continuing this conversation. Doctors would check her out and likely conclude, as Sundstrom suspected, she had stopped taking her medication.

I led them both back to their cell. After introducing myself to Deputy Thomas, I took her and Deputy Atkins to my office and filled them in on the details.

"We've got it from here," Atkins told me when we'd covered it all. "Any word on the victim?"

"She's stable as of yesterday. Her friends got clearance to visit her in the ICU today. They also have the good news of the perpetrator being behind bars."

"Positive news like that might make a difference," Deputy Thomas said.

Atkins agreed. "Let's get these four in the squads."

"Three," I corrected. "Kendra Grossman isn't guilty of anything but bad taste in men."

Deputy Thomas laughed a little too hard at that.

I went to Lindsey's cell and opened the door. "Ms. Grossman, you're free to leave."

She stood in front of Lindsey with her hand out. "Keys, please."

"You ain't taking my truck," he said flatly.

"How am I supposed to get home?" she asked.

"Not my problem." He looked away from her like a spoiled little boy. My guess was that they broke up last night.

"The keys are in with his personal effects." I went to the evidence locker and came back with four paper bags. I handed Kendra the one with her name on it and held up Lindsey's. "If you want, we can tow your truck. We'll put it in lockup. There will be a towing fee, of course, and a daily impound fee. Could get pricey. Especially if the courts don't get to you for a while."

He grunted. "Fine. But I better find it in my driveway when I get home or I'll send the cops after you for theft."

I walked Kendra to the front door. As soon as I opened it, Meeka burst out and headed for the trees. "Sorry your weekend was such a disaster."

Kendra shrugged. "It woke me up. Lesson learned, I

guess." She patted her front jeans pocket. "I've still got the number for your mom's spa. I'm going to pack up my stuff and then head down to Madison. Think I'll go visit my mom and get my hair fixed."

"Good luck." I turned back to find Atkins putting zip cuffs on Lindsey.

"Want to let the other two out?" he asked.

I cuffed them and walked them along with the two deputies to the squad cars in the station parking lot in the back.

"I got some news just before I left the station," Atkins said as he closed the back door of his car.

I paused, confused, and then my heart started racing. "News? On Donovan?"

"There was a reported sighting of him in Duluth yesterday." Before I could ask, he said, "Turned out to be false. It was a guy who looked an awful lot like him. Practically a dead ringer for Page."

Damn. I wanted this guy off the streets and behind bars where he could rot for the rest of his life.

"There's more," Atkins continued. "The guy says a woman asked him to pose as Donovan. She paid him to dye his hair and showed him a video of Page so the guy could walk the same way he does and mimic his mannerisms."

"Page is working with someone?" I concluded.

"Sounds like it."

"There's been nothing for months, and now this?" I didn't like it. "Sounds like he's getting ready to make a move."

"He might be close to Whispering Pines. Be on alert. I updated the APB and put out a BOLO to stations in the area." He stared at me, his expression serious.

"What?"

"What's going on with your deputy situation? If Page is getting ready to do something, you shouldn't be dealing with it alone."

I thought of Jagger, Emery, Schmitty, and Elsa. I could always call on Tripp, Gino, and the renovation guys. There were also some witches around the village that would be happy to help me take Donovan down.

"Reed getting back into the game would be the best option," I said, "but I've got other people I can call if necessary."

"And me. You know you can always call me."

"I do have your direct number now." I forced a smile. "Don't worry, I won't take chances."

As they drove off, I went back into the station and could've sworn the front door was closing as I entered the main room, as though someone had just walked out. Jumpy now after the report on Donovan, I unholstered my Glock.

"Is anyone in here?" I called out then waited a few seconds. "I repeat, is anyone in the station?"

No answer. With weapon in hand, I checked the interview room first as it was closest to the back door. Empty. Then I checked our small restroom. It was also empty. Finally, I stepped into my office. No one was there, but there was a crisp white envelope lying on my desk that hadn't been there before.

Dammit! The guy had been in my station while I was standing out back a few feet away?

I checked the front porch and scanned the surrounding tree line. Nothing. I locked the door and then checked behind the station. Also, nothing. I locked that door, returned my Glock to its holster, and rushed back to my office.

Using the same procedures as before, I put on gloves, sliced open the envelope, slid out the card, and put it directly into an evidence bag. This time, there was a picture as well. It was of Tripp taken at Grapes, Grains, and Grub Thanksgiving night.

Now I'm going to ruin yours.

Chapter 23

THE FOUR CARDS DELIVERED A full message.

I know what you did.
You know what you did.
You ruined my life.
Now I'm going to ruin yours.

This felt exactly like something Donovan would do. He'd been angry about how our father had abandoned him all those years ago. Gran had forbidden those villagers who knew what had happened to ever speak of the incident that resulted in Donovan's mother's death. Not a word. As far as the Whispering Pines history book was concerned, Priscilla Page died from a fall and her illegitimate son Donovan went to live with family. Poor parentless and forgotten Donovan targeted his anger on Gran.

Her death had been an accident, but he had caused that accident and then covered it up. He figured he'd simply be able to get away with it, never expecting anyone would put the details together. Especially not me, a silly little girl playing at being sheriff. But I did put it together and ruined his chances at a cozy little life in Whispering Pines among the unaware villagers.

Except, not all the villagers were clueless. A handful of the Originals knew the details surrounding the forbidden event. Flavia was one of them. Neither of them had admitted it, but I knew she had been in the house ten months ago, coaching Donovan on how to cover up Gran's death. She had to be the woman who paid the man in Duluth to act as him.

As I stared at the card on my desk, the picture he'd included with it came to the forefront. While I was sitting here, obsessing about Donovan Page, Tripp could be in danger.

I raced out the back door and leapt into my SUV. As I shoved the gearshift into reverse, I realized, "Meeka."

Where was she? She had raced out the front door approximately fifteen minutes ago when I sent Kendra on her way, but she hadn't come back in. Unless she snuck in when I opened the back door to escort Atkins and the others out. But I'd checked the entire station. She wasn't in there.

I got out of the vehicle and hollered, "Meeka?"

While straining my ears for some kind of a response, I scanned the trees behind the station, silently pleading for her to emerge. Where was she? Did he have her? Would Donovan seriously take his revenge on me by attacking both the man I loved and the dog that was practically my heart? Of course he would. I attempted to call for her again, but my voice stuck, and my mouth was too dry for a whistle. I cleared my throat and then tried again. "Meeka, come!"

This time, I heard a bark from the front of the building and nearly dropped to my knees. She rounded the corner to my left, running at full speed, clearly having heard the distress in my voice. She rushed to my side, and I plucked her up before she'd even come to a full stop.

"Thank God," I mumbled into her neck.

I had to get myself together. If Tripp truly was in danger, I needed to be the sheriff, not Tripp's hysterical girlfriend. On shaking legs, I reentered the station with Meeka in my arms and leaned against the wall to keep myself from falling. As I clutched my dog close, she leaned in to me, nuzzling her nose into my neck and helping me calm down.

Once I was back in control, I did a mental inventory of what I'd need. I patted my gun holster, ensuring my Glock was in place, and checked my pockets to verify I had a set of zip cuffs. Donovan had big hands, though. I grabbed a second set of cuffs.

"What am I doing?"

Meeka whined in response, verifying that I couldn't and shouldn't try and deal with Donovan on my own. He'd been eluding law enforcement officers across the upper Midwest and parts of Canada for four months. This was no time to be a hero. I needed help but didn't have time to explain the situation to Jagger or the others. I couldn't risk spending time begging Reed for help only to have him say no. That left me with one choice. I picked up the phone and called Atkins to come back.

"I'm only ten miles out of town," he said. "I can't come back with Stieber and Sundstrom in the back of my car." He paused, debating what to do. Suddenly, I heard his siren wailing and assumed his lights were flashing. "Here's the plan. I'll drop them off and let Deputy Thomas deal with booking all three. I'll call ahead and have them organize a team. We'll be there as fast as possible. All right?"

"Okay, sounds good." I relaxed a bit knowing he'd be back.

"One hour, tops. Stay where you are for one hour."

"No, I've got to get over to the B&B and make sure Tripp's okay. Donovan threatened him, not me."

He hesitated before saying, "All right, but don't go looking for Page alone."

"I won't but I've got to go. I have to get over to Tripp."

Two minutes later, we were in the SUV and racing toward Pine Time. The speedometer said I was going too fast, but it felt like we were inching down the highway. I took the corner at the campground a little fast and almost ran off the road and into the shallow ditch. Meeka scolded me with a bark from the back. She was right, I couldn't help Tripp if I got into an accident so slowed the vehicle a little. My racing heart calmed slightly when the garage came into view. Both Tripp's F350 pickup and River's Bentley SUV were parked there. Despite my earlier complaints about not seeing my boyfriend enough, I was suddenly grateful that the two spent so much time together.

I burst in the front door and screamed, "Tripp?"

Barking for him, Meeka ran to the kitchen, the place we almost always found him.

The house was silent, though. They had to be upstairs in the attic. I took a few precious seconds and made a loop around the main floor, ensuring that all the doors and windows were locked, creating a false sense of security. If someone wanted to get in badly enough, it didn't take anything to break a window or patio door.

I looked down at Meeka. "Go find Tripp."

The Westie ran ahead of me up the stairs and straight for the attic. My legs were ready to give out as I closed in on the top of the attic stairs. I had to brace myself against the handrail, my knees buckling when I saw both Tripp and River working together to put the texture coat on the walls.

"Jayne?" Tripp set down his spray gun and rushed to my side. "What's wrong? Are you okay?"

Nodding, I swallowed back the tears that wanted to burst free. I had to stay professional. I had to protect him.

He helped me over to one of the folding chairs and gave me a bottle of water from a cooler in the corner. The cold liquid soothed my throat and allowed me a few seconds to get myself together. Hiding the truth from someone was not the same thing as protecting them. In fact, keeping someone ignorant could have the opposite effect. I had to tell him what was going on.

"Remember the card I got at the pub?"

"I do." After a half-second pause, he added, "Is this guy still after you? Did you get another one?"

"I think I know who it is. Evan Atkins from the county station just told me that Donovan was spotted in Duluth. Except it wasn't Donovan."

I relayed all the information as River came close, projecting an aura of calm.

Tripp sprang to his feet from his crouched position next to me and started to pace. "What do you want to do? We can go somewhere and hide out until he's caught. Is Atkins coming back?"

"What I want," I said as calm as he was panicked, "is for you and River to stay together at all times. I'm not sure if it would be best for you to stay here or go to Morgan's place."

Tripp was shaking his head before I'd finished talking. "I'm not leaving you. If this guy is after you—"

"He's not after me." I shuffled through the evidence bags and found the most recent delivery. I held the bag up with the open card facing him.

"He's going to ruin your life?" Tripp demanded. "Where the hell is he? I'll tear him apart."

I turned the bag around so he could see the picture of himself and repeated, "He's not after me. He's planning to ruin my life by coming for you. I won't let that happen. You need to either stay in this house with River or go somewhere where Donovan can't find you."

He looked at me, mouth agape, like I was crazy. "You're going to protect me?"

I knew he didn't mean it, but it came across as the same type of sexist comments I'd been hearing for the last three days. *Little Jayne O'Shea. Isn't she cute with her badge and her gun? Thinks she can save the world when she can't even save this little village.*

"Protecting the public is my job. I know it's hard for people to believe, but I do know what I'm doing. I want you to stay in this house or go to Morgan's. Your choice." I turned to River. "I know he's worried about me, but I can take care of myself. I need to know you're with him and ensuring his safety, so I'm not distracted and worrying about him. Can you do that for me?"

River placed his hands on my shoulders and stared into my eyes with his black-brown ones. That same aura of calm encircled me like a forcefield, centering me almost as well as holding Meeka close did.

"Proprietress, I will stay with Tripp, but we need to know that you will also be safe. We are not doubting your abilities, but you should not be alone either."

"I won't be alone. Atkins is coming back with a team and they're going to search the village for Donovan. I'm going back to Reed's cottage and demand he comes back to work and partner with me."

Tripp laughed like this was a crazy idea. "You're going to put your safety in the hands of a man who's mentally unstable?"

"Reed isn't mentally unstable." I remembered the months after I'd ended things with Jonah. I could barely function. Of course, I'd quit my job, too, which was equally upsetting. "He suffered a devastating breakup. Haven't you ever had your heart broken that way?"

"Not yet."

"Tripp," River scolded instantly.

If he would've punched me in the gut, it wouldn't have

felt different. The breath left my lungs, and my vision narrowed for a second.

I looked to River and mumbled, "Keep him safe, please."

I spun and started for the stairs, but a hand on my upper arm turned me around. Tripp wrapped his arms around me.

"I'm sorry. God, I'm sorry. What a stupid thing to say. I'm just frustrated and scared something will happen to you."

I'd seen enough people in highly charged situations to know really stupid things could come out of their mouths when scared. Then again, words spoken when emotional were sometimes the truth.

"Remember how Donovan thinks," I told him. "Physically harming someone isn't his method for taking revenge. Emotional, long-lasting trauma is how he operates. He knows that hurting you would damage me for life." I looked up to see his eyes glistening, and my strength returned. "I'm not going to do anything stupid. I promise. If Reed still refuses, I'll stick close to Atkins. Okay?"

He hesitated before nodding. "Okay."

I pulled away from him, went directly to our bedroom, and to the nightstand on my side of the bed. I reached all the way to the back of the drawer to get to what I was looking for.

First, I found a small purple muslin bag, about the size of a deck of playing cards. Inside it were bits of basil, bay, cedar, thistle, lavender, and pine. Also in the mix were a golden pentacle charm, a small piece of quartz, and a shard of black tourmaline. This wasn't what I'd come for, but I shoved the protection bag Morgan had given me six months earlier into my front pocket anyway.

I patted around the back of the drawer until I felt a chain. Hanging from that chain was a small glass vial filled with tiny pieces of amethyst, black tourmaline, quartz, and amber. A small round apple-green peridot stone dangled from the bottom of the vial. Joining the amulet on the silver chain was a pewter pendant from Morgan's talisman collection. She'd called the quarter-sized pendant an Algiz and claimed it was a powerful protection rune.

As I slipped the chain over my head and then dropped the amulet and talisman beneath my shirt, I couldn't help but laugh. Six months ago, I'd looked at Morgan like she was loopy when she insisted this pretty necklace would protect me from the nastiness going on in the village. Perhaps it was time for me to put a little more faith in some things I didn't fully understand.

The hag stone Mallory had given me at the pub lay in the front of the drawer where I'd tossed it the other night. As far as I knew, the stone didn't offer protection for anything, but it would be good to know if people were telling me the truth. How exactly I was to determine that, I didn't know. Mallory never explained that part.

I added the stone to the other two items on my chain and slipped it back around my neck. When I turned away from the nightstand, Meeka was looking up at me with a curious expression.

"What? It can't hurt."

Time to go back to Reed's cottage. Surely once he understood what was going on, he'd come back to work.

Chapter 24

AS I WALKED THE SHORT distance from where I'd parked to Reed's front door, Meeka headed for the woods to explore. This time, I called her back.

"Sorry, girl. There's a crazy man wandering the village. You need to stay with me."

I got to the door, but Reed opened it before I could knock.

"I saw you coming," he said. "And I heard you. Might want to look into a new muffler for your Cherokee."

"I need a whole new vehicle. This one's slowly dying. Can I come in?"

He held the door open and stepped aside for me to enter. He'd started hanging drywall since the last time I'd been there.

"Got all your electrical done?"

"Yep. Mr. Powell signed off this morning." He sighed. "Drywalling takes forever."

"You don't have to tell me that. I didn't think Tripp would ever get done with the attic walls."

"Was there something you wanted, Sheriff, or did you just stop by to check on my home improvement skills?" He clearly didn't want me hanging around any longer than necessary.

Since we were being blunt, I didn't bother with a warmup. "Time to be done with your leave of absence. I need you to come back to work now." He started to object, but I talked over him. "Donovan is back in the village, and he's making threats."

I handed Reed the four evidence bags with the cards. He inspected them closely, his brow creasing as he did.

"What do you want me to do?" The statement was more dismissive than concerned. He held the bags out to me as though passing me a rag with which to wipe up a spill.

I looked at him, dumbfounded. "I want you to help me look for him."

"Have you gone door to door?" The statement was innocent enough, a deputy inquiring about the progress of an investigation. However, his uninterested tone made it obvious it was a recommendation, not a question, and was all the help he was going to give me.

"You do recall that this man is responsible for my grandmother's death. Now he's threatening Tripp. My own life could be in danger as well."

His response was to change the topic. "How did this last case turn out?"

Why was he being so cold to me? "You mean the stabbing? I closed that case this morning. Deputy Atkins took three people off to county."

"That's great. Seems you handled that one fine without me."

"Actually, I had help." I explained how I had recruited Jagger, Emery, Tripp, Gino, and other villagers to get it all done. "Atkins is coming back with a team to search the village."

"Sounds like you don't need me, then." He poured drywall screws into a suede pouch clipped to his belt.

"Others can do the legwork, Reed. You help me in a

different way. You work through the cases with me. Rather than simply following instructions, you know to question some things and to do other things without me needing to ask. I've come to count on and trust you a great deal."

He didn't respond.

"I've mentioned my old partner Randy Ketchum before. He and I started out a little rocky, almost as rocky as you and I did, but we got to the point of knowing each other's thoughts almost as well as we knew our own. I feel that kind of a partner connection with you too."

Reed picked up his cordless drill and ran a few screws into the drywall. "Didn't Randy end up shooting a civilian? Did you know that was going to happen? Is that how well you knew him?"

He was trying hard to pick a fight with me. Morgan, Briar, and Tavie all told me I needed to deal with my demons before I could help others. Maybe this was part of that.

"You know what?" I said, my patience starting to wane. "That was on me, I admit that. I knew Ketch was struggling with relationship problems, just like I know you're struggling. His wife didn't want him being out on the streets anymore. They had a toddler at home and a baby on the way. She was pushing him to quit the job he loved."

"Might want to reconsider your relationship with Tripp, then. Seems even in this dinky village, this job and relationships don't go together."

Considering the arguments I'd had with Tripp lately, Reed had no idea how close to my truth he was.

"Do you blame me for what happened with Lupe?" I asked. "Is that what this attitude is? Are you somehow mangling the facts and making it my fault that you ended up with a broken heart?"

He shook his head and turned away without offering a reply.

Is this how it would always be? By taking on the responsibility of being sheriff, would that mean I also had to accept a good deal of the blame for things that went wrong?

"You're far from the first to put everything on me," I told him. "Your mother has formed her own villager vigilante group. Did you know that?"

He paused for half a second before shaking his head again.

"When I took this job, I figured it would be an easy transition. Sure, things might be busy during the summer, but I'd dealt with Madison, which has approximately three hundred times as many people as Whispering Pines. I figured the non-tourist times here would be a cakewalk." I laughed and paced from his living room into his kitchen as I ranted. "That's what you'd think, but no, things just keep coming up. If it's not tourists picking fights and stabbing each other, it's villagers creating chaos instead of joining together to fix problems."

He drilled in two more screws, ignoring me.

"You know what, Reed? I'm done being patient." I gestured around his new home. "Not to sound like an old fogey, but you're entering the adult phase of your life now. That includes doing things you don't necessarily want to do. You made a commitment to the village and me. When you're not away at school, I expect you to honor that commitment."

He faced me, expression neutral, arms hanging at his sides.

Without begging or becoming emotional, I stated, "I need help. If you can't come back to work and do your job, then turn in your badge. I don't want to start over, but I'm getting pretty good at that. Jagger has expressed interest in helping me when you're not able to."

"Are you threatening my job?"

I guess I was, but I didn't mean to. Like Tripp's had not

even an hour ago, my mouth had taken over my brain.

"I told you how much I value you as a deputy and that I want you to come back to work. I meant both of those things. But I can't put my life and the life of the man I love in jeopardy while you keep moping around over the breakup of a two-month romance."

Dammit. The words were true, but I hadn't meant to say them. So much for not getting emotional. Before anything else stupid fell out of my mouth, I stormed out of his house and over to my vehicle. I sat with my hands on the steering wheel, so upset I was shaking.

I entertained the idea of going for a drive. That sometimes relaxed me. Driving while this upset wasn't a good idea, though. Besides, Atkins was on his way. I needed to get back to the station and wait for them.

The drive from Reed's place took six minutes, only because there were people shopping in the village today and the highway was a little congested. When the highway was clear, the drive took three.

Once at the station, I needed to do something useful while I waited for Atkins. I grabbed the fingerprint set from the crime scene kit and pulled on a pair of gloves.

Working on the stainless-steel table near the evidence locker in my office, I slowly and methodically dusted every inch, front and back, of each of the four cards and envelopes with black fingerprint powder. I even dusted the picture of Tripp. Donovan must have worn gloves, as had I, because there were no prints on the first one. I found my prints on the edges of the card delivered to my table at Triple G—I hadn't worn gloves when handling that one. The third one, the one he'd dropped off at the station when Tripp and Gino were doing guard duty, held a different set of prints. I could test them to be certain, and would if necessary, but it was a safe bet that those prints were Gino's. Donovan had handed the envelope to him when he dropped it off, and Gino had set it on my desk. The fourth card had no prints.

I'd just returned the cards to their respective bags when the back door opened and a flood of people entered my station.

Chapter 25

ATKINS HAD RETURNED WITH A team of a dozen women and men. An additional six deputies were also on their way to Whispering Pines. The variety of uniform colors told me they'd come from different locales. Either it was a slow day or they were all frustrated over Donovan eluding them for so long and were ready to bust him.

"We've all seen pictures of Page so know who we're looking for," Atkins addressed the deputies gathered in a half moon around Reed's desk. He was taking the lead since I was too close to the situation. "We all also know the details surrounding this case. Sheriff O'Shea, why don't you show us the cards you received and tell us what's been going on."

As the evidence bags with the cards circulated through the group, I gave a rundown on my history with Donovan, specifically the details of how we were related and what I believed happened with my grandmother.

"You all know he assaulted Deputy Atkins and escaped custody, which prompted the APB. There isn't much more to tell. I prevented him from getting what he wanted, and now he's taking revenge."

"Have there been any specific sightings of him in

Whispering Pines?" Atkins asked.

"No, but there is a man wandering the village wearing a brown jacket, aviator sunglasses, and a white stocking cap with a Minnesota Vikings logo. I've only seen this man in passing, not face to face, but believe he's Donovan Page." I paused to think if there was anything else that might help them. "Oh, there's a very unusual looking building almost directly north of here. It looks like a bunch of small buildings cobbled together and is called the un-church. I saw someone with white hair in the upper window of the tower although it could have been a white hat. Donovan has white hair."

"Un-church?" one deputy asked as another said, "Tower?"

"The woman who lives there used to be a nun." At their blank stares, I added, "She says the church excommunicated her, but she still considers herself to be a nun and calls her chapel the un-church." Unable to stop myself, I started giggling. "Sorry. She conducts un-masses and counsels people."

"Or does she un-counsel them?" someone asked.

"Around here," I said, laughing again, "that's entirely possible."

The group chuckled with me until Atkins cleared his throat.

I brought out a large map of the village and pointed out the location of the un-church. As I reviewed the layout of the rest of the village, I couldn't help but think of the search for Jacob Jackson last month. The hunt had brought the villagers together for a while. Now, they were pulling apart.

"You'll stay here?" Atkins asked.

"I'll stick to the immediate area."

Atkins shook his head before I could say more. Quietly, so the other deputies wouldn't hear him scolding me, he pulled me to the side and said, "Either stay here or go home. Or you can tag along with one of the teams. I don't want you wandering the village by yourself. We'll be out there for hours, and I won't check in with you until the end unless we find him. No news means we have nothing to report."

"I understand." As much as I wanted to help, it was best to let Atkins and his teams handle this. "I'll stay here."

It turned out, sitting in the station for hours with nothing to do except wait for the teams to report in was really boring. Meeka slept, inspected every corner of the station, slept again, went outside to do her thing, and then slept some more. I ordered lunch from Triple G, played a little online Solitaire, dozed in my chair for a while, then called my sister. When she didn't answer, I left a voicemail.

"Just checking in. We haven't talked in a couple weeks. How're you doing since the breakup?" She'd said when she left the village after Samhain that she would be ending things with her boyfriend, James. Turned out, she meant it and broke things off as soon as she saw him. "As usual, we've got a little drama going on up here." Damn. Why did I say that? It would just freak her out. "Nothing I can't handle, of course. Anyway, talk to you soon."

A minute later, she texted: *At a community Christmas play with Mom. I'm so bored! Points to the performers for trying, but only one of them can sing.*

I responded: *Why are you listening to voicemail and texting? You should be paying attention to the show.*

Told you, I'm bored!!!!! And if you want me to pay attention to the play, why do you keep texting?

I hated it when she was right. *Brat. Have fun. Talk later.*

She responded with a row of hearts and kissy lips.

Not knowing what else to do, I scrolled through the FBI's and then Wisconsin's Most Wanted lists. There were some scary dudes wandering the country.

Finally, after searching the village for six hours, Atkins returned with nothing to report.

"We went door to door." His voice held a combination of frustration, exhaustion, and annoyance. "The nun at the, uh, un-church let us in to search her place when I told her you reported seeing someone in that window. There was no one but her and a white cat with blue eyes." He dropped into one of the chairs across from my desk. "Are you sure it was Page who left the cards?"

"No, I told you we didn't have an actual sighting. You've got to admit, it makes sense. Activity relating to him was reported in Duluth. That's only ninety minutes away." I twisted to the left and then the right to ease the tension in my back. It popped five times. "Maybe he's hiding in one of the cottages?"

"We didn't get an answer at every door," Atkins said, "but everyone who was home let us in to look for him. Page is a big guy, and the cottages are small. If he was in one of them, we would've found him."

That should have made me feel better. Instead, it just created more questions. What about the cottages where they didn't get answers? He could have broken in and was hiding in one of them. He also had a way of hiding in plain sight. Or he could have left the village already. Was this part of his game? Slip into the village, torment me, and then leave? Now, I had to wonder if it really was him who'd left the cards.

"It had to be him. I can't even guess at who else it might be." My mind spun. "I can't think of anyone I interacted with here that I upset enough to . . ."

My voice trailed off and Atkins, naturally, caught it. "What?"

"Flavia Reed has been angry with me since the day I arrived here six months ago." An image of Sugar sitting in the corner with Flavia and her group at The Inn popped into my mind. "One of the owners of the sweet shop also runs hot and cold with me."

I described Flavia's cottage and one of the teams reported having searched there.

"She let us in," the mid-thirties deputy said and shook her head. "She had one question after another. Why did we think it was Page? Who said Page was in the village? Things like that. She was so interested in details about Page, we spent an extra-long time at her place."

That made it sound like if Donovan was in the village, she didn't know about it. Flavia only interacted like that when she was in the dark.

The team that covered the shops claimed no hesitation from any of the owners. "They all let us wander wherever we wanted. Even into their back rooms."

"We've done everything except search the woods," Atkins said. "We can do that if you want us to, but that will require more planning. We wouldn't be able to start until tomorrow."

"I'll let you know." With every "no" answer, more and more of my strength drained from my body. "If he was here, I think he's gone again. This is a game to him, just like it has been from the start. We interacted for the first two months I was here, and I had no clue what he'd done. I knew I didn't like the guy but never suspected him of anything illegal. He's playing with me."

"If you honestly think he's here, you need to be extra cautious," Atkins warned. "Don't be alone. The villagers know to be on the lookout for him and aren't happy that he might be lurking around. They're on your side and will help you."

That eased my mind more than I could say. In my gut, I knew most of the villagers were good people. It was amazing how just a few could ruin things for everyone.

"I'm mostly concerned about Tripp right now." Thank God River was staying with us. "If Donovan wants to do something to me, he'll go for those I love first and save me for last."

Atkins stared at me and blinked. "That's supposed to

make me feel better?"

"I won't take chances. Meeka is always with me." The Westie spun around with a bark of recognition from checking out something in the corner by the coffee maker. "She'll alert me to trouble."

"We're going to do a sweep of the circus grounds before we leave," Atkins informed, "and stop at a few of the outlying cottages you told us about. I'll be in touch if we find anything."

"I don't expect to hear from you." I gave him a tired smile. "Sorry to waste your time but thanks for coming."

"That's what we're here for. Call anytime."

I stood in the middle of my station after they'd left, deciding what to do next. I wasn't ready to go home. I couldn't deal with another fight with Tripp right now. Morgan and Briar, my usual go-to gals when I was upset, were too busy with Shoppe Mystique to comfort me. Besides, I wasn't sure I wanted to deal with words of advice at the moment. I just wanted to disappear. Figuratively.

Meeka stood at the front door, begging to go out, so I took her for a short walk down the Fairy Path, staying alert to my surroundings while weighing my options about what to do. I found myself in front of The Twisty Skein and thought of how I'd told Tripp I was going to take up knitting. I didn't really want to knit, but there had to be something that would interest me.

Ruby McLaughlin's shop had a slightly different feel than the others in the village. It had the same stucco and beam outside, but she'd painted the stucco a deep parchment-ivory instead of crisp-white like the rest. Two bay windows, each made up of five rows of six little panes, bulged out of the front wall on either side of the entrance.

I opened the door and poked my head in. "Are you still open?"

"Winding down but yes, still open." Ruby made a grand swooping gesture with her arm. "Come on in, Sheriff."

"Can Meeka come in too?"

"If she wipes her paws." Ruby laughed at herself. "Blue's here. They can keep each other company."

Blue was here? Didn't Atkins tell me she was up at the un-church? She never stayed in one place for long. Blue was a true community cat.

The inside of The Twisty Skein reminded me a lot of Shoppe Mystique. It was a big open space paneled with wood planks. Thick wood beams added interest to the tall ceilings as well as structure to the roof. It was very homey and welcoming.

"What can I help you find?" Ruby's smile faded. "Or are you here on official business. I heard Donovan might be in the village."

It both comforted and upset me that the villagers were concerned about this. "We thought he might be, but if he was, the deputies couldn't find him."

"Is he hiding?"

I stared for a second at Ruby, her short, choppy white-gray hair caught my attention. I'd seen a person with either a white hat or white hair in the window at Agnes' un-church. There were other people in the village with white hair and hats. Maybe Ruby or one of the other villagers had been there. It might have been Blue in the window. Or it could simply have been Deputy Atkins telling me about the Donovan lookalike in Duluth that made me think he was in the village and leaving me cards.

"Have you ever been to the un-church?" I asked.

The question caught Ruby off guard. She shook her head, her dangling turquoise earrings swaying as she did. "I've heard about it but never been there. Why do you ask?"

"No reason." I moved away from the Donovan topic.

Until I knew for sure that it was him, there was no sense upsetting people. "I was taking Meeka for a little walk and thought I'd stop in. I need something to keep me busy during the winter months."

"Good plan. Busy hands keep the brain working better." She spread her thin arms wide and spun in a slow circle. "As you can see, I've got a variety of options."

Determined to make sure I chose just the right craft, Ruby asked a hundred questions while walking me around the shop. To the right of the front door was the yarn section. Bins stuffed with different kinds and colors of yarn formed a rainbow on the wall. A spinning wheel and a weaving loom also sat in this area.

"That loom looks interesting."

"Oh, that's a lot of fun. Honey is in the middle of a table runner right now and then Gardenia wants to make a rug for her hallway. Gardenia is crazy-fast on that thing. You should see her when she's in the zone." She waved her hands back and forth as though shoving yarn through the loom. "I can put you on the list after her, if you'd like. Looming gets popular in the winter. I'm going to set up another one once the Yule season ends."

That would get me out of the house and encourage socializing with the villagers. "Sure. Add me to the list."

To the left of the door was the painting section. Wooden shelves held rows of paints in small bottles, pots, and tubes. Blank canvases filled a large steamer trunk. Easels for sale or rent were propped in the corner. Another four-sided rack held sketchbooks, pencils, charcoal sticks, and other drawing necessities.

Toward the back of the shop was a small section of quilting fabrics and supplies. There were also beads, embroidery kits, modeling clay, and a wall of scrapbook paper. At the center of the building was a circular stone fireplace surrounded by comfy lounge chairs, each with its own table. What a perfect spot to sit and craft with friends.

"Learning to paint is high on my list. I've got a nice set of watercolors I've never used." I could picture myself in the great room creating images of the lake and the pine trees.

"That," Ruby said, "will take more than the few minutes we have tonight. How about sketching? Similar concept without needing quite so much instruction."

We sat in front of that gorgeous fireplace, and Ruby gave me a very basic lesson on sketching while Meeka and Blue played hide-and-seek. Ruby showed me that holding the pencil an inch or so from the end rather than near the tip would give me more freedom of movement. She explained that each pencil lead had a different hardness which determined the amount of color they would leave on the page. Pencils with harder graphite produced a lighter shade. Softer graphite resulted in darker color.

"Use short, quick strokes," she explained while demonstrating. "That allows you to alter the shape more easily without needing to erase. Use a light pencil to create the basic outline of your object and then add definition with the darker pencils to make it all come to life."

She drew as she spoke, and I was in awe of how in a few short minutes, she had produced a simple image of Meeka.

"I imagine it will be a while before I can do that," I said, admiring the picture.

"I've been drawing for twenty-five years," Ruby said, "and I draw every day. While I'm winding down at night watching a show on TV, I keep my skills fresh by sketching something in the room. It relaxes me, especially because I never need to show anyone, so it doesn't matter what it looks like. Start with simple shapes and then add to them. I have classes throughout the winter. You should come. If you practice, you could be drawing Meeka by Beltane."

"When is that?"

"May first."

That gave me six months. Sounded like a decent goal.

She showed me a high-end drawing set with different kinds of pencils—graphite, colored, pastels, charcoal—multiple kinds of erasers, a sharpener, a sandpaper block for sharpening the pastels and charcoals, and a small posable mannequin. It was a beautiful set and maybe someday I'd be ready for it. For now, I chose a sketch pad and beginner's set of pencils, which still gave me twenty-five pencils to play around with.

Then I ran over to The Inn's restaurant to get takeout for dinner and returned to the station.

I sat at my desk, Meeka at my feet, and started drawing circles and squares, noting how the harder pencils seemed to almost tug on the paper while the softer ones glided across the page. Before long, I added diagonal lines to my squares and the combination started to resemble the evidence locker across the room. I was able to turn circles and triangles into a rough approximation of Meeka's head. Then I turned circles and swirling filigree shapes into a rather intricate Triple Moon Goddess symbol—a full moon with a pentacle at its center flanked by crescent moons on both sides.

I glanced at my watch and saw it was ten o'clock.

"We should head home soon," I told the furry one, now lying on my feet.

The next time I checked, it was nearly midnight. If this was what happened every time I sat down with a sketch pad, winter would be turning into spring before I knew it.

Chapter 26

I PULLED UP TO PINE Time to find the only lights on upstairs were the ones in River's room. The front and back porch lights were also on, and one of the back patio doors was unlocked. Any other time, I'd think it was sweet that Tripp left a door unlocked for me. Tonight, considering his life had been threatened, not so much.

"Do a quick patrol," I told Meeka as I waited outside for her. "It's late."

"Really late."

I nearly jumped out of my skin. Tripp was standing at the door behind me.

"Are you trying to scare me to death?" I asked.

"No. Are you trying to scare me? It's after midnight. Where have you been?"

His tone made me feel like a teenager who'd missed curfew.

"At the station," I said.

He pointed at the drawing set in my hands. "Doing arts and crafts? You raised hell earlier about Donovan and then you're gone this long without a phone call?"

I hugged my pencil set to my chest. "I needed something

to do while Atkins and the deputies were searching the village."

Not exactly the truth since the sketching happened after Atkins had left.

"Deputy Atkins stopped by here six hours ago. He told me they'd searched the village and found no sign of Donovan. That eased my mind for a while, but then a couple hours passed, and you didn't come home. Then a couple more. I've been sitting here worried that something happened to you."

I released my stranglehold on the box. "You couldn't have been that worried or you would've called the station to check on me."

Meeka slunk into the house like a kid trying to be invisible while Mom and Dad fought. I pushed past Tripp and went right to our bedroom. I placed my drawing set on one of the chairs by the windows and as I removed my badge and other tools from my pockets, I noticed that the covers had been thrown to the side of the bed. Tripp must've been lying awake and leapt out when he saw the car lights. Guilt stabbed at me over worrying him. I could have called.

Once he had entered the room and closed the door, I turned to him. "I'm sorry I worried you. I really am. This is why I didn't come home, though." I kept my voice even and nonconfrontational. "I knew we'd end up fighting again. I'm so tired of fighting all the time."

I stepped into the bathroom to change into a tank top and boxers. When I got into bed, Tripp said softly, "So you chose to avoid me instead? That's not the answer. Don't you think we should talk about what's going on?"

"Of course I do. Right now, or—"

"Tomorrow. Someplace neutral."

My mind spun for someplace in the village that was both neutral and private. "The campground? Or the Meditation Circle?"

"Either will work."

Finally, we agreed on something. We both rolled to our sides and slept back to back, but at least we slept in the same bed.

~~~

I woke the next morning with every muscle in my body aching. It might have been the stress over the possible Donovan threat. More likely, it was because last night had been awful. Not just the argument when I got home. I was feeling horrible for purposely avoiding Tripp. What was going on with me? I needed a therapy session with the Barlows.

After letting the hot water in the shower pound on my aching shoulders and back for a good fifteen minutes, I got dressed and smelled pancakes as I left the bathroom. Expecting to see Melinda and Gloria having their way with the kitchen again, I was surprised to find Tripp making breakfast.

I poured myself some coffee and went to his side. "Are we okay?"

He glanced at me as he added batter to the skillet. "We will be. If we talk. We can't keep ignoring this."

"Agreed. Tonight, for sure. Okay?"

He nodded and returned to flipping pancakes and tending to sausage links.

I found Tavie, Gloria, and Melinda in the great room.

"How are things with Silence?" I took a seat on one of the sofas.

Melinda and Gloria took turns explaining how things were looking hopeful, and that Silence wrote on her whiteboard that she wanted to go home.

"She's holding steady," Tavie said with a look of relief. "They agreed to transfer her to a hospital near home today. They still want to monitor her for infection for another day or
~~~

two, but if things continue as they are, they'll release her later this week."

"That's fantastic." I couldn't believe how relieved I was to have one Whispering Pines incident not end in death.

Tavie stood, pulled me to my feet, and then linked arms with me the way Morgan did when she wanted to have a chat. She led me down the hall to the sitting room across from the dining room.

"After breakfast, the girls and I will pack up our bags and head on out."

"I'll be sorry to see you leave," I told her. "Except for the obvious, I've enjoyed having you here."

"We'll keep praying for you and the village." She paused before asking, "Is everything okay with you and Tripp? If you don't mind me being nosey."

"You heard us arguing last night, didn't you?"

"No, but the air around here is thick with anger this morning. You told me a few days ago that it was growing pains because the two of you had recently moved in together." She stared at me until I looked at her. "Do you really think that's it?"

"No. This has nothing to do with different living styles. I lived with someone for many years, and he had a lot of quirky habits. Nothing Tripp does comes close to that."

"Then this thing runs deep. Whatever it is, it's not likely to work itself out. You two need to talk."

Maybe Tavie had a little fortune teller in her. "We will. We both agreed to have a discussion tonight."

I was about to tell her more when the phone rang. Good, I didn't necessarily want to tell her more. How did she keep doing that?

"I've got it," I called out to Tripp. I ran to the office, thinking it might be a reservation, and found it was Flavia's next-door neighbor.

"I'm sorry to be calling so early," began the woman with an unusually deep voice, "but you've got to come and do something. We can't take much more of this."

"Much more of what?" I asked.

"Come find out for yourself."

"All right, I'll be right there."

While I grabbed my Glock and essentials, Tripp assembled a breakfast sandwich for me to eat in the car.

"Be safe," he said and gave me a quick, albeit awkward kiss on the cheek.

"I will. Promise."

"River and I will be putting primer on the walls today."

"I can't wait to see it."

I gave Tavie and the girls goodbye hugs and asked them to keep me up to date on Silence's progress. Tavie assured me she would. Then Meeka and I rushed over to Flavia's street.

Flavia's witchy-looking cottage was right on the corner. Probably not originally positioned so she could stay on top of her neighbors' comings and goings, but it worked out that way. The other homes on the street were all different in structure, but all of the exteriors were either stucco with wood trim and thatched roofs or simple dark-stained wood like Flavia's.

I parked on the dirt road just before the bridge over the creek and immediately got an idea of what the neighbor lady had been talking about. A group of three guys, led by Brady Higgins, were parading up and down the street, loudly proclaiming that, "The people have had enough. It's time to take back the village."

"What exactly do you mean by that, Brady?" I called out, startling him and causing him to jump.

The color drained from his face when he saw me, and he stammered, "The village isn't safe. There's been too much death." He looked at the neighbors who had come out onto their front porches. "There's a dark cloud hanging over us. We all feel it."

I couldn't decide if his words were rehearsed or simply repeated too many times. In particular, I found the phrase "dark cloud" especially notable. It's exactly the one Sugar used when she told me she thought the drama here was my fault.

"Tell me," I moved closer to the trio, "what's the plan?"

A frown creased Brady's forehead. "What do you mean?"

"Well, most people who are unhappy about something have an idea of what they'd prefer. What's your plan to blow away this dark cloud?" Flavia, or possibly Sugar, must have put him up to this. Brady wasn't an activist, just a bored villager looking for a little excitement. After half a minute without a response from him, I said, "Brady, it's Sunday morning of Thanksgiving weekend. People are spending time with family and trying to relax."

Someone from one of the nearby houses called out, "Thank you, Sheriff."

Brady set his jaw and pushed his shoulders back. "I have the right to speak my mind."

The men with him replied with nods of agreement.

"You do have the right to your opinions, but you don't have the right to disturb people this way. Tell you what, why don't you arrange a village meeting? Laurel will probably let you hold it in The Inn's dining room. Sugar will surely provide scones and cookies. You can design, print, and hand out flyers. Make sure you put one on the commons' message board."

The more I spoke, the twitchier Brady became.

"I like this idea," I continued. "People who share your concerns can gather in one place and discuss a solution. Those who are fine with things as they are won't be disturbed. Make sure you invite me. I'm more than willing to come and talk to people. I'd like to know what folks are unhappy about." I paused as though ticking off items on a mental checklist. "It'll be a lot of work, but you're clearly passionate about this."

Brady took a few steps closer to me and leaned in. "This wasn't really my idea."

"I know that," I said, matching his confidential tone. "Let me guess, Flavia recruited you to stir the pot, so to speak?"

He didn't respond, but he did glance past me, presumably at Flavia's cottage.

"Go on home, Brady. You two as well," I told his friends. "You're upsetting people."

Flavia came storming out of her cottage then. "They have a right—"

I held a hand out to her. "You're a little late for that argument. Your neighbors don't want to be bothered this way. No one cares if you and your group want to discuss problems, just do it in an organized, non-invasive fashion. Call a meeting. Don't bother people in their homes."

"Why is it okay for *her* to bother people?" Flavia pointed past me with a bony finger. I turned to see Reeva carrying a large wicker basket.

"She's not bothering us," a neighbor called.

"Of course, I'm not," Reeva said as she got close to us. "Since I've decided to stay in the village permanently, I need to start earning a little money. I'm thinking about opening a business." She pulled back a black cloth covered with crescent moons and stars to reveal an assortment of chocolates. "Would you care for a sample?"

"I told you before, you can't trust her," Flavia hissed. "She always comes across as the innocent one, but she's not the victim here. It's all an act. She probably put something in those candies."

I blinked at her. "You're sounding a little paranoid, Flavia. Why would she do that?"

"Oh, in the name of the Goddess." Reeva blindly chose two candies from the basket and shoved them in her mouth and chewed, her cheeks bulging. "If I'd put something in them, would I do that?"

"Easy enough to deflect a hex off yourself," Flavia sniffed.

Reeva laughed. "That's absurd. I've done what I came to do, which was to hand out samples, and I'm leaving now." She turned to the gathering neighbors. "I've got oils and vinegars infusing with herbs. I'll have samples for you tomorrow."

While Flavia followed her sister down the street, continually hurling insults at her, a woman waved me over.

"See what I mean?" It was the woman who had called me, her deep voice instantly familiar. Although, I had a hard time reconciling it with her plump and petite frame. She introduced herself as LaVonne LeBeau. "If it's not Flavia having people warn us about the impending doom of the village, it's her arguing with her sister about . . . anything."

"How often does that happen? The arguing, I mean."

"Feels like every day lately. Reeva has been bringing around samples of things she's considering selling in her shop. Today it's chocolates. The salted caramel is fantastic. Yesterday it was yummy little meat pies that were three bites big. She claims that's all you need to get a good taste of something. I wanted more than three bites, though. A few days ago, it was just enough premeasured ingredients and instructions to make four spice muffins. Tomorrow, oils and vinegars." LaVonne smiled and shook her head. "Problem is, the poor dear is good at too many things. She can't decide what kind of shop to open. Something food-related, for sure. She's such a talented kitchen witch."

I seemed to remember Gran saying in one of her journals that Reeva was good at anything she touched, while Flavia struggled with everything. "Is this why you asked me to come over?"

She gave an embarrassed smile. "Guess that was a little extreme. We could have confronted Brady on our own. It's just that Flavia has been so unusual lately, we didn't know what might happen next."

I stopped myself from pointing out that Flavia was always unusual and instead asked, "What's been going on?"

"Well, there's the whole *the village is going to hell in a handbasket* thing." LaVonne sighed. "I think that's crazy talk. I mean, those of us who have been here for any length of time know weird things were going on well before you got here."

I nodded my thanks. "How long have you been here?"

"Twenty-five years. I met my husband in college. We're both computer programmers. His parents are Wiccan and moved here when he was a toddler. They passed on years ago and left the house to him. I love it here. Weird stuff or not. Besides that, there's the constant harassment of poor Reeva who's just trying to find her way. I mean, hasn't she been through enough? And there's also the man who's been hanging around her place."

A chill ran through me. "A man? At Flavia's cottage?"

Atkins said she let them in. Maybe she had Donovan hidden somewhere or shoved him out the back door when the deputies entered.

"I don't know what they're doing in there," LaVonne said with a slightly scandalous tone, "but he's been here for days. First time I noticed him was Wednesday night. He comes and goes, but I never see them together."

"Can you describe him?"

"Tall." She held her arm straight up, her hand hovering about a foot above her head, which put this guy at more than six feet. "He wore a brown leather blazer, and those sunglasses pilots like. Oh, a white Vikings cap." She curled her lip and flashed me the Packers T-shirt beneath her red fleece jacket.

This matched Tripp's description of the man at the station.

Donovan was staying with Flavia? That actually made sense. I suspected her of colluding with Donovan starting back at the incident with my grandmother.

I pulled myself back before I headed down that rabbit hole. "Did you see the man's face at all?"

LaVonne thought and then shook her head. "No, I never got a look at his face. I only saw him from the side. But his hair was medium-brown. Cut short on the sides but sort of curly on top." She twirled her fingers near the top of her head.

Short brown hair? That didn't fit. Donovan had white hair, always pulled back in a ponytail. Unless he changed it.

I pushed my shoulders back in a stretch and became very aware of the hag stone on the chain beneath my shirt. Did that mean I was closing in on the truth? Brown hair, leather blazer, aviator glasses. Oh my god.

"You said you saw him from the side. Did you by any chance notice a scar on his right cheek? It would've been fairly long." I indicated an arching line running from mid-cheekbone to my chin.

A jagged scar across a smooth plane, according to Lily Grace.

"Oh, gosh, I don't know." LaVonne squeezed her eyes shut, trying to picture him, then shook her head. "Maybe. Do you know this guy?"

"I might." But it couldn't be him. Why would he be in Whispering Pines? Even if he was in the village, why would he be with Flavia?

I swear, the hag stone was getting warm. Uncomfortably so. I tugged on the chain, pulling out the cluster, and held the stone. On a whim, I raised it to look through the hole the way Mallory did but before I could, a man appeared on Flavia's front porch. The exact person I'd been thinking of. My ex-partner, Randy Ketchum.

Chapter 27

I COULD HARDLY BELIEVE IT. I hadn't seen Randy in nearly a year. He looked awful. He'd lost probably twenty-five pounds, and he had always looked to me like he could stand to gain five. The weight loss combined with the circles beneath his eyes gave him a skeletal look. Even more upsetting than his presence was that he did not look happy to see me.

"Ketch? What are you doing here?" I meant specifically Flavia's house but also the village in general.

"I'm here for the anniversary. You know what this weekend is, don't you?" He didn't wait for me to respond. "It's been a year already. Can you believe that?"

"I do know. I've been thinking about Frisky a lot." As we talked about this very personal event, my vision tunneled to just Randy. Flavia and her neighbors seemed to vanish around me.

"A whole year." He paced the width of Flavia's creepy cottage with the same kind of twitchy movements of a crack addict needing a fix.

"But why are you here?" I asked again, grappling for some sort of solid ground here.

"To find you, of course. Who better to understand the significance than you?"

"When did you get here?"

He shrugged. "A few days ago."

"A few days? Why didn't you come find me?"

"Guess you could say I've been working on a project."

He took a white cap from his jacket pocket and tugged it over his head. I froze. My mind didn't want to accept it, but there was only one explanation—Randy had left the cards and threatened my boyfriend. And me.

"Ketch, did you leave those envelopes?"

"You got them?" This excited him, as though he'd been worried maybe I hadn't. "I know you got the one in the pub Thursday night. I saw you open it." He laughed and slapped his hand on the porch railing. "The look on your face. I can't believe you didn't see me in there. I was sitting two tables away. Sounds like Flavia is right. Your skills are slipping."

Nothing about this fit together. He was here because of the anniversary, that much made sense, but how did he end up with Flavia? How did they even know about each other? Had Reed betrayed my confidence?

No. More likely, Sheriff Brighton had relayed everything I'd said about my position with Madison PD and my partnership with Randy to Flavia. Had she contacted Randy?

All of that could wait. I needed to focus on the immediate problem.

"What do you think I did, Ketch?"

He went from laughing to dead serious in a blink. "You read the third card. You ruined my life. That's what you did."

"But how? What did I do?"

Then, as though we were old friends who met on the street and were catching up on news, he said, "You remember that Elena and I weren't doing so good, right?"

That was an understatement. They were a train wreck. He'd been on the edge over his failing marriage for months and had a huge fight with Elena before coming to work the day he shot Frisky. Elena threatened to leave him, and he was sure she'd be gone before he got home that night. It was a perfect storm kind of day. Frisky's erratic behavior was the tipping point for him. He should've called in sick. Or just not showed up for work at all. That would've resulted in a simple disciplinary meeting with Captain Grier.

"We tried the counseling stuff," Ketch continued. "That didn't work. It came down to what she'd been saying all along. She just didn't want to be a cop's wife anymore."

"Was there someone else?" I cringed as soon as the words were out of my mouth. The last thing I wanted was to escalate the emotions of an already upset man by insinuating his wife had been having an affair.

"You know, I wondered the same thing." His expression darkened. "She's got someone new now but swears there wasn't anyone before. I believe her. We're at the point where we don't need to lie to each other anymore." I was about to say that was promising news when he added, "If we want to hurt each other, the truth works way better."

My heart sunk. He really loved Elena and was crazy about his kids. "Are you officially split up then?"

"The divorce was final in August. She took the kids but didn't want the house." He made a disgusted *tsk* sound. "I don't want the house either. Needs more work than I can afford to do to it. Not sure I could even pay off the loan if I sold it as is." He shrugged. "Half my paycheck goes to Elena every month, so I can't make my mortgage payments anyway. The bank will likely make the decision on what I get to do with it soon."

"Are you still with the department?"

He looked at me like he couldn't grasp the question. "You didn't keep track of your brothers at all after you walked out, did you? Remember how you went into Captain Grier's office that day, spewing your version of the events, all full of confidence and righteousness?"

I remembered going into the captain's office, but it wasn't due to righteousness. It was because I couldn't handle the harassment from my so-called brothers anymore. They kept warning me . . . no, threatening me to not say anything, insisting I needed to keep my lips zipped and stand by my partner. In other words, blame everything on Frisky. I went into Captain Grier's office to quit that day but ended up doing exactly what they'd all warned me not to.

"Grier called me in the day after you left," Randy continued, "and recommended that I look for another line of work. He didn't want to risk the scandal the news of a cop shooting an unarmed woman would bring to the precinct." He locked his eyes on mine. It was the same threatening look the other cops had been giving me. "Even though my mistake was completely understandable."

He shoved his hands into the pockets of the leather jacket he always wore. It would be late May, far too warm for leather, and he'd still have that thing on. My gut told me to be on guard. Those pockets were plenty deep enough to hold a handgun.

"Understandable? Ketch, you knew Frisky as well as I did. You knew she wouldn't have hurt you. There's no way she would've had a weapon on her. Frisky was the biggest pacifist out there."

"Looked to me like she had a weapon."

"It was her cell phone." The memory of those fateful moments was forever burned into the front of my brain. "She had her phone in her hand. She'd been looking at pictures of her brother and her nephew. It was the anniversary of their deaths."

One had died that day, the other the next. And now it was the anniversary of hers as well. So damn much unnecessary death.

"Elena won't let me see my kids anymore. Not for even an hour on Thanksgiving. Not even in public. She thinks I'll hurt them."

The pained look on his face was heartbreaking. Ketch had been a good man, and a really good cop, who'd gotten off track. The pressure of supporting a family on a cop's salary got to be too much. I liked Elena, she was a nice woman, but she had champagne and caviar taste.

Ketch pulled one hand out of his pocket and put it over his eyes, the other still buried deep in the other pocket. When he covered his eyes, I unhooked and removed my gun from its holster. Prepared for whatever might come next.

"Sounds like you still need some help, Ketch. I know how devastating breakups can be."

"Oh, yeah." He laughed and dropped his hand. His eyes went straight to the weapon at my side. "I heard you broke things off with that whiner Jonah after you quit. Good for you." He gave me a nod and a wink. "Did you like the picture I took of your new guy? What's his name? Tripper Bennett?"

My blood ran cold. "What do you think I did, Ketch? How did I ruin your life?"

"You're not listening." He threw his arm out wide to the side, like a gangster. "I just told you. I lost my job because of you. I'm working at the corner convenience store now making minimum wage because of you. Elena didn't want to be a cop's wife anymore, but me losing my job was the last nail in the coffin for her. She took my kids and takes half my teeny tiny paycheck. No wonder she had to hook up with someone else. My support won't buy squat for our kids." He paused and then his voice broke when he said, "I can't support my family. I got no job, no wife, no life, and it's all because of you."

"So how did you end up here with Flavia?" My mind was scrambling for a way to disarm and subdue him. Ketch was almost a foot taller than me and had a good seventy-five pounds on me despite his weight loss. I was strong, but I couldn't do anything against him. "Did Flavia call you? Did she tell you the sheriff's position was yours if you could scare me out of the village?"

It was a ridiculous concept but might actually be possible. With Flavia, the further away from sense I went, the closer to the truth I got. Regardless of plausibility, I was desperate to distract him with anything I could.

"I did no such thing." Flavia moved forward, defending her own honor, stopping midway between Ketch and me. Brilliant. I was holding a gun, Ketch surely had one in his pocket, and Flavia puts herself right into the potential line of fire. "Whispering Pines does need a new sheriff, but the obvious choice is my son. Martin is superior to both of you."

Ketch stepped off the porch and closer to her. I tightened my grip on my gun. Meeka stood in front of me, prepared to attack if necessary.

"It was like I told you," Ketch said, hand back in his pocket. "I came up here because of Frisky and Elena. I thought it might be a good idea to be with someone who I wouldn't have to explain everything to first. You know?"

"I do." That was why I wanted Reed's help even though Jagger was capable. "Things got so messed up that day, Ketch. It still haunts me. I'd known for a while how stressed you'd been. I should've tried to help you sooner. I'm sorry."

"I have nightmares about that day." He stared at Meeka, his eyes vacant voids, not seeing anything but the past. "I swear, I thought she had a weapon. She was crazy that day. Remember?"

He was calming down. Good. I took a half step closer, my K-9 moving with me.

"She loved those two boys so much." Tavie's words echoed in my ears. *Anyone can fall on hard times, but that doesn't mean you need to let your life spiral or turn into a thug.* "She changed her life after they died. She transformed herself into the angel of her neighborhood." Another half step. "Remember how the kids talked about Mama Frisky?"

Ketch nodded, still in the past. "She was messed up that day. Sitting in her car and sobbing like they'd both just died in front of her."

"Frisky told me once that she'd go sit in her car, somewhere no one could find her, when she needed to be alone. She wanted to be strong for her 'cupids.' That's what she called the neighborhood kids." Another half step. "They made her fall in love with them, so they were her cupids."

He looked up at me. "I thought she was strung out on something."

"She might've been. She didn't have a weapon, though."

"I shouldn't have come to work that day."

"I should've said something sooner. I knew you were spiraling, Ketch."

Wrong thing to say. In the blink of an eye, he had one arm hooked around Flavia's neck and pulled the gun I'd known was there out of his pocket.

Without even thinking about it, I reacted and leveled my weapon on my ex-partner. Without even thinking about it. The same reaction he'd had that day a year ago.

"You never should have said anything," Ketch hollered. "You should've kept your mouth shut. It all would've gone away. Everyone would've forgotten about Frisky Fox, and my life would be fine." He nodded at my weapon. "You gonna shoot me, Jayne?"

"I don't want to. Why don't you lower your weapon and let Flavia go? You need help, Ketch." My mind searched for something, anything to distract him with. "Remember that missing UW student we found that time? My grandma's friend called and told me we'd find her in the duck blind in the woods across the street from her apartment. Remember her?"

He clutched Flavia tighter, and she closed her eyes, her lips moving silently. "I remember her."

"Her name is Jola Crain. She lives here now and works at our health clinic. She's really good, Ketch. Jola will find you the best possible care."

Again, wrong thing to say.

"You want my kids to think I'm mental?" He held the gun to Flavia's head, and she cried out in fear. A scream rose from the cluster of her neighbors behind me.

"You might as well shoot me." There was a desperate, pleading tone in his voice now. "I can't let my kids think I'm crazy. Shoot me, O'Shea. Tell them I went down fighting crime like a superhero." He blinked once, twice. "They love superheroes."

I had a clear shot. It would've been easy to put a bullet right into his abdomen. Too easy. He'd left his center mass exposed for me to hit. He was as worked up as Frisky had been that day, ranting and not making sense. Not that any of that mattered. I couldn't do it. Despite the risk to Flavia, an innocent civilian, I couldn't shoot my partner. More death wasn't the answer to the problems here.

"Randy, please. Let her go. We'll work this out. I promise."

Flavia called out, "Just shoot him. If anything happens to me, you'll—"

Before she could complete her threat, a man darted out of the crowd and grabbed hold of her. He yanked Flavia downward, freeing her from Ketch's arm, and tossed her aside. A half-second later, Martin Reed had Randy on the ground with his knee in the center of his back.

Chapter 28

THE CLUSTER OF NEIGHBORS WENT into action. The majority backed away, clearing a path for those most able to help. Someone pressed a foot to Randy's hand while another kicked the gun away. Someone else helped Reed hold Randy down by sitting on his legs. Meeka joined Reed on Randy's back.

"Got a pair of zip cuffs on you, Sheriff?" Reed asked.

I pulled them out of a cargo pocket, unsure which of the things that had happened in the last thirty seconds stunned me more. Ketch begging me to shoot him while holding a gun to Flavia's head. Flavia's unfinished threat to me if I didn't shoot him. Reed deciding to be a deputy again at just the right moment. Or the villagers, once again, coming together as a unit to make a difference. That last one didn't stun me. It made me proud.

"What are you doing here?" I asked Reed after we'd shoved Ketch into the back of the station van and zip tied one of his feet to a metal loop bolted to the floor.

"Aunt Reeva told me something was going down over here. She burst into my cottage and told me to get over here as quickly as possible."

She hadn't driven. How did she get to Reed so quickly? Maybe the Whispering Pines witches really could fly. Or Reeva Long could run a four-minute mile. At this point, neither situation would surprise me.

"Guess it's a good thing you hadn't turned in the van yet, hey?"

Reed shoved his hands in his pockets. "You knew I was coming back."

"Honestly, I wasn't sure. I'm really glad you did, though. For many reasons."

He kicked at a pebble with the toe of his boot. "I'm still stinging a little over the whole Lupe thing."

"I know—"

"But," he interrupted, "I thought about what you said. I made a commitment to you and the village. You didn't have to let me come back after Sheriff Brighton died. I don't take that second chance lightly. I won't let you down again."

"Good." A sense of relief flooded me. At least I was back on track with him. "You're a good man, Reed. I'm proud to have you as my partner."

The tops of his cheekbones flushed pink. "You want me to take him over to the station and start the booking?"

"Please. Call Deputy Atkins soon as you get there and tell him we caught the envelope guy." I glanced at Flavia, who was still brushing dirt off her cloak from when her son had thrown her to the ground. "I have to talk with your mother."

He rolled his eyes. "Better you than me."

I went over to the woman who had been like a splinter I couldn't dig out for the last six months. "Are you okay?"

"I'll have a few bruises, I'm sure, but I'm alive. No thanks to you."

Let it go, Jayne. Don't lower yourself to her level. "I need to speak with you, Flavia. Would you like to go over to the station, or should we talk here?"

She looked at me with pinched lips and then turned toward her cottage. "Here is fine. I don't need the neighbors gossiping about anything else today."

Inside, Flavia scowled at Meeka, who stared up at her from three feet away, as she waited for tea water to boil. Without asking, Flavia set a cup in front of me as we sat at her little dining table. In a very twisted way, Flavia and I had formed a relationship. It wasn't anywhere near comfortable, and we were far more antagonistic than friendly, but there was a familiarity between us now that meant we could do away with formalities.

Before I could say anything, Flavia blurted, "Were you going to let him shoot me?"

I wanted to say no. If Reed hadn't stepped in, I wanted to believe that the professional me would have risen above the me that felt constantly picked on by the schoolyard bully. If forced to be honest, I'd have to admit to an upsetting moment during the incident where I thought that if Flavia was gone, a lot of the darkness would lift from the village. That was a gamble, though. Nothing around here was certain. And I didn't really want Flavia dead, for Reed's sake if nothing else.

"You're fine, that's what matters."

A flash of pain shadowed her face. Apparently, she'd expected me to say, "Of course I wouldn't have let the bad man shoot you." Did she really think she could be so nasty and people would still want to come to her rescue? Pushed far enough, the bullied fought back.

"Tell me the chain of events with Randy."

She sipped her tea. "I met him at Ye Olde Bean Grinder."

I'd forgotten about that. It felt like it had been weeks since the sister altercation rather than only a few days.

"Planning ways to torment your sister, were you?"

"Perhaps." Flavia sniffed. "That's neither here nor there. Mr. Ketchum walked into the shop, ordered a coffee, and asked if anyone knew where he could find you. Basil gave him directions to both the station and Pine Time. Then Mr. Ketchum sat to drink his coffee."

"And you started a conversation with him?"

"I asked him what business he had with you, and he informed me that he used to work with you. That led to a discussion about where the two of you worked and when."

"Sheriff Brighton told you about how things had played out for Randy and me. Didn't he?"

"He did."

"So you knew we had parted on shaky terms."

"I was aware."

"Randy said he came here because it was the anniversary of Frisky's death. He has a conversation with you and suddenly changes direction? The first card was waiting for me at the station when I brought you there that day. There wasn't enough time for him to meet with you, print out that card, and deliver it before we got there. Your version of events doesn't add up."

Flavia focused on her tea and wouldn't respond. That's because, once again, she was involved with a coverup.

"What did you tell him, Flavia?"

I waited out the silence until she said, "I didn't intend for him to threaten Tripp."

But it was fine for him to torment me with creepy cards. I enunciated each word this time. "What did you tell him?"

"I explained that we all knew about the shooting because you told everyone he went off the deep end that day." The corners of her mouth turned up. "He didn't like that."

"I told very few people here about the incident. I certainly never talked with you about it."

She lifted her shoulders in a little *oopsie, silly me* shrug. "I told him I could only imagine what kind of a detective you must have been because you were a poor excuse for a sheriff.

The village has slid further and further into turmoil since you started wearing the badge, and you seem to feel that you can do whatever you want regardless of what's right." She paused, sipped, and smiled deeper. "Digging up long-buried things just so you can appear to be some kind of hero in the end."

I had unintentionally uncovered festering wounds from the past that needed healing. That certainly wasn't for my benefit. Priscilla Page had died, and the truth of how needed to come out. Same with my grandmother's death.

"I have no interest in being a hero, Flavia."

The statement didn't sound as strong as I'd intended, and Flavia picked up on that.

"Mr. Ketchum didn't seem very surprised by the revelation. Considering how you put your own needs above his last year." She added more tea to her cup, then sugar and a splash of milk, her infuriating little smile growing stronger by the second. "I guess it depends on the direction from which you're looking at things. You have a habit of doing whatever you feel is best regardless of which side of the line your actions land on. For the record, I had nothing to do with the envelopes or anything else he may have done after leaving the Bean Grinder that day. I mean, he has been staying in my guest room, so I knew what he was up to. I neither encouraged nor condemned his behavior, however."

"Just like you were innocent of Donovan's involvement in Gran's death? And Rae's in Priscilla's?"

She glared at me over her teacup.

"What were you expecting would come from this?" I asked. "Did you think threats would make me leave the village?"

"Not at all. I am curious where your breaking point is, however." Unsaid was that she planned to keep pushing. "I thought it might be Tripp. Seems I was mistaken. Of course, he is capable of fighting for himself." Her eyes lowered to Meeka.

I pulled my hands away from my untouched tea and folded them in my lap. I didn't want her to see how badly they were shaking with fury.

"You do understand that I'm the only person between the people here being able to stay in this village and everyone having to pack up and move. Don't you?"

She sighed as though bored. "I'm aware. You've told me before."

"And you still think it's a good idea to upset me?"

There was that annoying little shrug again.

"I won't let a handful of thugs in this village take everyone else down." I changed the topic before saying something I might regret. Such as reminding her about the fine print giving O'Shea family members the authority to overrule the council. Best to keep that little nugget tucked safely away. "Did you pay the man in Duluth to pretend to be Donovan?"

She tilted her head, confused. "I have no idea what you're talking about."

This time I believed her, which was frustrating. "Do you know where Donovan is?"

"Not at the moment."

"Have you known where he's been at any time since he escaped custody?"

She set her cup daintily on its saucer and clasped her hands on the table. "Yes."

I could start demanding she tell me where he was. I could threaten her with an obstruction of justice charge. I could have said or done a lot of things at that moment. Instead, I pushed away from her table and stood.

"This is good information to have, Flavia. As always, I'll be keeping an eye on you."

Chapter 29

IT WAS MID-AFTERNOON BY THE time Reed finished the paperwork on Ketch. I let him handle the interview on this one. I was far too close to it. I did sit in on it, though.

"When did you first come into contact with Flavia Reed?" he asked.

"A few months ago," Randy responded. "End of July, I think. She contacted me."

That was right after I'd exposed the truth about Priscilla's death and Flavia's involvement in it. The timing made sense. Flavia had been furious I'd resurrected the event. There was no way she would've been able to stop herself from retaliating somehow.

"Why did she contact you?" Reed asked.

Randy shrugged. "She said she knew about my history with Jayne and had some information she thought I'd find interesting."

"Meaning what?"

"Meaning the rash of murders Sheriff O'Shea seemed incapable of doing anything about."

Reed shifted slightly. "Is that why you came here? To help with the murders?"

Randy glanced to where I stood in the corner of the room. "No. I couldn't care less about your village's problems. I came here because *Sheriff O'Shea* ruined my life."

The spite and anger in his voice when he said my name chilled me.

"You wanted revenge," Reed supplied. Before Randy could respond, he asked, "What was the plan? Were you and Ms. Reed in on everything together?"

Randy snorted a laugh. "No. She wasn't interested in getting her hands dirty. She told me about the problems with your new sheriff and left it at that."

He locked eyes with me.

I'd never forget the blank look on his face the day he shot Frisky. His eyes had been empty hazel voids. At the moment, they were as cold and nasty as any I'd ever seen.

He turned back to Reed. "At the end of our first conversation, she gave me her phone number. I wrote it down but basically dismissed her as being some crackpot trying to cause problems. I already had more trouble than I could handle."

"What kind of trouble exactly?"

"Lost my job. Was about to lose my wife and my kids. And I'm probably going to lose my house any day now."

Reed leaned casually in his chair. "You don't really need to worry about that anymore. You'll be living somewhere else for a while." He tapped his notebook, returning to his questions. "You said your initial contact with Flavia Reed was in July. When did you next hear from her?"

Randy shook his head. "I called her."

"When was that?"

"Last month."

"Why?"

"The anniversary of the shooting . . . You're aware of what I'm talking about?"

Reed gave a crisp nod. "I am."

"Of course you are." Randy glared at me again.

"Let me guess," Reed began. "The anniversary was coming up and things were getting worse and worse for you. You decided Sheriff O'Shea was causing all your problems, so you needed to cut off the head of the snake."

"Snake." Randy chuckled. "Perfect way to put it."

"You said the anniversary brought you here. What happened when you arrived in the village?"

"Ms. Reed said there was only one coffee shop here and that she'd meet me there. I was to come in, ask about finding the sheriff, and she would initiate contact with me."

It's like they were playing spy games. Stranger comes to town, orders a coffee, says the code word "sheriff," and chaos ensues.

"How did you end up staying at her place?" Reed asked. "Was that the plan all along?"

"No. When we met at the coffee shop, she said if I had nowhere else to stay, I could stay in her guest room. You'd have to ask her why. I planned to stay at the hotel at the edge of town." He shrugged. "Figured I'd save some money and take her up on her offer."

Even if we got an explanation from Flavia for why she'd invited him into her home, it would surely only make sense to her.

"By the way," Randy continued, "Ms. Reed had no knowledge of what I was planning to do. She only knew that I was coming to the village to see O'Shea. She didn't know about the cards or my plans for Mr. Bennett."

I didn't know if he would've hurt Tripp or not, but my blood ran cold. Either way, I'd heard enough. If I stayed in the room any longer, I'd do something I'd get in trouble for.

I waited in my office for Deputy Atkins to return, for the third time in two days, to take yet another criminal away from

Whispering Pines. I thanked him and promised to not call him again for at least twenty-four hours.

"I'm just glad we got the guy," he said. "This guy was your partner?"

I nodded. That made two people in a row I thought I could trust who had betrayed me.

"You okay?"

"As okay as I can be," I answered.

Once they'd left, I was ready to go home. Reed had different plans, though.

"I'm going to hang out here for a bit and catch up on the things I've ignored for the last month."

"It's been slow. You haven't missed much."

Embarrassed, he avoided looking at me as he said, "I'll be heading back to Green Bay when I finish here. Classes start again tomorrow. I won't be back for a couple weeks since I made so much progress on my cottage, but I've got a long break for Yule. I promise to be available whenever you need me."

"Good. You may want to talk with your mother and aunt at some point too."

He nodded but didn't otherwise acknowledge the advice.

Meeka and I left Reed to do his thing. I put out a call via walkie-talkie asking if anyone knew where Lily Grace was. That led me to the massive deck behind Grapes, Grains, and Grub to take care of one last bit of business before heading home.

"Isn't it a little chilly to be sitting outside?" I asked the teen.

She was settled into what Maeve called The Love Nest, a raised platform at the very back of the deck that was only big enough for two people. She was once again staring intently at her laptop.

"It wasn't bad when the sun was shining on me." She

pointed at the outdoor heater standing next to her. "I convinced Maeve to let me drag that out here. I was trying to find someplace I could be alone that also had internet connection."

"Sorry. You're still looking at veterinary schools?"

"I am. Don't tell anyone, but I think I'm going to do like Jola did and go to school, then come back here once I have my degree. Igor might be ready to retire from the circus by then."

"I like that idea. But you do come from a long line of fortune tellers. Don't you think they'll know about your plan before you tell them?"

She sighed. "That's always a possibility. Did you want something?"

I sat across from her. "I need you to contact someone for me."

"Like a séance?"

"However you do it." As Reed was booking Ketch, it became clear to me how I needed to resolve this issue in my life. It wasn't Ketch I needed to close the loop with. It never was. "Her name is Frisky Fox. I need to ask for her forgiveness."

Lily Grace closed her laptop and placed her hands on the table, palms up. I placed my hands over hers, and a few minutes later, I had Frisky's response.

"She says," Lily Grace began in her trance voice, "that you don't need her forgiveness. She never held you responsible. She says you need to forgive yourself."

That would be a lot harder. The Frisky loop was almost closed, and at least now I knew which direction to head in to seal it completely. Sometimes that was half the battle.

~~~

As I pulled into my spot next to the garage, I was surprised to
~~~

find River sitting on the front porch. He was lounging in a pair of paint-splattered black khakis and black canvas work jacket, enjoying the trees and cool air.

"Where's Tripp?" I asked.

"We completed our daily task an hour ago, and he requested a reprieve from manual labor for the remainder of the day."

"What's he doing? Is he inside?"

"He was inside last I knew. What he's doing, I cannot say. He did mention taking a short walk along the lakeshore so he may be out for a stroll." River patted the Adirondack chair next to him. "Please, sit with me a moment." As I did, he said, "Morgan has requested that the three of us join her and Briar for dinner this evening. We are welcome at any time, but I wish to speak with you before we go."

"This sounds serious." As I settled into the chair and covered my legs with the blanket River offered me, Meeka ran laps around the football-field-sized front yard.

"Serious only in that I am concerned about you, Proprietress. You've had a great deal placed on your shoulders, have you not?"

The last thing I expected was a guidance pep talk from River Carr. Equally unexpected were the tears that suddenly started streaming down my face. Humiliated, I tried to wipe them away, but they wouldn't stop. "Sorry."

"There is no need to apologize." He touched the back of my hand resting on the chair's arm with the tips of his fingers. "Perhaps expressing these burdens will help."

Like Tavie, there was something about him that made me want to do exactly that, to tell him about my burdens. The melodic soothing baritone of his voice, his calm manner, the intensity of his dark eyes, it was all so hypnotic. Unlike Tavie, I didn't feel the need to hold back with him.

"I'm just trying to do my job. Everything started out fine

here. I was able to solve the murders of Yasmine Long and the two carnies up at the circus. Since then, though, it feels like with every step forward, something drags me back two. And now some of the villagers are turning against me. If it's not problems with tourists, it's ghosts from my own life coming back to haunt me. And the fact that Tripp and I are—" I paused to get control over my suddenly quivering voice. "The fact that we're fighting makes everything harder. I'm sure you've noticed we're not exactly getting along."

"It's been difficult not to since I reside in your house." He touched my hand again, to make sure he had my attention this time. "If it is any consolation, he is equally distressed by this turn of events."

I nodded and looked across the yard at the towering pines. "I feel like I was brought to this village for a reason. You know? Of course you do. You were too. I thought I knew what that purpose was, but I seem to be failing at everything I try. The one thing I've always been able to depend on is my instinct, but that seems to be failing me too. That leaves me with no idea what to believe. I mean, what if I've been wrong all along? Maybe my purpose was simply to come and get the house ready for sale like my parents wanted me to. Maybe Whispering Pines is meant to dissolve."

"Lady Jayne—"

"River, please." Even his chivalrous formality was stressing me lately. "Just Jayne."

"Very well. Jayne, I agree with you. I also believe you were summoned to this village for a purpose. That means you are fully qualified to fulfill that purpose." He paused to let that sink in. "The burdens upon you may be many, but they would not even be placed upon you if you were not capable of managing them."

In a very Whispering Pines sort of way, that made all kinds of sense.

"Oftentimes," he continued, "just as we feel we are coming to the conclusion of a task, we find there is still far more to do or something altogether new to accomplish."

"A speedbump?" At his confused look, I explained, "Briar says that just when we think the road is clear, the Universe tosses in a speedbump."

He considered this and nodded. "A fine way of looking at it. Rest assured, I have yet to see a speedbump so tall as to be impassable. And I drive a car with very low ground clearance."

I laughed at that. It felt good. "So suck it up and keep moving forward?"

He winked, his dark eyes gleaming. "Suck it up, Proprietress."

We watched Meeka drag herself back to the house. Her non-stop laps had finally worn her out.

"River?"

"Yes, Jayne."

"I think you were summoned here to do more than be with Morgan."

He looked pleased with this. "Are you implying I have offered comfort?"

"That's exactly what I'm implying."

"Most excellent."

Suddenly, a night with the Barlows sounded like exactly what I needed.

"I'm going to go change out of my uniform," I told him. "I'll be ready for a night with the witches in a few minutes."

"Very well. I will locate Tripp." He opened the front door for me, and as our paths diverged at the stairway, he said, "I nearly forgot. You are to wear something warm."

~~~
~~~

Before we left, I gave Tripp the ten-minute recap on everything that had happened over the last few days. I started with how I arrested the three vigilantes, moved on to why I stayed at the station to sketch last night, and blew him away by explaining that Randy was the one who'd been delivering the envelopes.

"Everything," I concluded, "to my knowledge, is back under control. The only issue is Flavia, but she's always an issue and not a direct threat."

At least I was pretty sure she wasn't a threat. She convinced others to do her dirty work.

Tripp sat without speaking on the foot of our bed the entire time, taking in every word. I waited a few seconds to see if he'd respond, but he remained mute.

"We can talk about this later if you want," I offered and waited for some kind of a response. "Have you got anything to say before we go?"

With hands folded in his lap, he looked up at me. "How did you decide on sketching for a hobby?"

I burst out laughing and then started crying.

He jumped to his feet and hugged me. "We'll talk more. I have a lot of questions, but for now, I'm glad you were able to wrap things up." He leaned back to look at my tear-streaked face. "Are you okay?"

"Shook up. Shocked to be threatened by someone else I knew and trusted. I'll be okay, though."

"You're sure?"

"I'm fine. Always am. Let's go do something normal."

He arched an eyebrow. "Normal? You remember that we're going to the Barlows', right?"

Chapter 30

MEEKA STARTED WHINING WHEN I slowed the Cherokee as we pulled up to Morgan and Briar's cottage. She was prancing her paws to be let out when I opened the back door.

"Little excited to see Pitch?" I teased.

She barked and pushed on the cage with her head.

"Okay, go play."

She burst out when the door was halfway open. Barking excitedly, she ran to the edge of the yard and slid between the bare bushes that lined the massive Barlow garden.

River knocked on the front door, and we were greeted first by Morgan and then by the mouthwatering aroma of Briar's cooking.

"Blessed be," Morgan greeted. "Come on in. Mama says dinner will be ready in half an hour."

She offered us chalices of mulled cranberry cider, patting her growing baby belly and assuring us it was alcohol-free when she sipped some herself.

"We want you to keep your wits about you tonight," Briar said, stirring at a cauldron of something bubbling on the stove. "Therefore, no booze."

Tripp and I looked at each other, and he asked me, "Why

do I think we're being set up for something?"

"Because you know the Barlows well?" I suggested.

Waving off our offer to assist with dinner, Morgan asked if River and Tripp would help with something in the atrium.

I could see myself spending all winter in that room if I lived here. The floor-to-ceiling windows let in sunlight that promised to keep the room warm and cozy even on the chilliest days. Maybe they'd let me come sit here and practice sketching. Between that and testing out the loom at The Twisty Skein, spring and the accompanying flood of tourists would be here before I knew it.

As we entered the atrium, I immediately noticed dozens of plants in pots gathered on the heavy wood table that served as both a potting station and altar.

"Wow," Tripp said. "Impressive collection."

"Mama has a special touch with her potted beauties." Morgan smiled at the display. "She likes to gather the bloomers in one spot."

"Lady Briar has a special touch with everything," River said, his gaze locked on Morgan.

Already glowing from pregnancy hormones, the blush on Morgan's cheeks from his words made her even more beautiful.

She pointed out a Christmas cactus covered in orange-red blossoms. A shamrock plant with deep-purple triangular leaves and tiny five-petaled pink flowers with white centers.

"Are these African violets?" Tripp inspected a collection of plants with velvety leaves and clusters of purple, pink, purple and white, or pink and white flowers. When Morgan nodded, he said, "Thought so. My aunt grows African violets. She has a huge bay window full of nothing but them."

At his nostalgic expression, I made a mental note to remind him to invite them for a visit. Other than a dozen or so bookings between now and New Year's, we had plenty of time to entertain.

“We need these two large potted trees to be placed onto plant dollies,” Morgan explained. “They always seem to want to be someplace other than where we put them. This way, we can move them easily.”

While Tripp and River took care of that, I asked her, “What’s going on?”

“I’m pregnant and not supposed to lift heavy items.”

“Not the plants. This whole evening. Why are we supposed to keep our wits about us? And don’t think I haven’t noticed the full moon.”

“Isn’t it glorious.” She clasped her hands together, her multitude of silver rings clicking as she did.

“You’re ignoring my question.”

“Answers will come in due time.” At my impatient expression, she added, “Relax and enjoy the evening, Jayne. Mama has prepared French onion soup, pot roast with carrots and mashed potatoes, and individual molten lava cakes for dessert.”

My mouth watered a little. “Sounds like comfort food.”

Morgan gave a happy sigh. “You’ll love it.”

And we did. The soup broth was salty, and the Gruyere cheese on top gooey. The meat fork tender. The little warm cakes rich and decadent.

“Most excellent meal, Lady Briar.” River pushed back from the table once we were all finished. “Allow Tripp and me to clean up.”

Tripp started gathering dishes. “I’ll be needing that soup recipe. If you’re willing to share, that is.”

“I could be persuaded.” Briar tapped her cheek and tilted it up to Tripp for a kiss. Grinning and satisfied with her payment, she said, “I’ll jot it down for you.”

As the guys washed the dishes, Briar copied the soup recipe onto a card and then dozed in a comfy wingback chair next to the kitchen fireplace. Meeka lay on the floor by her feet snoring contently while Pitch preened his feathers.

"Will you answer my question now?" I asked.

"Soon," Morgan replied and sipped more cider. "Deputy Atkins stopped by Shoppe Mystique looking for Donovan. That's very distressing. How did it turn out? And what happened with the stabbing? I haven't heard the latest on Silence."

Reluctantly, not wanting to break the cozy mood of the evening, I told her we thought it might have been Donovan because of the man in Duluth, but that it ended up being Randy causing all the problems.

Morgan frowned throughout my retelling but breathed a sigh of relief when I told her Silence would likely be fine. By then, the kitchen was back to its normal spotless condition, and Morgan woke Briar from her nap.

"Everyone, grab your coats," Briar instructed as she took her own heavy cloak from a peg by the back door.

"We're going to the garden?" I asked. "It's cold outside."

"That's why you need your coat," Morgan said, wrapping her own thick black cape around her shoulders and securing the deep-purple frog closure at her neck.

"Do you know what's going on?" Tripp asked River.

"Indeed, I do. We're going out to the garden," River answered and smirked.

Outside, we found a ten foot in diameter circle of stones near the fire pit where Morgan and Briar sat on chilly nights. Within seconds, River had a fire crackling in the pit. Between the flames and the full moon, the garden was so well lit I could have read a novel.

"Jayne and Tripp," Briar began, "come stand next to the circle."

"Do you know what they're up to?" Tripp asked me.

"Not a clue. It's best if we do as we're told, though."

"Please face each other," Briar instructed. When we were

in place, she said, "River tells us there has been a great deal of tension between the two of you lately."

River, standing next to Morgan, looked dark, mysterious, and totally guilty.

"The November full moon is known as the Snow Moon," Briar explained. "Rituals for ridding oneself of negative thoughts are especially effective at this time."

Morgan spoke next. "We all know how much the two of you care for each other. We want to help you get past this difficult patch."

"An intervention?" I looked from Morgan to Briar to River. "Is that what this is?"

"If that's how you prefer to view it," Morgan said. "We look at it simply as help. Even the strongest of relationships needs a little help at times."

"Wiccan couples' therapy," River mumbled, and I giggled.

"Arguments," Briar said in her Mama voice, "stem from either fear, misunderstandings, or anger. Are you angry about something?"

We both shook our heads.

"Has there been a misunderstanding?" Briar continued. "Perhaps about your respective roles within your bed-and-breakfast venture?"

We both paused before saying no, our roles with Pine Time were clear and we were happy with them.

"Then only fear is left." She placed her fingers beneath our chins and turned our heads until we were looking directly at each other. "There is no judgment in this space. River, Morgan, and I are here only to support you. Tell each other what these fears are."

Tripp and I glanced uncomfortably at and away from each other a few times. After what felt like an hour, he blurted, "I'm afraid I'm going to lose you."

I didn't even know how to respond.

"Until you," he continued, "I've only had casual relationships. There were women I liked spending time with, but no one I wanted to be with long term. For the first five months, we didn't move past that same kind of serious dating stage. We hung out, we had fun, but there was no commitment. Other than Pine Time."

"That's because—" I began, and he placed a finger over my lips.

"I knew I wanted to be with you right away. And now that we're together, the thought that keeps playing over and over in my mind is that the only woman to ever say she loved me, left me. That's why I made that boneheaded comment yesterday about not having had my heart broken yet."

I pulled his hand away from my mouth. "You're talking about your mother?"

He nodded. "Just saying it out loud makes me realize how stupid that is. I mean, you're not going to leave me, are you?"

He paled when I didn't respond right away. Before I could answer his question, I needed to tell him my fear. I knew exactly what it was. It had been playing in my head loud and clear for weeks.

"I'm afraid you're trying to change me."

He looked stunned. "Why?"

"Being sheriff and doing whatever it is I was brought to Whispering Pines to do is really important to me." I glanced at River who gave a single nod of encouragement. "Honestly, it's as important to me as you are." I held my hands flat, forming a smooth surface. "You and that need are on equal planes for me. I can't put one above the other, and sometimes it feels like you're either trying to set rules around that part of my life or make me choose. My job is what it is. There can't be rules around it."

He stood there, obviously searching for the right response.

"I'm not saying this right," I continued, "but what it comes down to is, if you force me to choose, I might not choose you." I shook my head as my voice strangled. Why couldn't I say this right? "Tripp, the last thing I want is to lose you, but I set my own needs aside for other people before. First, Randy, when I let my personal connection to him take precedence over what I knew was the right thing to do. And then Jonah. I let him slowly lead me away from what was important to me. By not saying no when he tried to mold me into the woman he wanted me to be, I almost lost myself. I can't risk that again."

Tripp cupped my face in his hands and turned it up to his. "You know that I love you."

"I do."

"Then trust me when I say, I'm not Jonah. I love you for exactly who and what you are. If I made you feel like I wanted you to choose, it's only because your job is so dangerous." He tapped his chest over his heart. "I have this need to protect you that I can't turn off, but I will be more aware of not trying to control your world."

I looked him in the eye. "Sounds like a fair compromise. I promise not to treat you like Jonah."

He smiled. "And I promise not to push my mother's mistakes onto you."

"Good." Briar clapped her hands softly. "This is very good. Your fears are intertwined with your love for each other."

Morgan stepped forward then and withdrew a small canvas bag from beneath her cape. "A full moon night is also an excellent time to perform a partnership or binding ritual."

Tripp and I looked at each other, and I said, "Woo-woo."

"Mindset and intent," Morgan corrected with narrowed eyes. She reached into the bag and withdrew two obelisk-shaped pink crystals. "Rose quartz heals both spiritual and physical ailments. It promotes self-love and inner harmony. And, among other things, it brings about forgiveness and opens the heart to give and receive love."

She handed each of us a crystal and then withdrew three lengths of leather cording, a small wrought-iron cauldron with a chunk of patchouli incense inside, and a folded paper.

"I would like to guide you through a binding ritual. It's nothing legal, of course. The intent is to bind the two of you spiritually and emotionally. To bring you closer in heart and mind." She paused for us to absorb that and then asked, "Would you like to proceed?"

"I would," Tripp said without hesitation.

I nodded. "I would too."

She handed us the other items from the bag and took a small burning stick from the fire. "Light the incense and cleanse your crystals with the smoke before entering the circle."

Tripp held the cords and the paper while I held the incense to the flame. Once lit, I returned the incense to the cauldron.

After holding our crystals over the incense smoke, Morgan instructed, "Enter the circle and place the cauldron to one side. You'll notice that two stones opposite each other on the circle are out of place. Each of you, take a stone and put it in place to close the circle." Once we'd done that, "Now sit cross-legged in the center of the circle knees to knees, one of you facing north, the other south."

I chose the north-facing position, and Tripp sat with his knees pressed lightly against mine. Next, we were to read the words on the paper out loud to each other.

Tripp went first. "On this night, beneath this Snow moon, in the presence of those who love us, I commit to you. I promise to always respect you for who and what you are and to never again reflect past hurts onto you. I love you with all that I am."

After I'd repeated the words to him, Morgan instructed us to secure a length of cord around each other's left wrists symbolizing our bond.

"Now take the longer cord," Morgan said of the remaining piece, "and tie the two crystals together as a further sign of your commitment to each other."

Tripp wrapped the crystals. As I tied the cord, I thought of Lily Grace's "two pink cylinders side by side" vision. That might be her best one yet.

"The final step," Morgan said, a smile brightening her face and happy tears gleaming in her dark eyes, "is to remove a stone together, breaking the circle and releasing your commitment into the world."

We did and as we stepped out of the circle, hands clasped tightly, Briar proclaimed, "So mote it be."

Pitch crowed and Meeka barked as our three friends wrapped us in a hug. We celebrated with sparkling grape juice, since Morgan couldn't drink champagne, and sat around the fire pit until Briar started dozing off again.

"Thank you." I wrapped my arms around Morgan, the baby preventing too tight a hug. "I'm so grateful I've got people who step in and rescue me from myself."

"The two of you are perfect for each other," she murmured in my ear. "You do realize that."

"I do." I pulled away and asked, "What about you and River? You must have more quartz and cording."

"Tonight is for you and Tripp. There will be other full moons."

Tripp and I didn't speak of our ceremony until we were home and tucked into bed.

"What did we just do?" he asked, pretending dread, but I heard the thrill in his voice.

I was lying contently in his arms with my head resting on his strong chest and shifted so I could look up at him. The light from the full Snow Moon illuminated the room perfectly.

"We proclaimed our intent," I said, smiling. "I'm sorry we've been fighting, but Briar was absolutely right. The arguments stemmed from our fears. I believe with all my heart that for as much as we were each drawn to this village, we were drawn here for each other as well."

"I think so too." Then he gave me a kiss that warmed every inch of me.

We debated about going out onto the patio to enjoy the crisp air and light from the full moon but decided it was much more comfortable in bed. Besides, we could still see the moon through the windows.

We stayed awake talking about everything—our recent fights, Randy threatening me, our binding ceremony, our bright and secure future—until three in the morning. I couldn't remember the last time we'd done that. It had to have been during my first week or two here, before I became sheriff and we got the go-ahead from my parents to turn this place into a B&B. Few and far between was better than never, though.

Meeka woke us at eight, needing to go outside.

"We should install a doggie door," I groaned.

"That would be great," Tripp agreed, "until the winter wind starts whipping across the lake and straight into the house."

"Always have to be practical, don't you?"

"One of us has to be." At my mock glare, he laughed and kissed my forehead. "Joking. I'm just joking."

He got up to let Meeka out and then started breakfast. I lay there a little longer, inspecting the leather cord tied around my wrist. We had guests coming tomorrow, so it would be back to normal B&B life for Tripp.

As for me, I'd take things as they came. Hopefully, I'd get a break from Whispering Pines' dark cloud for a few days, although I'd stay on guard for Flavia and her vigilantes. I had a sketchbook and plenty of places around the village where I could practice my new hobby. Yule was coming in a few weeks and there was a metric ton of Gran's decorations in the loft over the garage I should put out. Or I could help paint the attic. Or I could sit and sketch Tripp while he painted the attic. So many options.

Suspense and fantasy author Shawn McGuire loves creating characters and places her fans want to return to again and again. She started writing after seeing the first Star Wars movie (that's episode IV) as a kid. She couldn't wait for the next installment to come out so wrote her own. Sadly, those notebooks are long lost, but her desire to tell a tale is as strong now as it was then. She lives in Wisconsin near the beautiful Mississippi River and when not writing or reading, she might be baking, crafting, going for a long walk, or nibbling really dark chocolate.

Made in United States
Troutdale, OR
03/31/2024

18858993R00171